THE
LAST LADY
OF THE
SILVER SCREEN

DEANNA LYNN SLETTEN

The Last Lady of the Silver Screen

Cover Designer: Deborah Bradseth

Novels by

Deanna Lynn Sletten

HISTORICAL

Mrs. Winchester's Biographer
The Secrets We Carry
The Ones We Leave Behind
The Women of Great Heron Lake
Miss Etta
Night Music
Finding Libbie

WOMEN'S FICTION

Christmas at Mountain View Lodge
The Christmas Charm
One Wrong Turn
Maggie's Turn
Summer of the Loon
Memories
Sara's Promise

MURDER/MYSTERY

Rachel Emery Series
The Truth About Rachel
Death Becomes You
All the Pretty Girls

ROMANCE

Destination Wedding

Lake Harriet Series
Under the Apple Blossoms
Chasing Bailey
As the Snow Fell
Walking Sam

Kiss a Cowboy Series
Kiss a Cowboy
A Kiss for Colt
Kissing Carly

YOUNG ADULT

Outlaw Heroes

THE
LAST LADY
OF THE
SILVER SCREEN

CHAPTER ONE

TODAY

Kathleen Carver stood on the sidelines studying the studio with disdain. It was set up to look like a living room with fake walls, an imitation fireplace, cheap carpet, and strategically placed furniture. Two big cushy chairs were facing each other with small tables beside each one, meant to hold drinks for the interviewer and interviewee. Her nose wrinkled as she stared at the thick, cushioned chairs.

Don't these idiots know that elderly people have trouble getting in and out of cushy chairs?

Kath waved to her assistant and beloved niece to come over. "Darling. Will you please have them replace that big, fat chair with one I can actually sit in?"

Carolyn Gibson studied the situation, then nodded. "Of course, Aunt Kath. I should have noticed it myself."

Kath smiled for the first time since arriving at the studio. "Carolyn, dear. You can't be expected to do everything. But please have them switch it out."

Carolyn patted her aunt's shoulder and headed toward the director to make the change.

Kath watched as her niece took care of the matter efficiently, as always. Carolyn was sixty-seven, but she moved like a much younger woman and looked young too. She was as active as Kath had been at her age. Now, at ninety-eight years old, Kathleen Carver, the once spry and beautiful, or at least pretty, queen of Hollywood, was a mere shadow of her younger self. Still extremely thin, still wearing trousers—not pants or slacks, they were good old-fashioned wide-legged trousers—and still able to stare down even the most powerful person with ease, Kath knew deep down she was old and nearly useless. But she wasn't going to let these people see that.

Once the new, less padded, chair was in place, Carolyn helped her aunt walk to it and sit. Kath was relieved to finally rest her legs. Despite changing out the chair, she knew she wasn't going to feel relaxed throughout the entire interview.

Carolyn left to get water for her aunt, and the makeup artist once again approached Kath with brushes and palettes in hand. Kath waved her away as she had the first time she'd been approached. At her age, make-up would settle into her deep wrinkles, making her appear fake and maybe even a little crazy. Except for the creases, her skin tone wasn't bad for her age, and her eyebrows were well-shaped. She didn't need liner or color to make her brown eyes more expressive or blush to contour her face. Her square jawline and high cheekbones were all she needed for people to recognize her. The last thing Kath wanted was to look like a clown on television—or Netflix—or wherever this long, drawn-out interview of her life would appear.

"I finally found a mug to pour your water in," Carolyn said, approaching her aunt. "I know it's easier for you to have a handle." She placed the mug on the table and opened a water bottle to pour into it.

"Thank you, dear," Kath said kindly. "You always know what I need."

Carolyn smiled at her and then walked behind the scenes. A man asked for a sound check from Kath, who rolled her eyes and said a few words.

"Would you please speak up louder?" the burly man asked her.

"No," Kath said. "If I'm to speak for hours for the next few days, then I will not speak louder and tire my throat."

The sound man stared at her, looking astounded by her answer. "Yes, ma'am," he said. Then he returned to work, trying to get the mike to pick up her voice better.

Kath was getting restless waiting. This was worse than sitting around a sound stage, waiting for your turn while making a movie. She reached into her blazer pocket and pulled out a pack of Camels. In her younger days, she'd smoked the unfiltered Camels, but as she aged, she gave in to pressure from her niece and others to smoke the filtered ones. She also only smoked two a day now, but this incessant waiting was getting on her nerves.

Pulling out one of the cigarettes, she placed it in her mouth and lit it with the gold lighter her dear friend, Rock Hudson, had given her as a birthday gift decades ago. Inhaling deeply, she savored it before releasing the smoke from her lungs.

"Ma'am? Ma'am!" A young, short, skinny man-boy ran up to her, looking like the world was about to end. "I'm so sorry, ma'am, but this is a no-smoking area."

Kath took another long drag and slowly let the smoke out of her lungs. She stared at the man-boy with her eyebrows raised.

"Ma'am. I'm sorry," the nervous young man said, nearly

shaking in his loafers. "You just can't smoke in here."

"Justin, leave Ms. Carver alone," a tall man with perfectly groomed dark hair and wearing a navy blue suit said as he walked over to the chair opposite Kath's. "An icon of her ilk can do whatever she pleases here," the man said.

Justin, the man-boy, looked from the gentleman who'd approached them, then back at Kath. He looked like he was going to pass out from anxiety. "But Mr. Connally," he protested but was quickly waived away by the man. Looking petrified, Justin rushed away.

The man smiled over at Kath, his blue eyes twinkling under dark, groomed brows. "I'm Roger Connally," he said, extending his hand. "I'll be your interviewer for this program. It's an honor to meet you, Ms. Carver."

Kath reached up and shook his hand, then took another long drag of her cigarette. "Call me Miss Carver, please," she told him. "I never was a fan of that title, Ms. I was a liberated woman my whole life and didn't need someone to tell me I'd been liberated."

Roger smiled. "You are exactly as I expected you to be, Miss Carver. And I'm thrilled I'm working on this special interview with you."

Carolyn appeared with a clear ashtray just in time for the ashes to fall off Kath's cigarette. "That's number one," she told her aunt, lifting one finger.

Kath sighed as she snuffed out the cigarette in the ashtray. "It's already past noon. I've done well today."

Carolyn smiled and whisked the ashtray away.

Roger sat in the chair across from Kath, unbuttoning his suit jacket and adjusting his tie. "I have no problem with you smoking on set," he said. "But there is no smoking allowed on camera. I'm sorry. It's a different world from your days on a set."

"You're telling me," Kath said.

The makeup woman returned and did a few touch-ups on Roger, then the hairdresser did the same. Kath reached up to her own hair, now completely gray, that she'd had Carolyn pull up into a simple bun at the back of her head. The hair wasn't pulled tightly but instead was loose around her face. She always wore it this way. It was easier and more refined, as far as Kath was concerned.

"Are you ready?" Roger asked once the hair and make-up women left.

"I've been ready for two hours," Kath replied.

He smiled. "Then let's get started." He waved over a young woman who handed him a large, thick hardcover book. Roger turned it so Kath could see the front cover. "This was a fascinating read. I've marked all the places I want to ask you questions about."

Kath stared at the book in his hands. It was the biography she'd recently written for an insane amount of money. For decades, she'd turned down offers from the biggest publishers in the country to write her life story. Just as she'd never shared her life with the public throughout her career, she certainly wasn't going to share her secrets after retirement. She was a private person and had wanted to keep it that way.

But then she finally had to say yes. Not because she wanted the attention—but because she needed the money.

And when Netflix knocked on her door asking to do a documentary of her life, she'd grudgingly agreed again. Money was a powerful motivator. And she'd hated every moment of it so far.

"Shall we begin?" Kath said.

Roger smiled. "Yes."

Roger turned toward one of the three cameras, waited for the countdown—3-2-1—and began. "Kathleen Carver has graced the silver screen for over seventy-five years, entertaining audiences with dramas, comedies, and even Shakespeare. She's known for her simple lifestyle and sharp wit and is loved by generations of fans. But what do we really know about this incredible woman? She's kept her secrets close to the vest for years. Today, I'm deeply honored to have this time with this illustrious film star to discuss her amazing life as written in her own words in this new biography simply titled *Kath*. Please welcome Miss Kathleen Carver." He turned to Kath as the camera did also.

Kath sat and stared at him. She'd been told this was an impromptu interview where they'd casually discuss her book. But she'd immediately seen he was using idiot cards, or whatever they called it these days, on the screen underneath the camera. *He probably hadn't even written the words himself,* she thought scornfully.

Roger stared at Kath for a moment and then stumbled a little when he began to speak again. "Thank you so much for being here, Miss Carver," he said, then lifted her book for the camera. "Your biography is fascinating. I just couldn't put it down."

Kath only gave him a little nod of her head. *Let him work for this,* she thought.

"Tell me, Miss Carver," Roger continued. "What prompted you to write your biography after all these years of being so private?"

Kath raised an eyebrow. "Money."

Her answer seemed to startle Roger, but he slowly grinned. "And there's that sharp wit we all love you for," he said, chuckling.

"But there must have been another reason as well. Perhaps you wanted to share your legacy with all your adoring fans?"

Kath shrugged. She was having fun making this slick ex-anchorman sweat. "Quite frankly, if I hadn't needed the money for some nagging bills, I would have died keeping my life a secret. But when you live to be ninety-eight years old, the money comes in handy."

Off camera, Kath saw her niece smirk and shake her head. Carolyn knew her well and could see Kath was playing with the man like a cat playing with a mouse.

"At least you're honest," Roger said. He opened the book and looked at the page on which he'd placed one of many small sticky notes. "Shall we start at the beginning?" he said. "You say that you had a happy childhood. There aren't too many people who'd claim to have been happy children. Why is it you think your childhood was happy?"

Kath sighed, already bored with this tedious interview. "I don't *think* I had a happy childhood. I *know* I did." She stared Roger down a moment until she saw him squirm in his chair. Then she relaxed and continued. "My father and mother were the most amazing people, especially in a time when everyone was so rigid and uptight. They'd both grown up in the east, Connecticut, to be precise and attended college in Pennsylvania. My father studied at the University of Pennsylvania to become a lawyer, and my mother attended Bryn Mawr for two years. They met during the holidays at a mutual friend's house. My father always said it was love at first sight, although my mother, a very independent soul, only claimed to have liked him very much at first."

Roger gave a small laugh. "They must have been quite interesting people."

"They were," Kath answered. "Although my father believed in hard work to attain what you desire, he also loved to have fun. He was very athletic and taught us children how to swim, play tennis, golf, and various other sports. My father was also quite competitive, which drove some of my younger siblings crazy, but I loved every minute of it."

"What about your mother?" Roger asked.

"She was a beautiful woman and a liberated woman despite the times she was raised in. She was a strong woman and a kind mother. She believed children needed room to grow and develop character, and she let us run around the neighborhood like wild children." Kath laughed. "Neighbors would call her and say, 'Kath is up in a tree,' and mother would say, 'Good for her.'" They'd call to tell her that my brother Graham and I were miles from home, riding our bikes, and she'd tell them, 'Thank you. I'm sure they know their way home.'" She let us be as independent as we desired, and I adored her for that."

"Your mother didn't insist on you and your sisters behaving like young ladies?" Roger asked.

Kath laughed. "Absolutely not. We knew how to behave in polite society and did when it was expected, but otherwise, she let us be. Why, I remember when I was seven years old and saw the 1933 movie *Little Women* starring Katharine Hepburn as Jo. I was so inspired by her character that I went home and cut my long hair off to look like a boy. My sister, Katrina, screamed when she saw me, and my brother laughed. But my mother only shrugged. 'It's her hair and her choice,' my mother said. She was incredible."

"Your parents sound amazing," Roger said. "You wrote that your father was a lawyer for Warner Brothers Studios. You must have lived a high lifestyle."

"Not at first," Kath said. "My father worked for a law firm for the first few years after he and my mother were married. I remember moving out of the small apartment we lived in when I was about five years old. Three of my siblings were already born, and my mother was expecting my youngest brother. Father had been working for the studio for about six months, and we were able to move to the Toluca Lake neighborhood into a big Victorian house with a large yard. My siblings and I loved it there. It wasn't until years later that my father acquired the beach property in Malibu—but that was before prices were ridiculous and houses became mansions. My father loved the beach and ocean and decided we needed a weekend place away from the city."

"Wow. Malibu. And you still own that property, don't you?" Roger asked.

"Yes, yes," Kath said impatiently. "It's really the family's house. My youngest brother lives there permanently, but my nieces, nephews, and I use it too. It's the same lovely *normal-sized* home it was when my father built it on the ten acres he acquired."

"My goodness! Ten acres in Malibu, on the beach? The taxes must be extraordinary," Roger said.

"They are. Believe me. But I wouldn't sell it for the world. It's still paradise," Kath said.

"So, what did your father enjoy doing at the beach? Was he a swimmer? Or did he play volleyball with you children?" Roger asked.

"All of the above and then some," Kath said. She sat back and thought about her father and the many weekends he took them to the beach before they owned the Malibu house. She and her siblings loved it. But she believed that her father, Crandell, loved it the most.

CHAPTER TWO

1934

Eight-year-old Kathleen Carver screamed with delight as her father sprayed water in her face. They had been having a swimming contest—and of course her father won—and now, as they headed toward shore, he sprayed her. She splashed him back and soon he, Kath, six-year-old Katrina, and five-year-old Graham were having a water fight to see who gave up first.

After a time, Crandell called for a truce. Laughing, he said, "We'd better be on our way home for lunch, or your mother will skin us all."

Kath laughed along with him. "Mama would never touch a hair on our heads."

"Don't be so sure," her father said. "Sometimes, she even scares me." He shivered as he toweled off.

The crew hopped into their father's 1930 Chevrolet Universal 4-Door Sedan and began the long ride from the beach to their Toluca Lake home. Crandell didn't mind the distance to the beach, although he always said he wished they had a weekend house on the ocean. He loved spending time with his children in the water and playing in the sand.

"There are my ragamuffin children," Catherine said as they piled through the back door, leaving sand in their wake. She smiled as she said it, which made Kath smile back. "Off with you to your rooms to change for lunch. Mrs. Cray has been working hard to feed you lot of miscreants, and we don't want the food to get cold."

Kath led the way through the kitchen to the back staircase and called out a hello to Mrs. Cray as the other children followed her upstairs. They lived in a large, three-story Victorian home. Kath had her own room on the third floor, while her sister Katrina shared a room with their three-year-old sister, Lillian, on the second floor. Graham shared a room with their baby brother, Daniel, who'd just turned one. The other children rushed to their rooms, and Kath went up the narrow stairs to hers.

Kath loved having the space upstairs to herself. Her father had even put in a tiny bathroom for her. It felt like her own little apartment, and sometimes, she'd invite Kat to come up and spend the night so they could talk and giggle and share secrets.

The entire crew filled the large, polished walnut table as they sat down for lunch. Kath's mother believed in eating the biggest meal of the day at noon and then a smaller meal for supper. That routine suited Mrs. Cray well. She left supper in the oven or on the stove for them before she left for the evening.

Kath recounted their morning at the beach to her mother, who sat feeding Daniel, the baby.

"Well, it sounds like you had a boisterous time at the beach," Catherine said, wiping sweet potatoes off little Daniel's face. "So, what are your plans for the afternoon?"

Kath's eyes lit up. "Could we play tennis at the courts?" she asked her father. "Just you and me?"

Kat and Graham complained loudly, but Crandell quieted them by raising his hand up in the air. "I'm sorry, Kath. I have to run into the office for a short while this afternoon. But you and Graham could practice tennis at the courts."

Kath sighed. Graham was three years younger than her and not nearly the competitor as her father was.

"Sorry, dear," Crandell said, smiling at Kath. "Work always comes first, play comes second."

Kath nodded. Her father worked as a contract lawyer for Warner Brothers Studios, and he took his job seriously. He loved it there more than when he'd worked at a law practice. He met interesting people and was held in high regard. And in the current Depression economy, he felt lucky that his job allowed his family to live as well as they did.

Kath studied her father as he finished his lunch. He was a handsome man, perpetually tan, from all the time he spent outside with his kids. He had the same thick, wavy auburn hair as Kath and her brown eyes as well. When she'd accompanied him to the studios, she'd overheard someone asking if he was a movie star. It had made her laugh, but then she realized he was as good-looking as any of the movie stars on the screen.

Kath glanced over at the other end of the table where her mother sat. She was beautiful. Her mother still had a slender figure despite having had five children and always looked perfectly groomed. At times, she'd catch her parents staring at each other, her father with a twinkle in his eyes. They were truly in love, which made Kath feel safe and secure.

After lunch, Kath, Kat, and Graham decided to ride their bikes around the neighborhood streets, leaving Lillian behind because she still couldn't ride a two-wheeler. They went to their favorite tree that stood tall in the empty lot beside old Mrs. Landon's house. Dropping their bikes on the ground, Kath and Graham scaled it like monkeys, leaving Kat on the ground, whining. Finally, Kath climbed down and helped boost her little sister up while Graham held on to her tightly so she wouldn't fall.

The kids could play in the old oak for hours. They pretended they were pirates, sailing across the rough ocean. Then, they were great hunters in Africa, hiding from a pack of lions below. Kath had a wealth of imaginative ideas that the kids could feed off of for hours. Her father always told her she should be a writer when she grew up because of her vivid imagination.

As the sun fell low in the sky, their father's maroon and black car came chugging up the street. He parked and walked casually over to the tree.

"Hm. I could have sworn I saw a pack of monkeys running this way," he said loudly, glancing around. "I suppose they'll have to go hungry for the night since they can't be found." He slid his hands into his trouser's pockets and slowly made his way to the car. Suddenly, the children all called out to him to wait.

"Papa! We're here! Don't leave without us," Graham yelled, scrambling down the tree.

Crandell turned, grinning, and walked back to the tree. "Graham? Where on earth were you? I thought for sure the pack of monkeys had eaten you."

Graham laughed. "I was in the tree, Papa. So are Kath and Kat." He pointed up. "See them?"

"By Jove, I do see them now. Way up in the top branches," Crandell said, playing along. "Are you girls ready to come down and head home? We'll all need to eat a hearty supper if we're to have more adventures at the beach tomorrow."

"Coming Papa!" Kath yelled, swinging her way down. But when she heard Kat cry for help, she climbed back up and helped her younger sister down. Crandell reached up and grabbed Kat when she was within reach, and Kath jumped to the ground.

"My goodness, Kat," he said, staring at his second daughter. "I had no idea you could climb as high as your sister and brother."

"They helped me," Kat said proudly.

Kath rolled her eyes. She and Graham always helped Kat. Kath couldn't wait for Kat to grow bigger so she could keep up on her own.

"Well, kids. Follow along behind my car with your bikes," their father announced. "It's been a long day, and I'm tired."

Kat chose to load her bike into the back seat and ride with her father. Kath didn't want to be seen as a baby and rode her bike home along with Graham.

"My goodness, what a commotion you children caused today," Catherine said, standing at the door with young Daniel on her hip. "Mrs. Landon called here at least five times to tell me you were stuck in the tree. I told her you were fine, but at one point, she threatened to call the fire department to get you three down." Their mother shook her head. "Old busybody."

Kath laughed. She loved her mother's confidence in them. Her mother was busy with several women's organizations that encouraged the empowerment and better treatment of women and children. She was influential in getting women out to vote in the last election. And she was also a mother who was very hands-on with her children. She didn't have time to fuss with the Mrs. Landons of the world.

That night, Kath generously invited Kat upstairs to her room for a sleepover. Lillian had been very put out, but Kath had said it was for big girls only. They put on their night-clothes—Kath insisted on wearing flannel night pants and a shirt like Graham while Kat wore a long nightgown—turned Kath's radio on very low and sat in bed, looking at Kath's collection of movie magazines. Kath saved her allowance to buy the magazines, which her father thought was a foolish way to spend her hard-earned money. But Kath didn't care. She adored movies and the Hollywood stars—especially all the pretty ladies—and loved reading about their lives.

"Look at this one with Katharine Hepburn on the cover," Kath said, carefully handing it to her sister. "Don't rip it."

Kat gently opened the magazine. It was the April issue of Photoplay which had cost Kath a whole twenty-five cents. "She's so beautiful. And so thin," Kat said. "Do you think she ever eats?"

Kath rolled her eyes. She had the January issue of New Movie Magazine open in her lap. "Of course, she eats. But movie stars have to be thin. Papa says they look even thinner in person."

"I wish I could go to the movies with you and Papa," Kat said, sighing. "But Mama says I can't go until I'm eight."

Kath sat up taller on the double bed. This had been the first year she'd been allowed to go to a Saturday matinee with her father. They had watched a funny comedy starring Hepburn and from that moment on, Kath wanted to be just like her. She read everything about her that she could, not understanding, because of her young age, that all the movie magazines were as much fiction as the books her father sometimes read aloud to them.

"You'll be eight soon enough, and then maybe you, Graham, and I can go to the movies every weekend," Kath said.

This made Kat smile. Even at six years old, she loved being included in everything Kath did.

Their father made the trek up the two flights of stairs to say goodnight to the girls. "Lights out soon, girls," he said, poking his head inside the room. Kath's room was large, with two dormer windows to brighten it. She had her bed, a nightstand, a desk on one side, and a dresser on the other. Her mother had it painted yellow years ago, but Kath would have preferred blue.

"Oh, my," Crandell said, coming closer to the bed. "Are you wasting your time with those silly movie magazines again?"

"It's not a waste of time, Papa," Kath said quickly. "It's fun to read about everything the movie stars are doing."

Crandell shook his head. "They aren't any different from you or I, dear. They're people first, movie stars second. Remember that. Not everything that glitters is gold."

Kath laughed. "Oh, Papa. You just say that because you see the stars around the lot every day, and it feels normal to you."

Crandell bent to kiss first Kath and then Kat on the cheek. "Maybe so, my little dreamer, but people are people. Never put anyone on a pedestal. Goodnight, darlings. Get some sleep so you have the energy to beat me in swimming tomorrow."

"Goodnight, Papa," the girls said in unison, then laughed.

"Do you think papa's right?" Kat asked. "That movie stars are nothing without their beautiful clothes and hairstyles?"

"I think they'd still be special, even if they wore no makeup or glittery dresses," Kath said. "Mama's special without all that stuff. I think they're special because they're in the movies." Her eyes turned dreamy. "I'd love to play different characters in the movies. It would be so much fun."

Kat yawned. "You'd make a wonderful movie star," she told her sister as she slid under the covers and closed her eyes.

Kath watched her little sister fall instantly asleep. She carefully piled her magazines onto the nightstand and turned out the light. She agreed with Kat. She'd be an amazing movie star someday.

Chapter Three

TODAY

Carolyn drove Kath to the family's Malibu house after her day of talking with Roger Connally. Kath wanted to spend the weekend at the ocean before continuing the blasted interview on Monday. At least she'd have two days to enjoy cool breezes off the ocean and sleep to the sound of the waves caressing the sand.

Nearly all of the beach houses in Malibu were crammed next to each other, but Kath's father had the foresight to buy enough acreage to place the house in the middle and have land on each side. He'd purchased the ten acres on the ocean in 1941, a year after the original owner, May Rindge, died. Rindge's daughter was happy to sell it to him because it helped her pay the taxes on the large amount of acreage the family still owned.

As Carolyn drove the car down the shrub-lined drive-way, Kath smiled. She loved this place. It was still the original house that her father and mother had built—not one of those awful, showy beach mansions everyone had these days.

A simple two-story Cape Cod style with dormers upstairs and large windows downstairs to enjoy the view. Two additions were added on, one on each end. A sunroom and an additional bedroom. The house was cozy and comfortable, with hardwood floors that the sand could easily be swept up from and slip-covered furniture they could simply toss in the washing machine as needed.

Kath's father had wanted an escape from the city so he and his family could play all weekend, and that was exactly what he'd built. Throughout the decades, houses had been built along the beach, then torn down for the new monstrosities. But their simple, elegant home had remained the same. Unfortunately, the property was worth a fortune, and the yearly taxes were outrageous.

They parked at the back of the house and Carolyn ran around to assist Kath out of the car. Carolyn drove a small SUV, so it was easier for Kath to step in and out of than in a small car. Since the death of Carolyn's husband nine years prior, she'd worked for her aunt. She hadn't needed the money because her husband left her well-off, and they'd had no children. When Kath had asked if she'd become her assistant and companion, Carolyn had agreed. She'd always adored her outspoken aunt and was happy to spend more time with her.

"Thank you, dear," Kath said, standing up to her full five-foot, six-inch height. In her youth, Kath had been two inches taller, but time and age had shortened her stature. Just one more aspect of aging that riled her.

The two women went in through the back door with Carolyn carrying their small weekend bags. As they entered the kitchen, a voice called out.

"Who's there?"

"Just me," Kath called back, irritated. "And Carolyn. I told you we were coming."

A tall, elderly man, slightly stooped, with very little gray hair left on his head, entered the kitchen. He had a cane to steady himself but otherwise got around well for a man of ninety-one.

"Hello, Carolyn," he said cheerfully, showing crooked aging teeth. "How much trouble has this one given you today?"

Carolyn laughed at the sneer on her aunt's face. "Oh, Uncle Daniel, you know Kath is always sweet."

"Humph!" Daniel's watery blue eyes twinkled with mischief.

"Stop being a jerk, Daniel," Kath said sharply. "I've had a long day, and I need a good rest this weekend to put up with that slick anchorman again next week." She walked past her brother toward the kitchen staircase to go up to her bedroom. Technically, she should have the downstairs bedroom since she paid most of the house's expenses, but since Daniel now lived at the beach house full-time, he'd claimed it as his own.

"Ah, yes, the interview. How did that go?" Daniel asked his sister's retreating back.

Carolyn made a face, and Daniel grinned as Kath turned around.

"Terrible. Horrendous. And it's not over yet," she said. "But it'll pay to keep this house going until you and I are put in the ground, and that's all that matters." Kath turned again toward the stairs.

"Such a positive attitude," Daniel said.

"Oh, shut up," Kath told him, walking up the stairs.

Carolyn hurried to follow Kath up the narrow wooden staircase which was painted sage green decades ago. They walked down the hallway and into Kath's bedroom—the room she'd had since the house was built in 1941.

"Let me hang your things," Carolyn said as Kath sat down in a padded wicker chair next to the large dormer window.

"Thank you, dear," Kath said, then sighed loudly. "It's so good to be home—even if Daniel is here."

"Oh, he's not so bad," Carolyn said as she placed Kath's blouses on hangers and put them in the tiny closet. She folded her aunt's sweaters and slipped them into the drawer of the high-boy dresser. "He's always been full of mischief."

"He was the baby of the family, and he's still a baby." Kath huffed. "He never settled down or had any responsibilities in his life. His job at the post office in Beverly Hills was the only thing he ever kept for any length of time. No wife, no children, no dedication to anything."

Kath caught her niece side-eying her. "Yes, yes. I know. I've never been married or had children, either. But my career lasted decades, and I had a purpose. His purpose was to live off our father's money, then mine."

Carolyn pushed her thick shoulder-length auburn hair behind one ear. At sixty-seven, she still had her hair dyed to its natural color. Carolyn wasn't chasing youth—she just didn't want to have gray hair until she felt old. "Well, I still like Uncle Daniel despite all that," she said. "Do you want to rest before dinner?"

"Yes, I think I will lie down for a bit," Kath said. More and more, she tired easily. But she guessed being ninety-eight did make a person tired. "First, though, I want to talk to you about your interview tomorrow."

Carolyn sat in the other wicker chair next to Kath's. "I know what I should or shouldn't say," she said gently. "Some secrets should remain private."

Kath nodded. "Yes, I know you understand that. But that slick Roger Connally could easily trap you in a corner. Since you typed up my book, you know what stories I told—and didn't tell. Please just keep to what's in the book."

"I completely understand," Carolyn said. "Besides. I don't know most of your real secrets." She grinned.

"Let's keep it that way," Kath said, giving her niece a mischievous smile. Sobering, Kath said, "I just can't wait for this to be over. I hate selling my life story so the media can have a field day with it. I hope the friends I mentioned in the book will forgive me."

Carolyn patted her aunt's hand. "Sadly, all of them have passed, so it really doesn't matter anymore."

Kath nodded. All her old friends had passed. Rock Hudson, Grace Kelly, Tony Curtis, Susan Hayward, Betty Bacall and Bogie, and even sweet, beautiful Marilyn Monroe. So many more could be added to that list. One name, however, she couldn't bear to think about because she missed him so much.

"You rest while I cook dinner," Carolyn said as she stood and headed for the door. "Does chicken and seasoned rice sound good?"

"Yes, dear. That will be fine." Kath moved to the double bed and lay down on the old quilt. Just a little rest, then she'd deal with Daniel again. She sighed and closed her eyes.

* * *

Later that evening, Kath, Daniel, and Carolyn sat at the kitchen table to eat dinner. The kitchen hadn't been remodeled in years and was small like kitchens used to be. No big island or granite countertops in their beach kitchen. Good, durable Corian countertops sat on painted white wood cabinets. The kitchen had last been remodeled in the mid-1970s, and recently, they'd had to buy new appliances. Carolyn had talked them into a stainless-steel stove and refrigerator and also had a dishwasher installed. Kath had scoffed at the dishwasher—people could wash the dishes. But now, she realized what a timesaver it was.

"You should come live with me full-time," Daniel said to Carolyn. "Then I could enjoy your home cooking more often."

"You couldn't afford to pay her what she's worth," Kath said sharply.

"Old grouch, that's what you are," Daniel said, but he was smiling.

"Humph."

After dinner, Carolyn went up to her room to read. "Call up to me if you need help, Aunt Kath," she said before heading up the stairs.

Kath and Daniel went to the sunroom for a last cup of decaf and to watch the sunset over the ocean.

"I want to talk to you about the interview you agreed to," Kath told Daniel. "I wish you'd said no, but now it's too late."

"Are you going to tell me what to say?" Daniel asked. "Like I'm sure you told Carolyn what to say."

Kath turned her brown eyes on her brother. "No. I'm going to tell you what not to say. After all, you weren't even around for most of my movie career. You know nothing about my private life back then, and I don't want you repeating old gossip."

Daniel chuckled as he sipped his coffee. "Come on, Kath. We all know that old gossip is mostly true. Dating Howard Hughes. Long-time love affair with a married man. It's all true. Why not just own up to it?"

Kath's blood boiled. "Don't share anything that I didn't

put in the book. Do you understand?"

"Who said I read your silly autobiography?" Daniel said.

"I mean it, Danny. Don't share anything you know I don't want to be made public. I gave enough of myself in that book. I don't need more said." She paused a moment. "And don't talk about Graham—at all! I don't want all those nasty rumors swirling around about him again."

Daniel stared hard at her. "Yes. We all know Graham was your favorite brother. But I wouldn't doubt if some of the rumors were true."

"Daniel, I swear, if you malign Graham in any way, I'll make sure you never live in this house again," Kath said.

Daniel studied her for a moment as if trying to figure out if she could kick him out. "If you're so intent on staying private, why did you bother writing the book and doing this ridiculous Netflix documentary?"

Kath scoffed. "Really, Danny? You know exactly why I agreed to do all this. Your mishandling of money that was supposed to go toward taxes for this house put us in a bind. I refuse to lose our family beach house for unpaid property taxes. You live here full-time. The nieces and nephews and I all gave you our portion of the tax money—and you didn't pay it! You used it for yourself." Kath was yelling at this point and stopped because her throat was sore.

"You know I used that money to fix a few things in this house. And to pay the insurance. I didn't waste it," Daniel said.

"Then you're going senile because fixing the house wasn't as important as paying the taxes," Kath spat out. "The money from the book and this awful Netflix interview will pay the back taxes and future taxes for several years. And you won't have any control over that money."

Daniel glared at her. He leaned forward in his chair. "It's ridiculous that we keep this old house anyway. The taxes on this land are insane. We could sell this property for millions, and each of us—you, me, the nephews, and nieces—would be set for life. I don't understand why you think you have to keep this place."

"Because it's Dad's place," Kath said. "He bought this land and built this house so generations of our family could enjoy it. And I am bound and determined to continue the legacy."

Daniel shook his head. "Ridiculous. The moment you're buried in the ground, the family will sell this land and enjoy the money."

"Maybe," Kath said, turning to stare out the window at the ocean under the night sky. "But I'll be dead then and won't care."

"Fine." Daniel stood slowly, lifted his empty mug, and walked toward the kitchen.

"Don't forget," Kath called after him. "Stay on script when they interview you. Don't offer any information they don't already know."

"Yeah, yeah," Daniel said before disappearing.

Kath sighed. She couldn't wait until all this nonsense was over.

Chapter Four

Summer 1943

Seventeen-year-old Kath sped along the coastal road in her father's Chevy Sedan to their family's Malibu beach home. The top was down, and the day was glorious. She'd never felt so free.

"Slow down, Kath!" prissy twelve-year-old Lillian said from the back seat. "Or I'll tell Dad you were speeding."

"Go faster!" Graham, now fourteen, yelled with a smile on his face. "Ignore the little twerp."

Kat giggled from the front seat. At fifteen years old, she was still small and petite—the exact opposite of Kath's tall, thin, leggy frame. But she and Kath were now as tight as sisters could be, and Kat loved that.

"When will we get there?" ten-year-old Daniel shouted from the back seat, squeezed between Lillian and Graham.

"Soon enough," Kath said, pushing down even harder on the gas pedal. They took the curves at a dangerous speed, but only Lillian complained.

Soon, they drove up the driveway of their Cape Cod-style

beach house. Kath loved this home her father had built two years before. The trees and bushes that lined the driveway were still small, but she knew they'd grow tall and lush. Spending weekends at the beach was her favorite thing to do, especially now when her new friend came to visit.

"I'm going to tell Dad you didn't drive safely," Lillian whined as she slid out of the back seat.

Kath stuck her tongue out at her little sister. "You lived, didn't you? So, stop bellyaching and enjoy our extra day here." Crandell had allowed Kath to drive the kids to the house on a Friday. He and their mother would join them on Saturday. Her father had recently purchased a second car, a 1938 Packard Twelve Roadster, and he loved driving his sports car. Kath's mother wasn't as excited about riding in the convertible, but she indulged her husband's sense of fun.

"Everyone, grab your suitcase and put it in your room before you do anything else," Kath ordered. She opened the back end, and each child lifted out their suitcase. She and Kat took out their own, plus each carried a bag of groceries they'd picked up before heading there.

"I'm in charge, so you all better listen to me today," Kath told them once they entered the kitchen. "No one goes out to the beach alone, and definitely not in the water alone. Wait until either Kat or I are outside. Understand?"

"Yeah, yeah," the other kids mumbled as they headed for the back staircase.

"Who's going to make sure you follow the rules?" Lillian said.

"Never you mind about me," Kath said sternly.

Soon, the groceries were put away in their cozy white kitchen, and Kath and Kat changed into swimsuits. Kath envied Kat's curvy, petite frame, although she wouldn't trade her long, shapely legs for anything. But Kath was slender and had a small bust and wished it was larger. Still, boys noticed her just the same.

"Let's go!" Daniel yelled impatiently up the stairs.

"We're coming," Kath yelled back. She grabbed a white cotton blouse to wear over her swimsuit, then ran down the stairs behind Kat.

It was past noon by the time the group ran out onto the beach. The day was warm, but the ocean breeze felt cool and inviting. No one else was around as they headed for the waves and swam and splashed around. The Malibu Movie Colony that had sprung up slowly in the 1920s and 30s was farther down the beach from their property. Important people like Jack Warner, Gary Cooper, and Barbara Stanwyck had homes there, along with other Hollywood stars, producers, and directors. Crandell had made sure he owned enough land so his house wouldn't be crowded in among the many new ones popping up.

Kath had recently cut her hair to shoulder length, and when it was wet, it turned into spiral curls framing her face. Kat's blond hair wasn't as thick as her sister's, and she wore it long, so she'd put it up in a ponytail to keep it out of her eyes.

After a time, the group came out of the water and ran to the cooler for bottles of Coca-Cola. Then Kath grabbed the volleyball from the front porch. "Who's up for a game?"

Graham, Kat, and Kath were always ready to compete, but the two youngest ones shied away.

"You're all taller than we are," Daniel whined. "We never get a chance to hit the ball."

"Aw, come on, Danny," Graham said. His dark, wavy hair fluttered over his forehead, and his blue eyes sparkled. Even at the young age of fourteen, it was obvious Graham was going to be a looker. "We'll split it up so Lillian is on one team and you're on the other."

"Let's make it three against two," Kath offered. "That'll be fair."

"I'll play and even it out," a voice called out.

They all looked up at the tall, muscular figure walking toward them. Kath grinned widely.

"Grant!" She ran over to him, conscious that her tight swimsuit was wet and clung to her narrow figure. Grabbing her shirt, she slipped it on as she reached his side. "This will be great. We can have even teams."

Grant Kirby smiled down at her. Even though Kath was tall at five feet, eight inches, Grant towered over her. He was six feet, one inch tall, with sandy blond hair and gorgeous blue eyes. His tan, muscular physique didn't go unnoticed by Kath either. She'd met him two years ago when they'd first built their house in Malibu. Grant's parents had a house down at the Colony, and he'd grown up there and in the Hollywood Hills. Grant had instantly become a favorite visitor at the Carver household ever since.

"Great! Grant's on my team!" Graham said enthusiastically.

Lillian's face turned sour. "I don't want to play volleyball. I'm going to sit on the porch and read." She turned and headed for the house.

"Be sure to rinse the sand off your feet with the hose first," Kath yelled after her. As the oldest, she was responsible for keeping the house clean while they were there.

The group assembled—Kath, Kat, and Danny against Graham and Grant. They played a lively game, with Danny crying only once because the ball hit him on the head. Then, they finally gave up and headed for the front porch.

"I have to make dinner for this crew," Kath told Grant. She'd tied her shirttails up in a knot around her waist. On the porch, she grabbed a pair of shorts and slipped them on. "Do you want to join us? I'm making spaghetti."

"Actually, I'm making spaghetti, and Kath is helping," Kat said, giggling. She was the domestic one of the bunch.

Grant laughed. "Sure. I'll stay."

After washing the sand off their feet, legs, and hands with the outdoor hose, Kath and Kat worked in the kitchen. Kath had brought a jar of Mrs. Cray's homemade tomato sauce, and Kat mixed in spices and heated it in a pan on the stove. They boiled the noodles and made garlic butter to spread on the French bread they'd bought that morning. Soon, dinner was ready, and the group sat around the large dining room table and ate hungrily.

"This is fun," Grant said, smiling over at Kath. "I can't believe your parents let you all come here alone."

"They'll be here tomorrow," Kath said. "Our parents trust us."

"Kath drove like a maniac on the way here," Lillian said. "Dad shouldn't trust her."

Grant laughed, and Kath threw a piece of garlic toast at her.

"Lilly. How can a girl who looks like a little angel be such a sourpuss?" Kath said.

The kids erupted in laughter as Lillian's face grew pinched.

After cleaning up the kitchen, everyone except Lillian played gin rummy until the younger kids began to yawn.

"Off to bed with you two," Kath told Danny and Lilly. "It's already past your bedtime."

Kat offered to take them up to bed, and Graham wandered off to the living room to read a book.

"Finally," Kath said, grabbing Grant's hand and pulling him out to the front porch. They sat on the padded wicker sofa and enjoyed the cool breeze coming in through the screened windows.

Grant moved closer to Kath and kissed her deeply. She felt a wave of excitement run up her spine. "I'm going to miss you while I'm away," Grant said as he pulled away.

Kath sighed. "I wish I were going off to college this year. High school is so boring."

"My dad wants to make sure I'm not drafted to go overseas, at least for a while," Grant said. "I know it sounds unpatriotic, but I don't think I'm ready to be shot at yet."

"My parents are pushing me to go to Bryn Mawr out east after high school," Kath said. "It's not far from Harvard, I'm told."

"No, it's not. You could visit me, or I could come to see you there," Grant said hopefully.

"If you haven't found a new sophisticated girlfriend by then," Kath said.

"Me? With a sophisticated girl? Nah." Grant grinned. "I like girls like you."

"Hey! Are you saying I'm not sophisticated?" Kath hit him on the shoulder.

"Not at all. You're the prettiest, most athletic, and lady-like girl I know."

She laughed. "That's definitely not true. I suppose that's why my parents want me to go to Bryn Mawr. So they can turn me into a lady. Ugh!"

"Well, a little refinement wouldn't hurt," Grant said,

chuckling. "But I do like you exactly as you are."

"I hope this horrible war ends soon, and you won't have to go overseas," Kath said, turning serious. "A few of the boys from high school went over right away and have died. It's terrible."

"Honestly. I hope I don't have to go either. But I'll go if I have to," Grant said. He leaned down and kissed her passionately. Coming up for air, he said. "What were your parents thinking letting you come here unchaperoned?"

This made her smile. "They know they can trust me. And that I'm able to fight you off with my bare hands if need be."

Grant leaned down and kissed her again. "Do you want to fight me off?"

"Hmm. Not quite yet," she said.

Later that night, long after Grant had left, Kath lay in bed thinking about him and her future. Kath knew to be careful with boys. Her parents were liberal but not *that* liberal. She wanted so much out of life and wasn't interested in being tied down with a husband and children immediately. She wanted to go to college, have a career, and travel the world. But someone as delicious as Grant was hard to resist.

Kath also worried about what she wanted to do with her life after high school. She still dreamed of acting and becoming a movie star. Her father used to scoff at her aspirations, so Kath had learned not to talk about them anymore. He was so proud of her grades and how intelligent she was that he wanted her to take business classes or study law.

"You could be one of the few female lawyers," Crandell told her. "You're bright enough and a good student. Wouldn't that be incredible?"

Kath always nodded politely, but she knew she didn't want to be a lawyer.

Her parents arrived the next day, her mother a bit disheveled from having the car's top down. All the kids were already outside, swimming and playing in the sand under Kath and Kat's watchful eyes. Graham had run down toward the homes in the Movie Colony to visit a friend for the afternoon.

"Well, all seems to be well here," Catherine said as her husband carried in their bags.

Lillian had rushed up to the house the moment she saw her parents. "Kath drove too fast on the way here," she said, looking smugly at her older sister.

"Seems to me you are all alive and well," Crandell said, smiling. "No need to worry."

Lillian pursed her lips and ran back outside while Kath laughed.

Crandell soon joined the children on the beach, and Grant dropped by and joined in on all the fun. They had swimming races and played an aggressive game of volleyball. Graham returned and joined in. As usual, their mother kept watch from the front porch with iced tea and a good book.

That evening, after dinner and after Grant had left, Kath helped her mother clean up in the kitchen. Kat was folding beach towels she'd washed earlier that day in their brand-new washing machine and had hung outside to dry.

"Grant is a nice young man," Catherine said while she wiped down the counters. "I hope you two are being very careful."

"Mom!" Kath said, heat rising to her cheeks.

Her mother chuckled. "Don't be silly, Kath. I know you two have become serious this summer. I just want you to make good choices."

"I am making good choices," Kath said. "I'd never do anything to ruin my future."

"Well, according to a certain little blond girl I know, you and Grant were out on the front porch smooching late last night." Catherine grinned at her daughter.

"Oh, that nosey little twerp," Kath said, irritated. "It was just some innocent kissing, nothing more."

Kat giggled behind them as she folded the towels.

"Don't you start on me now," Kath fumed at her sister.

Catherine sat at the small kitchen table and motioned for Kath to do likewise. "Sweetie, I'm just teasing you. But I do want you to be careful. I'd love to see you have a wonderful last year of high school and then go off to college. Girls today have so many choices compared to my day. Don't get involved with a man too soon."

Kath nodded. "I know, Mom. Grant is leaving next week for Harvard, so I won't see him for months—if ever. He'll probably fall in love with a Radcliffe girl. Or worse, a debutante."

Catherine raised her brows. "I was a debutante."

"Sorry, Mom. I didn't mean anything by that. I'm just glad we don't follow those old-fashioned standards out here anymore."

"I would love to be a debutant," Kat said, her eyes shining. She danced around the kitchen with a towel raised high. "All those dances and soirees. They're so romantic."

Kath and her mother laughed. "Yes, I could see you as a deb," Kath said. "Frilly dresses and fancy hairdos would suit you. Give me a good game of beach football or volleyball any day instead."

Catherine reached over and patted her daughter's hand. "Just be careful. That's all I ask. I'd love to see you go to Bryn Mawr next year and flourish. I do hope you are still considering going there."

Kath studied her mother and realized she now had to live her life through her daughters. Even though Catherine had been involved in many causes to promote better lives for women, she still lived a very conventional existence, being married and raising children. Kath wanted to make her mother proud.

"Yes. I think I'd like to go there," Kath lied to her mother. And honestly, she thought to herself, did it matter where she went to college?

"I'm happy to hear that," Catherine said, smiling. "And your father will be pleased too."

Later, Kath and Kat were up in Kath's room, sitting on the bed, looking through all her old movie magazines.

"Why did you tell Mom you wanted to go to Bryn Mawr?" Kat asked. "You've said many times you didn't want to go there."

Kath shrugged. "It will make Mama happy. She's worked so hard all her life trying to push women forward. If she thinks Bryn Mawr is the best place for me, then I'll go."

Kat stared at her sister for a moment, her head cocked.

"What?" Kath asked, annoyed.

"I've never known you to give in to anyone, not even Mama or Papa. I'm just surprised," Kat said.

"Well, I'm full of surprises," Kath said dramatically, making her sister laugh. Then she smiled. "Bryn Mawr has a drama department. I thought I could study English and Literature and add drama in as well."

"Ah. Now I understand," Kat said. "And isn't Harvard just a short distance from Bryn Mawr?"

Kath grinned. "Why yes, little sister. It is." Both girls giggled as they continued looking over the glamorous lives of movie stars.

Chapter Five

TODAY

Kath took her seat on set on Monday morning, glancing around the fake living room. It really was a boring room. There was nothing in it to give it character, like photos or treasures from a life well-lived. It would have been more personal to have filmed this documentary in the living room at the beach house, but Kath had nixed that idea. That would be too personal.

Carolyn walked over with a mug of tea for her aunt and placed it on the small end table beside the chair. "If you want a cigarette, you'll have to be quick about it," she told her.

"I had my morning cigarette earlier," Kath said. "As you well know. Are you testing me?"

Carolyn chuckled. "Why, I'd never do that," she said innocently, then hurried out of the frame.

Kath smiled to herself as she thought how very much Carolyn was like her.

"Well, good morning, Miss Carver," Roger Connally said with a large grin. He set a tall stainless-steel mug of coffee on his end table. "I hope you had a restful weekend."

Today, Mr. Slick wore a navy suit with a pink and navy striped tie. Kath stared at the tie, wondering what her beloved Gordon would have thought of it. He would never have even thought to wear a pink tie.

"I had a restful weekend, as I always do when I'm at the beach," Kath said.

"Wonderful," Roger said. He stood while the hairdresser fussed with his greased-down hair, and the make-up woman took the shine off his forehead. Finally, he sat. "I had an excellent interview with your niece on Saturday. You'll be happy to know she didn't give up any family secrets."

Kath raised one perfectly tweezed gray eyebrow. "If they are secrets, then how do you know she didn't give any up?"

"Hm? Oh, yes," he said, looking a little embarrassed. "I was only joking." Roger cleared his throat. "I'm looking forward to interviewing your younger brother Daniel. I hear he's quite a character."

"Humph," Kath said. "Are we ready to begin?"

"Of course." Roger pulled note cards out of his pocket and shuffled through them. Kath couldn't understand why since he had a prompter telling him what to say.

"Are we ready?" he asked the crew. They mumbled and moved around, then a man behind a camera motioned and counted down with his fingers—3, 2, 1.

Roger smiled into the camera. "Miss Carver. We covered your childhood, so let's move on to your college years. You went east for school, didn't you? To Bryn Mawr. How did you enjoy your years there?"

"I loved my college years," she said smoothly. "It was my first time away from home, and going to school with so many wonderful young ladies was exciting."

"What did you major in?" Roger asked.

"Well, as I said in my book," she said pointedly. "I majored in English and Literature, which included several creative writing courses. Although I'd always wanted to be an actress, I also thought I might enjoy journalism." Kath chuckled. "You know—a sort of Lois Lane-type character running about writing newspaper articles about crime."

"Oh yes. I could see that. I suppose many young women wanted to be like Lois Lane in your day," Roger said conspiratorially.

"I'm not sure about that, but I always loved to dramatize my life, so that's how I saw myself," Kath said. "Thus, drama also became an interest."

"And Bryn Mawr is where you became interested in acting?" Roger asked.

Kath wanted to roll her eyes. Hadn't she already explained this? "I was always interested in acting, even though my father was against it. He worked around actors at Warner Brothers and didn't have a high opinion about them. But yes, Bryn Mawr offered a drama course, and I jumped at the chance to be included. I had to audition and, luckily, was accepted."

"How did your father feel about that?" Roger asked.

"He thought it was a waste of my time but also felt it might be a way to get it out of my system. He was just happy I was in school and working toward a degree," Kath said.

"Do you remember what plays you were in?" Roger asked.

Kath glared at him. Of course, she remembered the plays she was in. It was her first chance to act, and she was thrilled. Did he think she was dotty and didn't remember those years?

"Yes, I remember them well," she said but didn't elaborate. *You should have read the book!* she thought.

Roger cleared his throat again and took a sip of coffee. "There was one play that was especially important to you in your second year of college. Would you like to tell us about it?"

Good, she thought. *He's finally doing his job.* "Yes. I was delighted to land the role of Jo in *Little Women.* I had adored the movie when Katharine Hepburn played that role, and I was honored to do it myself. It was that role that changed my life."

SPRING 1946

"I loathe Bryn Mawr," Kath complained to her friend, Jane Audrey, for the thousandth time. It was their second year of school, and Kath and Jane were walking, actually running, to their science class.

"You say that every day, Kath. Give it up," Jane said, laughing. The two met on their first day at the college, bumping into each other in the residence hall dining room. Jane was shorter than Kath but slender, and her brown hair was cut in a short bob style. She wore trousers like Kath did, and the two bonded immediately.

"I swear. If it wasn't for the drama classes, I couldn't stay here. It's suffocating. The rules, the curfews, the limited classes. I feel like I'm in prison."

"Yes. A very high-brow prison," Jane said. They'd reached their classroom only to find the teacher hadn't returned yet from his lunch. "You're only upset today because you learned that your crush, Grant, has found himself a Radcliffe debutante and is madly in love."

Kath grimaced. "I knew that would happen. His father is new money in Hollywood and his family would want him to marry well so they'd be better imbedded in society. It's all so stupid, these old-fashioned ideas. But I don't need a man. I'll make my own money."

"Well, you need your father's money until you can make your own," Jane reminded her.

"Pish!"

The teacher arrived and let them into the classroom.

"At least you got the best part in the production of *Little Women*," Jane whispered. "Everyone wanted to be Jo, and you got her. Aren't you lucky I get to play Laurie to your Jo?" She giggled.

Kath rolled her eyes. "These all-girl plays are silly too. But yes, you'll make a great Laurie, and I'm thrilled to play Jo. I've loved that part since I was a child."

"That's because you are Jo," Jane teased. "An outspoken tomboy."

This made Kath smile. "So true."

Kath was ecstatic to have been chosen for Jo's part. And rehearsals had gone well, giving her confidence she was growing as an actress. When she'd first started drama class, the elderly woman teacher had constantly picked at her about her voice, her movements, pretty much everything. "Speak up, Miss Carver," the teacher would yell. "Speak from your diaphragm, not your throat. Why do you sound like a cat bellowing?" It went on and on. But Kath had worked hard to do as she was told, and now she'd earned the most coveted part in the play.

As opening night drew near, Kath wished her parents could come out east to see her in the play. She believed that if her father saw her acting, he'd understand how important it was to her. But a long train ride across the country wasn't going to happen, especially when her younger brother and sisters were still at home.

On opening night, flowers arrived for Kath backstage. "Good luck, my darling," the card read. "Love, Mom and Dad." It wasn't the same as having them there, but it lifted her spirits that they'd thought of her that night.

"Ready?" Jane asked, dressed in a suit and wearing a wig to look like a boy.

"As ready as I'll ever be," Kath said, hugging her friend. She wore a long dress and a dark wig. Her hair was too short now to play Jo for the first half of the play. She'd change into another wig after Jo revealed she'd cut off her hair and sold it.

Kath peered out the curtain and was shocked to see that every seat was taken and people were standing in the back as well. Word had spread around the campus that this would be the best play of the year, and everyone came. At that moment, her heart pounded in her chest. She'd never experienced stage fright in the past because the theater had never filled up like this before. Her stomach rolled and lurched, and she ran as fast as possible to the bathroom and lost her lunch.

"Kath? Are you all right?" Jane asked, pounding on the bathroom door. The rest of the cast came over to see what all the commotion was. They'd all seen Kath race to the bathroom.

Kath came out a moment later, patting her face with a wet paper towel. "I'm fine," she said, as if nothing had happened.

Jane looked at her like she didn't believe her, but they all went to their designated spots to prepare for the opening scene.

The play went well—extraordinarily well—and Kath was proud of her performance. The entire ensemble had done an excellent job and the audience clapped with glee at the end.

"We did it!" Kath exclaimed to Jane after their last curtain call. "You were wonderful! Everyone was. And I felt like I was really Jo, and everything was real."

Jane was all smiles. "You were definitely the star. You did shine up there."

Kath didn't want to sound obnoxious and agree, but secretly, she did. This was her best performance ever, and she realized that. "All I had to do was lose my lunch, and then everything was good," she said, laughing.

As the actors changed and took off their heavy make-up, a portly gentleman came backstage asking for Kath.

"I'm Kathleen Carver," she said, quickly pulling on a robe.

"Ah, yes. It's so good to meet you," the man said. He was balding and had combed his hair over as men did. His dark suit was a bit wrinkled but looked expensive. "I'm Oliver Kramer," he said, offering a pudgy hand to shake.

Kath shook his hand and forced herself not to wipe her own on her robe. The man's hand was sweaty. "Nice to meet you," she said.

"I always come to watch the last play of the year at Bryn Mawr, as well as the other area colleges," he explained. "You did an excellent job up on stage tonight. I was quite impressed."

"Thank you," Kath said as Jane came up behind her to see what the man wanted.

"I'm an agent in New York City, and I'd be interested in representing you when you finish school," Oliver said. He handed Kath his card. "I hope you'll come to see me if you decide to pursue acting as a career."

Kath stared at the card. An agent. She couldn't believe it. "Why, thank you, Mr. Kramer. I certainly will consider it."

The man smiled and nodded, then left.

Kath turned to Jane, and both girls screamed excitedly.

"What on earth is all this nonsense?" the drama teacher

asked, looking perturbed.

"So sorry," Kath said and pulled Jane into the room she'd been changing in. They jumped up and down like children, then calmed down. "An agent is interested in me," Kath said. "Imagine that."

"It's incredible," Jane agreed. "And you deserve it. Your performance was amazing."

Kath was all smiles when they left the building to eat a late dinner with the cast. An agent was actually interested in her. She could go to New York and become an actress. A real actress. Right then and there, Kath made up her mind.

Once school was finished that spring, Kath talked Jane into going to New York City with her and trying their hand at acting. Kath had a terrible argument with her father over the phone about her plan.

"I will not pay for you to live in New York and hustle yourself as an actress!" Crandell bellowed, furious that his daughter would even think of doing such a thing.

"But Papa," Kath said, nearly in tears. "An agent wants to represent me and send me on casting calls. It's all on the up and up. Please, let me try it this summer."

After much back and forth, Crandell finally agreed Kath could stay for a summer, but only after he'd checked out Oliver Kramer's reputation and Kath agreed to stay at the all-women's hotel, the Barbizon. "Three months!" Crandell said. "Then it's back to school with you if you've not found success in acting."

Kath knew she had to make those three months count.

Jane, who was from a middle-class family that could barely pay her Bryn Mawr tuition and lived in Ohio, found nothing wrong with her living with Kath in the city in an all-women's hotel. As long as she helped to pay her way, her family said yes.

The first day Kath and Jane walked into the lobby of the Barbizon, wearing their usual attire of a shirt and trousers, they were immediately told to change into dresses or leave. Kath was taken aback, but the two went into the ladies restroom and changed. No pants were allowed, ever.

"Well, this is going to cut my wardrobe in half," Kath complained to Jane as they were shown to their room.

The room was minuscular, even compared to the dormitory room they'd shared this past year. Two narrow twin beds with one nightstand between them, a high-boy dresser, a desk, and a dressing table were the only furniture in the room. There was a shared bathroom down the hall. None of that bothered Kath, though. She would do whatever she had to do to follow her dream.

The day after checking in, Kath and Jane went directly to Oliver Kramer's office and asked to see him.

"He gave me his card at my performance at Bryn Mawr," Kath said haughtily to the secretary guarding the door.

The older woman sniffed. "He gives out a hundred of those every spring. Sit down, and I'll ask if he'll see you."

All of Kath's bravado left her as she and Jane sat in the red-padded chairs. The office was small, and the furniture wasn't new. Maybe Oliver Kramer was a hack.

"Don't worry," Jane said, as if reading Kath's mind. "He's been in business a long time and is too busy to worry about how his office looks.

"Well, that's one way to look at it," Kath said.

"Mr. Kramer will see you now," the secretary said.

Kath and Jane stood, both taking a breath for courage and walked through the door.

"Well, well," Oliver Kramer said, standing behind his

cluttered wooden desk. "I hadn't thought I'd see you so soon, but I'm happy you're here. Please, sit down."

"So, you remember me?" Kath asked, encouraged by his greeting. She sat in one of the two chairs facing his desk.

"Of course," he said, sitting also. "You played Jo in *Little Women*. It was a wonderful performance. And I believe this young woman with you played Laurie, right? I didn't catch your name."

"Jane Audrey," Jane said, looking flushed. "I'm just here for moral support."

Oliver laughed. "You mean you aren't looking to become an actress too? I could certainly find work for you."

Jane looked over at Kath, who wasn't particularly happy to have the attention taken away from her. But Jane was her good friend.

"It would be wonderful if Jane wants to pursue acting too," Kath said, smiling at her friend.

"Good." Oliver grabbed a sheet of paper and handed it to Kath. "Write down your names, addresses, and phone numbers. When I find auditions for you to go on, then I'll call you."

Kath wrote down her name, address, and the phone number for the hotel, and Jane did the same.

"Are there any auditions we can go on today or tomorrow?" Kath asked hopefully.

"Hm. You're a go-getter, that's for sure." Oliver dug around his desk and found another sheet of paper. He wrote down two addresses and handed them to Kath. "If you need work just to pay the rent, this department store is always looking for models to show off their designer clothing. They pay you by the day. The other address is for a very off-Broadway play, but it's a good part. The auditions are tomorrow at two." He glanced at both women. "You should both try out because you never know who they'll hire."

"Thank you so much," Kath said, standing. Jane stood, too. "We'll do our best. Should we call you if we get the part?"

"Oh, yes. Definitely. Tell my secretary. And also make sure they know who sent you to the audition," Oliver said. "Good luck."

"Thank you," Kath said again, and the two women exited the office. They held in their excitement until they were out in the hallway.

"Our first audition!" Kath said, trying not to squeal. "We're on our way!"

Chapter Six

TODAY

"And how did that first audition go?" Roger asked Kath.

Kath had been reminiscing about her first days in New York City, and she was lost back in time for a moment.

"Hm? Oh, yes. That first audition was terrible. And so were the next several auditions. Starting out as an actress was much harder than I'd originally thought." She chuckled. "I was sure they'd see me as the great actress I was and want to sign me on immediately. But the truth was, Jane got a couple of small parts before I was hired for anything."

"Oh, that must have hurt," Roger said with an understanding grimace.

Kath shrugged. "It did at first, but then I realized my time would come eventually. So, to earn food money, I started modeling each day at one of the high-end designer clothing shops. I was tall, thin, and had an attitude. They liked me."

"I can only imagine," Roger said. "Were you able to prove to your father that being an actress was a lucrative career choice in that one summer?"

"Yes. The first two plays I was in started and ended in one night. Then, I was hired as the understudy for a semi-famous actress in a good play. It ran for several weeks and had promise to continue throughout the fall. Jane also had a tiny part in that same play. I just had to wait for my big break. Of course, that meant the star had to get sick or hurt so I could have my chance. But as luck would have it, the star tripped over her long dress after the late show, and the next day, it was my turn to shine."

FALL 1946

"I can hardly believe she tripped on her dress," Kath said to Jane as they walked to the Barbizon after the late-night show. Even though their curfew was ten o'clock, they were given special permission since they worked in the theater.

"Yes, it was quite unexpected," Jane said, looking sideways at Kath and grinning.

Kath stopped walking and stared at Jane. "What does that mean?"

Jane smiled.

"You? How could you have tripped her? You weren't anywhere near her."

"Let's just say her dress hem fell out halfway through the show. Such shoddy sewing, wouldn't you say?" Jane said.

Kath laughed out loud. "You little conniver! I hope she isn't too hurt. That would be bad karma for me."

"Mostly for me," Jane said. "You didn't do anything. And besides. She still should have been able to walk in that dress despite the hem falling out. How clumsy is she?"

Kath shook her head and laughed again. She'd thought of a

million ways to get the lead actress to miss a performance, but she never would have acted on any of them. How lucky she had a friend with less scruples than her.

"I'm sure she only pulled a muscle or something," Jane said as they continued walking in the warm New York night. "So, you'd better make your chance count. Act the hell out of that play. Show everyone what you're made of."

"I'll try," Kath said, beginning to feel nervous. "That's the best I can promise."

The next evening, Kath prepared to go onstage. She made sure the hem of the dress was sewn up correctly, and the shoes fit perfectly. The last thing she needed was to fall on her face. Five minutes before the curtain went up, she rushed past the cast to the ladies' room and lost everything in her stomach.

"Are you ready now?" Jane asked her friend as she emerged from the bathroom.

Kath nodded. "I guess tossing my cookies is starting to be a routine for me."

"You'll be great. Go get ready." Jane left to wait for her walk-on part.

Kath took a deep breath, straightened her shoulders, and walked onto the stage as if she'd done it a hundred times before. She spoke clearly and moved smoothly, all the things her drama teacher had taught her. The audience laughed at the funny parts and gasped at the big reveal. When the curtain came down, the applause was more thunderous than it had been on previous nights.

"They loved you!" Jane said, coming across the stage to hug her friend. "Get back out there for a second bow. The audience wants you."

The entire cast walked out and bowed as the clapping

continued. Kath felt like she was floating on air as the curtain closed for the last time.

"You did amazing," her on-stage husband said. "Bravo!"

"You were incredible," the actress who played her mother told her.

The entire cast praised Kath for her excellent acting. Even the director told her it was the best acting he'd seen in years.

The next day, Kath and Jane were awakened by a pounding on their door. Grumpily, Kath pulled open the door. "What?"

The young woman—one of the Power's Agency models—looked startled at Kath's anger. "There's a phone call for you," the girl said, then walked away haughtily.

Kath headed to the phone in the hallway dressed in only a long shirt. "Yes. This is Kathleen Carver," she said brusquely.

"Kath. It's Oliver. You sure aren't a morning person, are you." The older man laughed.

"Oh. Mr. Kramer. What can I do for you?" she asked, shocked to hear him calling her.

"It's what I can do for you," he said cheerfully. "The director of the play you're in just contacted me with a new contract for you. He'd like you to star in the play. Did you hear that? Star!"

"Oh, my goodness," was all Kath could manage. "What about the other woman?"

"She's history. The director had never seen the audience respond to her as magnificently as they did to you. You're in, she's out. Congratulations! Come to my office later today and look over the contract. You'll make three times the money, and hopefully, the play will go on for a while."

"Thanks, Mr. Kramer," Kath said before hanging up. She stood there a moment, staring at the flowery wallpaper. She was going to be a star. Amazing. "Jane!" she yelled, running back to her room. "Jane! I'm going to be a star!"

The next few weeks proved that Kath had the potential to pursue a career as an actress. Her father wasn't one hundred percent convinced, but he had to admit that her securing the leading role was a good sign. He agreed to her not returning to Bryn Mawr that year and paying her rent for one more year until she got on solid footing.

For Kath, it was a great win. She was heading toward the future she wanted, and she couldn't wait to see where it led her.

The play ran until the winter, then slowly fizzled out. But by then, she'd had a few positive reviews under her belt, and when a lead in a comedy production came up, she auditioned and got it. Jane was thrilled for her and was getting tiny parts here and there for herself. Kath knew Jane was just having fun, but for Kath, this was all serious business. She wanted it as a career while Jane was just passing the time.

The new play was funny and smart, and they rehearsed for several weeks. The man playing opposite Kath was Randall Cooper—a twenty-five-year-old Harvard graduate with wavy dark hair and gorgeous blue eyes. He was tall, which was good since Kath was tall for a woman. He was also athletic. It wasn't long before Kath fell head over heels for Randall.

"Shall we grab a drink after rehearsal?" he asked her one night in his smooth, deep voice, and Kath couldn't say no.

"It's so nice to work with a professional actress," Randall said after they sat in the lounge of an upscale hotel. "I've worked with so many women who only get parts because they have large breasts or sleep with the producer."

Kath laughed. "And we both know neither of those things applies to me."

Randall chuckled. "I didn't mean it that way. You're a beautiful woman and a hell of an actress."

"Thank you," she said, feeling a blush creeping up to her face. Randall was much too handsome for his own good.

"So, some of the girls in the play say you're living at the Barbizon with a girlfriend," Randall said. "Is she a girlfriend or a *girlfriend?*"

Kath frowned. What on earth did he mean? Then it hit her, and she laughed out loud. "Oh, my goodness! We're friends, not lovers," Kath said. "We went to Bryn Mawr together and came to New York to try our luck. I can't believe people are spreading that rumor."

Randall laughed along and shrugged. "Everything goes in the theater world, so one never knows."

Randall and Kath became the talk of the town soon after that, as they went everywhere together when they weren't working. Soon, photographers were waiting outside his apartment building to catch a photo of Kath entering and leaving. The matron at the Barbizon was livid the first night Kath returned way past the time her play was over.

"If you continue this behavior, you'll be asked to leave," the tight-lipped matron told her. Of course, Kath didn't care what the woman thought.

"We're being kicked out," Jane told Kath one morning when she returned to their room after spending the night at Randall's place. "I just got the notice." Jane was nearly hysterical. "Where will we stay?"

"We'll find a small apartment," Kath said, waving her hand through the air as if it were no big deal. "I'm making more money now, and you're working too."

"Then you'd better find something soon because we have to

be out at the end of the week," Jane said.

Kath called Oliver and asked if he knew of any apartments she and Jane could afford to rent. "The Barbizon has become stifling."

"That may be," Oliver replied. "But you won't find a place that nice for that cheap. I'll see what I can find." What he found was an old brownstone several blocks in the wrong direction and very far from the theater where Kath worked. "It's the best you can do. You need money for food, too, you know."

Jane and Kath moved in the next week. It was as small as the Barbizon's room, except they had their own bathroom, although everything was old and dirty. The bed was so ratty Kath had the building's janitor take it out to the trash and she bought two twin beds for her and Jane.

"No bedbugs for us," Kath said, chuckling, but Jane didn't find any of this humorous.

"We were living in a safe, clean place before. This is horrendous."

"I'm sorry," Kath told her friend. "But we have our freedom, and that's all that matters, right?"

Jane shrugged.

Not long after their move, Kath's play closed. Randall moved on to another play and another girl. Kath didn't mind losing Randall—after all, they were just having fun—but she needed to work. She had to beg her father for a loan to keep the apartment. "I'm sure I'll find another play soon, Papa," she told him.

"I hope so," Crandell said sternly.

Kath hit the pavement and auditioned for every part available. Big or small, it didn't matter. She needed money. She also modeled for designers and even ended up in a couple of fashion advertisements in Harper's Bazaar and Mademoiselle magazines. Her look was different from most women of her day—her body was long and lean, not curvy. But she looked elegant and sophisticated in anything they put on her.

Kath was almost ready to give up when she auditioned for the lead in a drama cat-and-mouse-style play. After her audition, the director came up on stage and asked her, "Aren't you the woman from the advertisement in Harper's Bazaar?"

"Why, yes, I am," Kath said, hoping being a model wouldn't be a mark against her. Many of the theater people believed models were brainless.

"I've heard good things about you from previous directors. I'll be in touch," he said.

Two days later, when Kath called Oliver's office, he told her she got the part. "This is a good break for you. I hope you work hard on this play," Oliver said.

Kath was ecstatic. "I will. I want to get out of that rat-trap apartment. I'll work my butt off!"

Kath played her heart out in the murder mystery play, and the audience loved it. Critics praised her acting abilities and called her a breath of fresh air in the theater world. Her name was on the marquee, and her picture was in the paper often. Kath was on her way to being the celebrated actress she had always craved being.

Kath and Jane rented a better apartment with a doorman—it wasn't the Ritz, but it was nice and in a safe neighborhood. Jane had gotten a few bigger roles in plays, too, and was contributing to the rent. The women from Bryn Mawr were on their way.

In the spring of 1948, a man wearing an expensive-looking striped suit came backstage after the evening showing to see Kath.

"What can I do for you?" Kath asked. She was still in costume and had made sure to leave her dressing room door open so tongues wouldn't wag.

"My name is Jeremy Holt," the man said. He had a round, kind face, and a sincere smile. He handed Kath his card. "I scout out actors for MGM."

Kath's heart pumped faster. "Really? Are you scouting me?"

Jeremy laughed. "Why yes, in fact, I am. Would you be interested in going to California and doing a screen test? Mayer is looking for fresh faces and new talent, and I think he'd be interested in you."

Interested? I'd be crazy not to be interested, Kath thought. "Yes. I'd be very interested. But I'm in the middle of a play, and I can't leave them high and dry."

"We'll pay your train fare there and back along with a traveling companion. It's important that you go soon, though. Wouldn't a chance to do pictures be worth leaving a small play like this?" Jeremy asked.

Small? Kath hadn't thought of her play as being small. But maybe he was right. It might be her only chance. Kath agreed to go out west the following week. When she told her director, he was upset but understood.

"Hollywood is the dream, isn't it?" he asked. "Your understudy will be thrilled to get a chance to play the part."

That night, Kath went home and told Jane her news. "Any chance you want to go to Hollywood with me next week?"

"Is that even a question?" Jane asked. "Of course, I want to go."

The next week, the two women boarded the train and Kath headed back home with great hopes of beginning a career in films.

Chapter Seven

TODAY

After a long day of talking about herself, Kath rode home with Carolyn to her little home tucked away in the hills of Bel Air. As they pulled up the long, private driveway, Kath sighed.

"It isn't the beach, but at least it's home," Kath declared.

"It's not too shabby of a neighborhood, either," Carolyn said with a grin.

The house was once a guest house on a larger property belonging to Kath's good friend and favorite director, Scott Coolidge. He'd had a large home, an outdoor and indoor pool, and two guest houses on nine acres. He'd been her very first director and had offered Kath the guest house when she'd been looking for a place to rent.

"As long as I don't have to sleep with you to rent it," Kath had joked.

"Sweetie, I'm afraid you're not my type," Scott had said with a grin, and from that moment on, they became great friends.

Kath entered the home through the side door that went into the kitchen. It was small and was still styled in the black and white check from the 1940s. The counters were white tile, and the sink was porcelain. Painted white cabinets sat under the tiled countertops. An old-fashioned Formica and chrome table sat in the middle with black padded chairs. It was a room that took you back to another era, and it reminded Kath of all the good times she'd had in this cottage.

The home had three bedrooms and three bathrooms, along with a kitchen and living room. Carolyn ran upstairs to put her purse away in her own bedroom while Kath went to sit in the living room. On her way to the sofa, she passed Gordon's corner—his favorite spot in the house for twenty years. There was an old gold-colored chair there with a tall light hanging over it and an end table that held his beloved paperbacks. Gordon had been a voracious reader, and after he'd died, Kath had kept his corner and books just as he'd left them.

"I can't stand the thought of returning to that studio for two more days," Kath told Carolyn as her niece brought her a glass of iced tea. "You know how much I hate talking about myself."

Carolyn sat on the small sofa and sipped her tea. "Yes, I do. You hate talking at all. But it will be over soon."

"Danny will be there this afternoon," Kath said, her face pinched. "I dread what he'll tell Mr. Slick. Tomorrow, I'll have to unravel everything Danny said."

"It might not be that bad," Carolyn told her. "He knows what not to talk about."

"Which will be the exact things he'll talk about," Kath said. "Some things should just be put to rest."

"Everyone's gone now, Aunt Kath. What are you afraid of?" Carolyn asked.

"Just because they're gone doesn't mean their lives should

be upended and talked about," Kath said. "We kept secrets in those days for a reason. Why upset their families with new revelations now?"

"Would any of them be that surprised?" Carolyn asked. "Maybe the secrets weren't so secret after all."

Kath studied Carolyn. Did she know all the secrets? Or even suspect them? "Still. I don't want to be the one to share everyone's dirty laundry. They were my friends."

Her niece nodded. "I'll be in my room if you need me," she said, then left the room.

Kath stood and walked into the kitchen and outside onto the small patio deck. From here, she used to have a view of Scotty's pool and house. There'd been crazy parties almost every Sunday, and many men who came and went. Would Scotty want her to tell those secrets? He'd spent his entire life hiding his sexuality. Who was she to tell?

The most recent owner of the property had torn down Scotty's house—a beautiful Spanish-style mansion with a red tile roof, arched entryways, and gorgeous red-tile patios near the pool. There had been arched doorways inside the house and that old plaster on the walls that gave the house character. Now, there stood a mansion made of glass where you could see every movement of the owners at night when the lights were on. Who wanted to live in a glass house? These people carried just as many secrets as the past owner—they only pretended to be transparent. Everyone had secrets.

Walking back inside, Kath made her way past Gordon's chair, patted the back of it, and headed for the staircase. Turning, she said, "We had our secrets, didn't we, Gordon old boy?" Then, she slowly made her way up to her bedroom.

* * *

The next day Kath was dressed in her usual trousers and flats and wore a blue cashmere sweater set. Kath couldn't remember the last time she'd bought new clothes. She really didn't need them. She loved her old clothes because they were comfortable and familiar. And she was never one to care about style anyway. She'd worn the necessary evening gowns and dresses in her day but had always gone back to her trousers after work.

Now, she sat again across from Mr. Slick. Kath had a mug of water by her side as she waited impatiently to get started. She would have loved to have a cigarette, but she'd already had her morning smoke earlier. It would have been fun, though, to piss off the man-boy again.

"All ready, Miss Carver?" Roger asked as he sat in the seat across from her.

"Yes. Let's begin," she said tartly.

He smiled. "Your brother was a fun person to talk to yesterday. We got a lot of entertaining footage from him."

Kath narrowed her eyes. "Such as?"

"Oh, that will be a surprise," Roger said, winking.

Kath wanted to knock that grin off his face.

"We're ready in 3-2-1," the stage manager said, then pointed to Roger to begin.

"So, in the summer of 1948, you returned to California for a film test with MGM Studios," Roger said smoothly. "That must have been exciting. And your friend, Jane Audrey, accompanied you. How did it go?"

Kath relaxed her face even though she wanted to glare at Mr. Slick. "It all went fine. I did a scene from the play I'd recently left, and they liked me. They also allowed Jane to do a screen test, too. It was all quite exciting."

"And they hired you?" Roger asked.

"Oh, yes. They hired me," Kath said, remembering that day well.

1940

"Mr. Mayer will see you now," his secretary said to both Kath and Jane. The two women looked at each other and then stood. It felt like they'd been told they could see the King of England.

When they entered the inner sanctum of Louie B. Mayer's office, Kath let out a long breath. Standing behind the enormous desk was a short, chubby man whose vest on his expensive suit strained not to pop a button. He smiled and motioned for the two women to sit down. At that moment, Kath thought she couldn't be afraid of this grandfatherly-looking man.

"I'm so happy to meet you both," Mr. Mayer said. "Who knew when I asked for one girl, I'd get two?" he chuckled.

"It's very nice to meet you, sir," Kath said, taking the lead. "I'm Kathleen Carver, and this is Jane Audrey. We're thrilled to be here."

Mr. Mayer nodded. "Yes. Well, I saw your screen tests and you both show quite well on film. I know my scout sent only you, Miss Carver, but I'm interested in hiring you both."

Kath smiled, and Jane did, also. They couldn't believe their luck.

"So, tell me," Mr. Mayer asked. "How do you two know each other?"

"We went to Bryn Mawr together," Kath offered. "We were both in the theater program there. After I was recruited by an agent, we both moved to New York City to pursue acting."

"I see." Mr. Mayer studied them for a moment. "Well, what you do in your personal life is no business of mine but make sure I never hear any rumors, understand? My secretary will have you sign contracts out at her desk. I hope you'll both be happy here at Metro." He stood, and the two women understood that was their cue to leave.

"Thank you, Mr. Mayer," Kath and Jane both said, then exited the room.

As the women waited for the secretary to pull out the contracts, they stared at each other.

"What did he mean about our personal lives being our own business?" Kath whispered to Jane.

Jane grinned. "I think he thought we were a couple."

Kath's eyes widened, and it was all she could do not to laugh out loud.

Later, back at Kath's parents' Toluca Lake home, she watched her father's eyes widen when he looked over her contract with MGM.

"Five hundred dollars a week to act?" he asked.

"Isn't that good?" Kath asked him. She knew her father made up contracts for actors at Warner Brothers and was afraid she'd been cheated.

"Good? That's wonderful, considering they didn't hire you for a particular film," Crandell said. "And for two years. I'm impressed."

"They can break the contract at any time, though," Kath said. "Let's hope they put me to work immediately so I can prove I'm worth every cent." Kath knew that Jane's contract was for two hundred and fifty dollars a week and felt lucky hers was twice that amount. But Jane hadn't minded.

"It's not bad considering I never planned on becoming an actress," Jane had said.

The two women shared Kath's old room on the top floor of the house until they could find an apartment of their own. That meant Kath could catch up with her siblings, who she hadn't seen in four years. Although, Kat, now twenty, was living at the beach house and working at a dress shop in the little Malibu town.

"Why didn't Kat go to Bryn Mawr?" Kath asked her mother as the two women set the table for dinner. "And why is she living at the beach house?"

Catherine carefully folded the cloth napkins and placed them around the table. "Katrina wasn't interested in an education out east, so we didn't push it on her. And she has a beau at the beach. So, she lives there and rides her bike back and forth to her job."

Kath frowned. "I didn't want to go out east, but you and father made me."

"It worked out well for you, didn't it?" Her mother smiled. "Your father and I knew you wouldn't be happy with a quiet job or getting married right away. And we were right, weren't we?"

"Yes, you were," Kath said grudgingly. "I just can't believe that's all Kat wants. There is so much out there for women to choose."

"Yes, there is. But that's the point—it's her choice. We are all about women choosing their own path," Catherine said.

Kath couldn't argue with that.

Mrs. Cray still worked for the Carvers, and Kath helped her in the kitchen. Kath loved learning to cook and Mrs. Cray was the best to learn from.

That night, as the entire family sat down at the large table to eat, Lillian, now seventeen, spoke up. "Did anyone tell Kath who Kat is dating?" Lillian was still very cute with long blond hair and large blue eyes, but she was also still a little brat.

"Lilly," her mother said, staring daggers at her. "Let's not worry about that right now."

Graham laughed.

Kath looked around the table, frowning. "What's the matter? Who is Kat dating?"

Crandell and Catherine exchanged looks while Lilly grinned mischievously.

"She's been seeing Grant Kirby since last summer," Lilly blurted out.

Kath couldn't believe her ears. "My Grant?"

"Well, dear," Catherine said calmly. "He's not really your Grant anymore. You two broke it off when he left for Harvard."

Kath thought for a moment. "Wait. I thought he married a Radcliffe debutante. They were engaged the last I heard."

"He was engaged," Crandell said. "But they broke it off. Now he's here, working at an office job at Paramount Studios. His father got it for him."

Kath was about to protest more, then stopped. Her mother was right—Grant wasn't her boyfriend anymore. Still, it bothered her, but she wasn't going to give Lilly the satisfaction of seeing that it bothered her.

The summer weeks went by and on one Friday, Kath was given a script to study. "Be ready for rehearsals on Monday," she was told by the young man handing out the scripts.

"Which part?" Kath asked. She figured it was a tiny part she'd barely have to study for.

The young man looked at the clipboard he was carrying.

"The lead," he said, then left.

Stunned, Kath looked at the top sheet of the script. The title was *Grab a Good Woman,* and it was a comedy. The director was Scott Coolidge and she was playing opposite another unknown by the name of Rock Hudson.

That weekend, she and Jane borrowed her father's car and went to the beach house for some peace and quiet so she could study the script. When she arrived Friday night, Kat was there cooking dinner for Grant.

"Well, don't you two look cozy?" Kath said, glancing between Kat and Grant. "I hear you two are an item."

Kat jumped up and gave Kath a hug. "I'm so happy to see you! Are you staying the weekend? We have so much to catch up on."

Kath was taken aback by how happy Kat was to see her. Maybe she was being petty about her sister dating Grant. Kat was much shorter than Kath and curvier, and she looked beautiful and so grown up since she'd last seen her. "I'm glad to see you, too," Kath said. "This is Jane Audrey. I've written you about her when I was at school."

"Oh, yes. Jane. It's wonderful to meet you," Kat said, offering her hand. "I'm so glad Kath has such a good friend to do everything with."

"It's nice to finally meet you, too," Jane said.

Grant stood and walked over to Kath, giving her a friendly hug. "It's great seeing you, Kath," he said. "I hear you're working at MGM now. That's amazing."

Kath pulled away and smiled. "Yes, I am. I was just handed a script today, so I thought I'd come out here and study it for the weekend. I hope we won't be in your way." She raised her brows.

Grant chuckled. "No. This is your family's home. I'll try to stay out of your way."

"What is the script about?" Kat asked excitedly. "I'd love to hear about it. Are you two hungry? I'm sure we have enough to share."

Kath looked at the kitchen table where they'd been sitting. Kat had made shrimp scampi and garlic bread, and it did look good. "Sure. If you have enough. Let's break out one of Dad's wine bottles, too. I'm home! Let's celebrate."

Kath and Jane went upstairs to put their suitcases away and change into more comfortable clothes—which for them were trousers and oversized sweaters. By the time they'd returned to the kitchen, Kat had reheated dinner, and Grant had opened a bottle of white wine. They'd moved the dinner into the formal dining room.

"This is really good," Kath told Kat after taking a bite of her dinner. "Where did you learn to cook?"

"I helped Mrs. Cray in the kitchen a lot after you left for school," Kat said. "I had no one to do things with anymore. Lilly was still young and annoying, and the boys were into their own things. It was like everything changed after you left. I'd never realized you were the one who came up with all the fun things to do."

Kath was surprised. "What about dad? He's the one who loves to keep busy. Didn't you all spend time here at the beach swimming and playing games?"

"Oh, yeah, we did." Kat glanced over at Grant and smiled. "We still had volleyball games and swimming contests. But it was never the same after you left."

Kath took a sip of wine and considered this. She supposed she had always been the leader of the group. But she'd never realized it before. She turned her attention to Grant. "What about you? You must have graduated from Harvard a year ago."

He nodded. "I did. I came back here and interned at the studio for the summer, and now I work in the office. It's an entry-level position, but at least I'm not starting in the mailroom." He chuckled.

Kath took another sip of wine, and the warmth coursing through her gave her courage. "What happened to your Radcliffe deb? I heard you were engaged."

Grant's eyes slid over to Kat, then back again. Kath had to admit Grant had become even more handsome over the past four years.

"We broke it off after a year," Grant said. "I guess I got caught up in all that high society stuff and lost my way for a while. She ended up marrying a distant Astor relative, so she didn't do too bad."

"How wonderful for her," Kath said, sipping her wine.

Later that evening, Kath took her new script out to the front porch to enjoy the cool breeze while studying it. Kat and Jane had both gone up to bed. As she studied the script, there was a knock on the screen door. Startled, she looked up and saw it was Grant.

"Come on in," she said. "I half expected to see you."

"Really? Why?" Grant sat in the chair opposite her.

"I was sure you'd want to explain yourself."

Grant let out a sigh. "I guess that is why I'm here. I didn't want you to be angry with your sister about me. She adores you, and I'd hate to come between you two."

"So, you decided to date my sister as a way to not come between us?" Kath said.

"In my defense, you and I hadn't seen each other in three

years by the time I started dating Kat," Grant said.

"That's because I learned you were engaged. Otherwise, I would have gone to see you at Harvard," Kath told him.

"Really? I figured you were done with me." Grant looked genuinely surprised.

"Well, I'm done with you now," she said tightly.

Grant placed his elbows on his knees and moved closer to Kath. "Please don't be upset. I didn't plan on falling in love with Kat—it just happened. Last summer, when I came home, I came to see your family and, as usual, was drafted into a volleyball game and swimming matches. The more time I spent with your family, the closer Kat and I grew. I'm absolutely in love with her."

"Is that supposed to make me feel better?" Kath asked.

"No, but I wanted to ensure you understood my intentions toward Kat. This isn't a fling—it's the real thing." Grant looked her in the eyes. "We've been talking about marriage."

"I see," Kath said. She was shocked to hear it, but then she still thought of her sister as the young girl she'd been when Kath left for college and not the woman she'd grown into. "Well, it's not up to me to stop you, is it? If you two are in love with each other, then there's nothing I can say."

Grant stood and slid his hands into his pants pockets. "I just wanted to make sure you understood. I thought I at least owed you that."

"You don't owe me anything, Grant. Marry Kat and be happy. All I ask is you treat her like the incredible woman she is," Kath told him.

Grant nodded. "I will."

After he left, Kath was no longer interested in her script. It was strange, having been away so long that everything had changed so drastically. But she also knew Grant was a good man, and he'd be a good husband for Kat.

With a sigh, she gave up on reading the script and headed off to bed.

CHAPTER EIGHT

1948

Filming *Grab a Good Woman* only took three weeks after two weeks of rehearsals. Kath didn't think it was the best movie ever made, but it was a cute romantic comedy. Rock Hudson, who'd told her to call him Roy, was a joy to work with. He was still unpolished and needed several takes to finish a scene, but he was always on time and sweet to her. They had a lot of fun on set and became close friends by the end. One of the extras, a pretty blonde going by the name of Marilyn Monroe, had also struck up a friendship with Kath. The girl was shy and endearing, and that came across on film. Kath liked her immediately, and the three had lunch together almost every day.

What Kath enjoyed the most about making the film was watching Scott Coolidge direct. He was sensitive to each of the actors' needs and was able to get the best performance out of each of them. She hoped she'd get to work with him again in the future.

Once the film wrapped and went into editing, the director invited everyone to his house for a big party. Rock told Kath that Scotty did that after every film, good or bad, and encouraged her to come.

"What does one wear to a Hollywood party?" Kath asked.

Rock laughed. "Wear a pretty evening dress, heels, and get fancy with your hair and make-up. There will be a lot of producers and directors there so you want them to see you at your best. It's a great opportunity to be seen."

Kath was excited to go and invited Jane to come along. They went to the designer dress section of Bullock's Department Store and bought the most expensive dresses each had ever owned. Jane's was a black dress with a fitted bodice and a full, black tulle skirt with a satin skirt underneath. It had rhinestone buttons all the way down the back. Kath went all out and bought a red satin dress with a draped neck and a slim skirt down to just below her knees. The back of the dress was open in a V-shape halfway down her back and came with a red satin wrap. They felt like kids playing dress-up and hoped they didn't look that way at the party.

Rock borrowed a studio car and picked up the women at the house. Kath had to beg her father not to make him come inside and introduce himself. "He's a sweet guy who'll look after us, I promise you," she told Crandell.

Crandell fussed, but Catherine reminded him that the girls were twenty-two and could make their own decisions. He did, however, stand outside the door and glare at Rock as he got out to open the car doors for the ladies.

"I wouldn't want to battle your dad, that's for sure," Rock said as they pulled away from the house. "He looks like he's in great shape."

Kath laughed. "My father would never fight you. But he would talk you into a game of basketball or volleyball and wipe the ground with you."

Rock was a tall, broadly built man, but he shuddered just the same.

He drove them into the Bel Air neighborhood and up the curvy road toward the top of the hills. He had to park the car a block away from the house because of all the other cars there and escorted the women up to Scott Coolidge's house.

Kath gasped when she saw the house after walking up the long driveway. It was tall, with several floors and had large windows that overlooked the Los Angeles skyline. The pool water sparkled from the underwater light, and twinkling lights had been strung around the entire patio. The downstairs windows were ablaze with lights, and a piano could be heard playing from inside.

"This place is beautiful," Kath said as they drew nearer.

"It is," Rock agreed. He pointed to the right of the house. "Way over there, he has two guest houses, but don't let the name fool you. They're as big as a regular home."

"So, you've been here before?" Kath asked.

Rock nodded. "My agent has invited me to several parties here." He grinned but didn't elaborate.

If Kath had thought the lights were bright inside, they certainly didn't outshine the many sparkling movie stars that filled Scott's living room. It was as if every MGM actor had come to the party. Judy Garland stood by the piano with a crystal glass in her hand, looking melancholy. Fred Astaire was leaning down, talking quietly to her. Cary Grant was playing bartender behind a long, wood-topped bar, pouring a fresh drink for Barbara Stanwyck, and Jack Lemmon was cozying up to the beautiful young starlet from their picture, Marilyn Monroe. The room was filled with famous celebrities and those looking for their big break.

"Welcome to Hollywood," Rock said, guiding the ladies inside. "I'll introduce you around."

Kath had never experienced anything like this before. All the beautiful dresses and well-dressed men, diamonds sparkling on necks, ears, and fingers, and everyone already a little too lit up with alcohol and who knew what else.

"Be careful not to drink too much," Kath told Jane. "I have a feeling things could go south pretty quickly if we aren't careful."

Jane agreed.

Kath wasn't much of a drinker, so she ate hors d'oeuvres instead that were brought around by waiters in black suits. She sipped a little wine here and there to look sociable. In the backyard, she heard Rock's deep voice above all the rest, laughing and teasing and having a good time. Men and women surrounded him—he was that handsome and appealing.

Kath tried to act calm, like she belonged in this throng of famous people, and didn't gush over Judy's singing voice or Fred Astaire's dancing. She casually said hello or nodded to those she passed as she mingled but her heart was doing flips with each celebrity face she encountered.

"Are you enjoying yourself?" Scott asked Kath. He wore a black tuxedo and looked quite handsome. Kath was used to seeing him in his shirt sleeves and slacks while he worked.

"Yes. Thank you for inviting me," she said. She and Scott had gotten along well while making the movie and she felt comfortable around him. "There are so many interesting people here."

Scott laughed. "Yes, and most of them think they're interesting," he whispered to her. "But it's fun to get everyone together once in a while. Hollywood is a small community when it all comes down to it. We all have to stick together."

Kath found that interesting. It felt like there were actors and actresses everywhere in Hollywood, but perhaps he was right. The big-name celebrities were a small group.

"Wait until Judy gets another couple of drinks in her," Scott said conspiratorially. "Then she'll have enough nerve to sing and entertain us."

It didn't take long for Scott's prediction to come true. When Judy belted out the new song from her latest picture, *Easter Parade*, all the party guests pushed their way into the room to listen. Then, she sang the old blues song, *The Man I Love,* and the emotion she evoked seemed to cut everyone to their core. Even sweet young Marilyn Monroe had tears in her eyes.

As the evening wore on and many of the people began to leave, Kath found Jane. "Ready to go? I don't want to be the last one here."

"I'm ready," Jane said. She glanced out to the patio by the pool. "But I think Rock is three sheets to the wind. Last I saw him, he was passed out in a chaise lounge chair by the pool."

Kath rolled her eyes as Jane led her to the passed-out hunk. There he was, lying dead to the world in the lounge chair. "I guess I'll be driving tonight," Kath said.

The two women pushed and nudged Rock, but he wouldn't wake up. Finally, two very strong men that Kath had seen as extras around the lot offered to help them get him to the car. Kath went to the car and pulled it up the driveway now that there was room. The two men unceremoniously dumped Rock into the back seat.

"See you two ladies on the lot," they said as they left.

"Hm. They were kind of hunky," Jane said as Kath circled

the large fountain in the middle of the driveway and headed back to the street.

"This town is full of hunks," Kath said. "It just depends on if they prefer women or men."

Jane laughed. "Sometimes it's hard to tell."

It was past one o'clock in the morning when Kath pulled up to her parents' house. "How are we going to get Rock inside? Do we dare leave him out here?"

"We'd better take him in. What if he gets sick?" Jane said.

The porch light popped on and Kath's father stood in the open door.

"Oh, oh. He's not going to be happy," Jane said.

"Too bad. He can help us." Kath got out and told her father Rock was passed out in the backseat. Crandell looked peeved but didn't say a word. He followed her back to the car and pulled Rock out as if he was a feather. Then he put Rock's arm around his shoulders and half-walked, half-dragged him into the house, dropping him on the living room sofa.

"Let's hope he doesn't get sick all over your mother's nice rug," Crandell said.

Kath laughed, and Jane tried not to. Crandell finally laughed, too. "At least you're home safe and sound. Some escort he is."

"Oh, Dad. You know I can take care of myself," Kath said. She kissed her dad on the cheek and said goodnight.

Rock was utterly embarrassed the next morning and apologized to Crandell repeatedly. Crandell softened up to the farm-boy turned actor and finally told him all was well. He invited him to breakfast and they all sat down for eggs, bacon, and toast.

"Join us at the beach some weekend," Crandell told Rock

before he left. "We'll tear you down a notch or two with a tough game of volleyball. I'm sure Kath could outswim you, too."

Rock laughed. "I have no doubt about that. And I'd love to join you all."

After he left, Graham, now nineteen, said, "He sure is a good-looking man. Is he really as strong as he looks?"

Kath studied her little brother for a moment. "I suppose he is. He's a nice guy and was always respectful and polite on set. Maybe you can get to know him better if he comes to the beach house."

Graham suddenly turned red. "Oh, I didn't mean anything by what I said. I just meant he seemed nice." He hurried out of the room, making Kath wonder what he'd meant.

"Graham has a crush on Rock," Danny sang out. Then he laughed. Kath turned and glared at him. "Don't say that! What would you know, anyway? You're still a kid."

"Yeah, but I've been around here these past few years, and you haven't," Danny said. "I know what I see."

Kath went into the kitchen to help her mom. Since it was Sunday, Mrs. Cray had the day off, so her mother was cleaning up after breakfast. "Mom. Why didn't Graham go to college after high school?"

Catherine's brows shot up. "What made you think to ask that now? You've been home for weeks."

"I guess I've been so busy, I didn't have time to think about it," Kath said.

Her mother sighed. She was scrubbing the egg pan in the sink. "Your father and Graham had a huge fight over him not wanting to attend college. Graham said he didn't want to spend years in school just to sit in an office all day. That didn't go over well with your father."

"So, what is he doing?" Kath asked.

"He works as a stagehand and basically a gofer around the Warner Brothers lot. Your dad told him he had to work somewhere, so he got him the job there. Graham seems to like it. He's been used as an extra in a few films, too. With his height and good looks, he could be an actor like Rock, don't you think?"

Kath believed Graham was handsome enough, but it kind of peeved her to think he might get acting jobs with no experience at all. She'd worked hard to become an actress. She didn't say that, though, and instead told her mother stories about the party from the night before while she helped her with the dishes.

* * *

As Kath waited to hear when her new picture would hit the theaters, she was sent to work on more bit parts in different movies. She played a small background part in a movie with Lucille Ball and Bob Hope in the lead roles, and also as a pub vixen in the movie *The Three Musketeers*. Finally, Scott approached her in the studio commissary to tell her that the film she and Rock had made together had been canned.

"Canned? You mean, they're not going to distribute it?" Kath was heartbroken.

"Sorry," Scott said. "It happens often. The bigwigs watched it after editing and decided it wasn't worth pushing. But they loved you in the role. Mr. Mayer said you project well on screen and told his staff to find you something bigger to work on."

Jane, who'd been having lunch with Kath, patted her arm.

"That's good news, isn't it?"

Kath nodded. "Yes, I guess so. At least he doesn't want to tear up my contract."

Scott chuckled. "No one is tearing up your contract, believe me. They like you. I hope we get a chance to work together again."

"I do, too," Kath said. "I love working with you."

"Thanks," Scott said. "Well, I'm off to tell Rock about the movie. He'll be heartbroken. Maybe I'll invite him to the house for a swim to lift his spirits." Scott winked at them and headed out of the commissary.

Kath frowned and stared at Jane. "What did he mean by that?"

Jane laughed. "You still haven't figured it out yet? Rock likes men."

"No." Kath shook her head. "No. He was so kind and attentive to me when we worked together. Women all swoon when he walks by."

"Have you ever seen him make a pass at a woman?" Jane asked.

Kath had never seen him flirt with women. She thought he was just being a gentleman. "I guess I have to start paying more attention to what's happening around me," she said, then chuckled.

For the next few weeks, Kath was at the studio taking dance, voice, and singing lessons. She laughed about singing because she couldn't carry a tune. The studio was ramping up her experience and wanted her ready for when they had the perfect role for her. Mr. Mayer also sent word to the hairdresser to have Kath grow her hair out to at least shoulder length and add red highlights.

Kath just did as they wanted. She was hungry for success and hoped the studio knew what they were doing.

As promised, Rock came to the family beach house the last weekend in September. The whole family was there, and he got along well with everyone except Lilly, who, at seventeen, should have been drooling over the heartthrob but instead found him annoying.

"How on earth could you find Rock annoying?" Kath asked her younger sister when Lilly told her that. "He's the nicest person you'll ever meet."

Lilly scrunched her nose. "He's always complimenting everyone, and it's so phony. And does he ever wear his shirt? It's been off since he got here."

Kath laughed. "We're at the beach, little Miss Priss. And I've noticed that other women on the beach have no problem with him being shirtless."

Lilly sneered at her and walked away with a book. Kath knew Lilly was dating a young man in high school whose father was a Lutheran minister. She had the feeling that Lilly thought she was above everyone because of that.

Graham, however, was having a great time with Rock at the house. They had swimming races and played volleyball as a group. Occasionally, Graham and Rock were off alone by the water, sitting in the packed-down sand and talking. Kath watched with interest, wondering what they were discussing. She guessed it wasn't any of her business.

"Your family is amazing," Rock told Kath the night before they had to leave and return to work. "Everyone was so welcoming. You're lucky to come from such a good family."

"Thanks, Roy," she said, using the name he'd told her to call him. "Wasn't your family life as good?"

Rock shook his head. "No, it wasn't as nice. I couldn't wait to leave home and joined the Navy right out of high school."

"I'm sorry," Kath said quietly. She knew she was lucky to come from a big, supportive family where she felt safe.

"Kath, can I ask you to do something for me?" Rock said shyly.

She smiled. "Sure. What?"

"My agent, Henry Willson, thinks you and I would look like a believable couple going out to premieres and parties. Maybe even a dinner date once in a while. He told me to ask you if you'd pretend to be my girlfriend for a few months."

Kath was taken aback. "Roy, you can date any girl you want. I mean, look at you. Why on earth would you want to pretend I was your girlfriend?"

He bit his lip. "Henry thinks it will look good for me and you. If people think we're dating, they won't start rumors about our lifestyles."

Kath tilted her head, confused. "Lifestyles?"

Rock blushed. "You know. You and Jane. Me and…well, other men."

"Oh." Kath sat back, completely stunned. "Okay. Well, just so you know, Jane and I aren't a couple. We're just best friends who went to college together. I like men."

Rock's eyes grew wide. "Really? Mr. Mayer told everyone to leave you alone since you're in a 'female relationship.'" He broke out laughing. "This is hilarious. Everyone on the lot thinks you two are a couple." His deep laughter made Kath laugh, too.

"Well, I guess I don't have to worry about the casting couch around there, huh?" Kath said. Her words only made Rock laugh harder.

"As far as you and I pretending to be a couple," Kath said. "Sure, why not? It would be fun going out to places with you for a while."

Rock gave her a big, white-toothed grin. "Thanks, Kath. You're a true friend."

"And it's just between you and me, right?" Kath said.

He nodded. "It's our little secret."

After Rock left, Kath thought about their conversation. She thought it might be fun pretending to date a hunk like Rock. And he was so sweet. She couldn't wait to run upstairs and tell Jane what everyone thought of their "relationship." Kath knew she'd get a kick out of it.

CHAPTER NINE

TODAY

Kath awoke the next day, thinking of her first year in Hollywood and her friendship with Rock Hudson. They had remained friends until his death in 1985. All those years, she'd never breathed a word that she knew Rock was gay. Why would she? They were friends and friends didn't tell each other's secrets. But because he'd shared his secret before his death, she'd felt it was fine to include what she knew in her biography.

Getting up slowly out of bed, Kath searched for one of her old scrapbooks. She liked to keep them nearby, to look at old faces she'd once cared about. She found the book she wanted, marked 1948-1950, and sat on the bed to open it. There, staring back at her, was the handsome face of Rock Hudson.

She smiled when she remembered how much fun they'd had pretending to be a couple. The studio put them on the list for movie premieres, award shows, and celebrity parties that the studio planned and made sure the tabloid photographers would be at. She could borrow beautiful gowns from the wardrobe department and even had hair and make-up women and men at her disposal to look stunning. It had been a blast attending functions with the up-and-coming Rock Hudson, and they both had a great time.

God, how she missed him. And all the other people who'd gone before her.

Finally, Kath put the scrapbook away and dressed for another day of interviews.

When Carolyn and Kath arrived on set, Roger seemed eager to begin immediately. Kath sat in her chair, wondering what Mr. Slick had up his sleeve today.

"Miss Carver," Roger began once the cameras were on. "From reading your book, I understand you dated Rock Hudson for a year, right before you both became famous."

Oh, great, Kath thought. *He's going to delve into this!* She nodded. "Yes, we did. In fact, I dated several men over the course of my many years in Hollywood."

"Yes. But Rock Hudson. Tell us, what was he like? Was he everything we've been led to believe?" Roger's eyes shone brightly.

Kath frowned. She wondered if Roger knew he was a complete ass. "I actually made my very first movie with Roy— that was his real name—and we had a wonderful time. Roy was kind, polite, and sweet. Unfortunately, the movie was canned, but Mr. Mayer saw that I could act and put me in a better movie the next time. Roy went on, as we all know, to have an equally successful career."

"That's interesting, but what was he really like? You know, as a boyfriend." Roger watched her expectantly.

Kath seethed. She knew what Roger wanted her to say, and she wasn't going to give him the satisfaction. "As I said in the book, he was a very polite, shy, kind soul. I enjoyed his company very much."

"Come now, Miss Carver. Are you telling us that you didn't know Rock was gay while you were dating him? Everyone in Hollywood knew."

"Really?" Kath said, raising her eyebrows. "Well then, I guess that was his business, wasn't it?" Kath knew they'd have to edit out this entire section because it would make Roger look like a jerk.

Roger sat back, annoyed and defeated. "Okay. Play it coy. Let's move on to your first big movie, *Until Sunset*. It was a suspense/thriller. How did you get that role?"

Kath relaxed. Finally, they were talking about something she enjoyed. "Mr. Mayer wanted me for that role. He said he wanted an actress who reminded him of Lauren Bacall or Katharine Hepburn. When he chose me, I was stunned. To be compared to that kind of talent was a great compliment."

"Oh. So, you and L.B. Mayer were close?" Roger asked.

"No, not in the way you're suggesting," Kath snapped. "He ran MGM, and I was an employee. He had the last say in which actors played what roles. Period."

"Well, yes," Roger said, his cheeks flaming. "Anyway, your co-star in that picture was the dashing Stewart Douglas. He was already a big star, and you were an up-and-coming starlet. How was it to work with him."

"Stewart was wonderful to work with, as I said in my book," Kath said. "Always the gentleman and quick to see when a scene wasn't working well. His charm and wit also played well in making the audience love him even though no one knew until the end if he was the good guy or the bad guy."

"Was there a romance between you two after the picture was finished?" Roger asked, grinning.

"Absolutely not," Kath said, indignant. "Stewart was very loyal to his wife and family. He adored them. I even spent an afternoon at their home, and their children were adorable. I never saw him stray once in the years we both were at MGM."

"Oh, I see," Roger said, then smiled again. "But I have a feeling you wouldn't tell us if you did have any dirt on any of the men you knew. You seem to be very loyal to your friends."

Kath's hackles rose. "Mr. Connally. Just because you want parts of my life to appear unseemly, it doesn't mean that anything you're fishing for is true. So, I'd appreciate it if you'd stick to what I wrote in my book and stop hinting at scandal."

Roger tightened his jaw and sliced his hand through the air to tell the cameramen to stop filming. "I think we need a break for a moment," he said tightly. "Excuse me." He stormed off the set.

Kath's anger abated, and she smiled. It was lovely seeing Mr. Slick angry.

"Aunt Kath. I think you made him angry," Carolyn said, walking onto the set with fresh water for her.

"He deserved it," Kath said softly. "He's trying to turn all my words around to make the story more interesting. Isn't it enough what I've shared of my life? Why does everyone want to make everything so unseemly?"

Carolyn sighed. "That's what people want. Scandal and dirt. It's sad."

Kath stood and stretched, then walked to the ladies' room. Carolyn helped her smooth her hair and fix what little make-up she wore. Once she felt refreshed, Kath returned to the set and sat down.

Roger returned, looking calmer. The two gave each other phony smiles and began again.

"You say in your book that 1949 was a banner year for you," Roger began. "Was that because of all the hit movies you had that year?"

"Of course," Kath said. "After *Until Sunset* was a hit, I did four more movies back-to-back. Every one of them did quite well. Suddenly, I was recognized by fans on the street and people were standing outside my parents' house, just waiting for me to come outside. Rock was also doing well that year and since we attended events together, the fans went crazy. I loved it, but I think it made Rock a little nervous. It bothered my parents, too. So, it was finally time for me to find a place of my own."

1949

Kath smoothed down her satin dress as she sat on the sofa at Cary Grant's house. He was having a small party with some of his closest friends and she and Rock had been invited. Kath knew many of the guests from previous parties, but tonight, she didn't feel like mingling.

"It isn't good to drink alone," Scott Coolidge said, sitting beside Kath. "Mind if I join you?"

Kath smiled. She adored Scotty. They'd made a second movie together—a comedy—and he'd been brilliant at directing it. "Of course, you can join me," she told him. "And you know I'm not much of a drinker."

He grinned. "Everyone in Hollywood drinks except you," he said. "So, why are you hiding over here, away from everyone."

"I guess I'm just tired. I've been working so much," Kath said. "Not that I don't want to work, but it's been tough. And

I need to find a place to live now that people recognize me. It's driving my father crazy having cars and people hanging around outside the house."

"I might be able to help you with that," Scott said. "Would you be interested in renting one of my guest cottages?"

"Really?" Kath was thrilled. "I'd love to if I can afford it."

Scott brushed his hand through the air to wave away her worry. "How does $200 a month sound. You can use the pool anytime you like, and the tennis court. I'm rarely home anyway. And if your friend, Jane, wants to stay there too, there's no extra charge."

"Oh, Scotty! That's wonderful!" She reached out and hugged him. "Thank you so much. Your house is private, and no one will know I'm there."

He hugged her back and then pulled away. "You're welcome. I do have to warn you, though, that I tend to have guests on Sundays when I'm not working." He cleared his throat. "Male guests. That will have to be our little secret."

Kath wasn't surprised. She already knew Scotty's preferences. "Absolutely. I'll stay in my own space on those days. Thanks, Scotty. I'm so excited."

"You'll be doing me a favor. Those houses should be used, and you can watch my house when I'm working on location."

"I'll be happy to," Kath said.

Rock came over and pretended to be jealous. "Scotty! Are you trying to steal my date?"

Scott laughed. "Of course, Rock. You have the prettiest girl here." He vacated his seat, and Rock fell into it.

"Do you mind driving me back to your house?" Rock asked. "I had a little too much."

Kath laughed. "You always have a little too much."

He went off to the bathroom while she went to find her wrap. Cary came up to her with a tall, good-looking man in tow.

"You're not going already, are you Kathleen?" Cary said in that lovely accent of his. "I have a friend here who is dying to meet you."

Kath turned and looked at the man. He seemed familiar. "Rock and I were on our way out, I'm afraid. Rock has an early morning shoot."

"Well, before you leave," Cary said. "I'd like you to meet Howard Hughes. Howard, this is Kathleen Carver."

Kath's mouth nearly dropped open, and she forced herself to keep it closed. So this was the famous aviator, producer of films, and philanthropist. "It's nice to meet you, Mr. Hughes," she said steadily, offering her hand.

He tipped his head and shook her hand. "Please. Call me Howard. I've been wanting to meet you since I saw *Until Sunset*. You're a very gifted actress, Miss Carver."

"Thank you. Just call me Kath. Everyone does," she said.

"Howard! Are you trying to steal my date?" Rock grinned, coming up beside Kath. "I seem to be fighting off throngs of men tonight."

"Not tonight, Rock," Howard said. "I wouldn't do that to a friend. But you never know about tomorrow." He winked at Kath. "It was nice meeting you, dear. I hope to see you again soon."

Kath nodded and Howard and Cary were off to the other side of the living room.

"Watch out for that one, Kath," Rock said as they made their way to their car. "That man is a scoundrel."

"Aren't you all?" Kath asked. She drove the car back to her

parents' house and Rock took up residence on the sofa as he usually did on the nights they went out.

Kath was excited to tell Jane the next morning about renting Scotty's guest house. She, too, was excited. Jane was dating an executive at MGM, and their relationship was getting serious. She told Kath that having the freedom to come and go without her parents' watchful eyes would be a relief.

Kath agreed. She was nearly twenty-four years old, and even though her parents treated her as an adult, they were still nosy about her comings and goings.

The two women moved into the guest house in the hills of Bel Air on a gorgeous day in December. The house was furnished, so all they had to bring were their personal items. Kath had also bought her own car—a black 1948 Ford hardtop convertible Roadster with cream interior—so she could drive back and forth to the studio. Scotty had offered to let her use one of his many cars, but she didn't want to take advantage of their friendship. She was already grateful for the low rent on his beautiful guest house.

The home had three bedrooms, each with its own bathroom, a large living area, a kitchen, and a dining room. There were patios in the front and back to sit on and enjoy the view. The back patio overlooked Scotty's backyard and pool. It was the perfect spot for two young women to enjoy privacy and feel safe.

The first day Kath moved into the house, a large bouquet of pink roses was delivered. She didn't have to see the card to know who'd sent them. Ever since she'd met Howard Hughes at Cary's party, he'd sent her flowers daily.

"I see Howard has already found you," Jane said when Scotty's butler delivered the flowers to their door. "He's quite persistent."

Kath smiled. She hadn't even thought twice about the handsome aviator after meeting him until the first box of two dozen red roses arrived at her parents' house. She wrote a thank-you note but hadn't had a chance to send it before the gorgeous white calla lilies arrived the next day. And so it went, flowers every day with a card stating, "With great admiration, H.H." It was very flattering, but Kath wasn't sure what to do about it. Howard Hughes was twenty years her senior, although he was still a very handsome man. Was she interested?

"Be prepared," Jane told her. "He's bound to ask you out very soon."

Kath had expected that, too, although she still wasn't sure how she'd respond.

Kath celebrated the New Year of 1950 with Rock at Scotty's big party. Celebrities filled the house and the pool area—everyone from MGM was there, with a sprinkling of stars from the other studios. Kath had also invited her brother, Graham, who had begged her to include him. At almost twenty-one, he was tall and handsome, and in a tuxedo, he fit right in with the gorgeous stars. He charmed young women and men alike and seemed to be having a great time.

"Hm. Your brother fits right in," Rock said, handing Kath a glass of champagne. "Should I keep an eye on him?"

Kath studied Rock for a moment. "You mean in a brotherly way, right?"

"Of course," Rock said, looking offended. "This crowd will chew him up and spit him out. I'll make sure he gets back to your house safe and sound."

Kath chuckled. "Can you say the same for yourself?"

"Sheesh. You get drunk a few times." He laughed and made his way into the throngs of people.

"You and Rock are very good friends, I see," a man said from behind Kath. She spun around, and there in a black tuxedo stood Howard Hughes.

"You snuck up on me," she said, sipping her champagne. "And yes. We are good friends."

"Not too good, I hope," Howard said, grinning.

"Just friends," Kath said. She studied him as he sat down beside her. He was tall and lean, which was why he looked so handsome in a tux. His hair was swept back from his face, and he sported a thick mustache. But it was his eyes and expressive eyebrows that caught her attention. His eyes were so dark and intense she could see her reflection in them.

They sat together on a chaise lounge outside, away from the ruckus, and talked well past midnight. He told her about his businesses and the things he was most passionate about, and she talked about how she'd made her way from Bryn Mawr to Hollywood.

"I'd love to spend more time with you," Howard said when Kath finally told him she had to get some sleep. "How about dinner at the Beverly Hills Hotel tomorrow night?"

Kath smiled. "Okay, as long as it's in the restaurant and not your bungalow." She knew Howard had purchased several bungalows at the hotel and stayed there periodically. Everyone in Hollywood knew that.

He stood and bowed. "As the lady wishes. I'll send a car for you at seven." Then he left.

Kath smiled to herself. Dating Howard Hughes might prove interesting.

Chapter Ten

1950

Kath's whirlwind romance with Howard began after a lovely dinner at the Polo Lounge and weeks of him wining and dining her. He took her up in his small plane, and they flew over the ocean and around Los Angeles. They golfed at the Bel-Air Country Club even though Howard couldn't swing a club as well as he used to because of injuries from a plane crash in 1947.

"I hate playing anything that I can't do perfectly," Hughes told Kath. She understood the desire for perfection because her father had the same driven nature, but she simply enjoyed being outside and hitting the ball around.

When the tabloids got wind of Kath and Hughes dating, the press was on their tail every moment of every day. Kath was only safe at her house and at the studio. Hughes came and stayed with her at the beach house a couple of times since the press couldn't follow them onto the private property or beach.

After one such weekend when Kath's entire family was at the beach house too, her father commented after Hughes had left. "He's a rather odd duck, isn't he?" Crandell said. "I mean, he's nice enough for a rich guy, but have you noticed some of his strange habits?"

Kath had, and she bristled at her father mentioning them. "He's a bit of a germaphobe, but so what?" she said sharply to her father. "We all have little quirks."

Her father shrugged and let it go, but it still bothered Kath. She'd noticed how Howard would do something several times in a row or constantly clean the silverware with his napkin, or refuse to take seconds at dinner without getting a clean plate. But he was also considered a genius, and she understood that people like that could be odd.

During this time, Kat and Grant became officially engaged and Kath wasn't sure how she felt about that. She was happy for her sister, and she knew Grant would be a good husband for her, yet she felt somehow that Grant still belonged to her.

"Get over it, Kath," her mother told her one Sunday at the beach house after Grant had left, and Kat wanted Kath to look at wedding magazines with her. Kath was drying dishes as her mother washed them.

"Get over what?" Kath asked stubbornly.

"Get over Grant. I know you want Kat to be happy, and she is. But I can tell you still harbor feelings for Grant," Catherine said. "He's not yours anymore, nor has he been for years. Let your sister be happy."

Kath knew her mother was right. And besides, she was dating Howard Hughes. Why did it still bother her? Even though Kath never dreamed of getting married to anyone, she had to admit that she was a little jealous of Kat for having someone who wanted to marry her. And it didn't help that her youngest sister, Lilly, was also on her way to marrying her minister-to-be boyfriend, too.

Between dating Howard and making movies, Kath was constantly busy. That year, she made five films, and in between, she attended weddings for both Kat and Jane. Jane and her executive boyfriend, Kirt Williams, tied the knot in a small civil ceremony in June 1950. Kath was her maid of honor, and Kirt's good friend was his best man. Kath was sorry to see Jane leave the house. She knew she'd miss her after years of living together. But she was happy for her as well. Kirt had a great job at MGM and would provide well for Jane.

By the time Kat married Grant in September of that year, Kath and Howard had called it quits. Mostly, they had grown apart since they were both so busy. Plus, there were times Howard would retreat into his own little world for weeks at a time, and Kath found that disturbing. But they had a great time together, and she didn't regret their relationship. He'd also taught her a lot about the movie business and said he'd always be there for her if she needed him.

Kath threw herself into her work, and by the end of the year, she was preparing for another drama/suspense movie to start filming in January 1951. Her films that had been released so far had been great successes, and she was excited about this new one. She'd be playing opposite one of Hollywood's most famous leading men—Gordon Quinn.

TODAY

Kath waited impatiently for Roger's next question. It turned out to be a long day, and she was sure he'd be prying into her personal life even more than he already had.

"So, let's talk about Howard Hughes," Roger said, smiling wickedly. "That must have been an interesting relationship."

Kath took a breath, then let it out slowly. Since the press had known about their relationship, she had written a short chapter about it in her book, so talking about him was fair game.

"Howard was an incredibly interesting man. So intelligent, yet so kind and thoughtful. We dated for a few months in 1950, and then it ended. He was busy with his businesses—especially his work with RKO Studios—and I was making one movie after another. There wasn't time for a relationship."

"Ah, but you two did spend a lot of time together. Tell us what he was like. Did his quirky personality traits start revealing themselves when you two were together, or did that start later?"

Kath hated the tone Mr. Slick used every time he tried to get her to give dirt on the people she knew. "Howard was a genius. Of course, he had a few different habits. But he was always fun to be around and interesting as hell. We'd fly out over the ocean in one of his seaplanes, and he'd land it far away from shore and anchor it so we could sit inside and enjoy a peaceful lunch his cook made. We'd swim sometimes, and it was quite exhilarating, being out in the middle of the ocean like that. I never had a boring minute when I was with him."

"So, you saw no sign of his mind deteriorating while you two were together?" Roger asked.

"No. None," Kath said sharply. "In fact, he was as sharp as a tack. He taught me a lot about the movie business and gave me tips on how to ensure I received the money I deserved. He also once bought the film rights to a play I had great success with later in my career and gave them to me. I was able to sell it to a studio for twice the amount Howard purchased it for, and I controlled the entire picture. Howard was generous that way, and we remained friends until his death."

"I see," Roger said, looking bored at her praise of Hughes. He glanced at his notes, then smiled that evil grin again. "After your great success in 1950 with several movies, you were given a choice picture in early 1951 that all the major female stars were clamoring for. You starred opposite the man who would become your leading man in both film and in life for the next twenty years—Gordon Quinn."

Kath sat still in her chair, one eyebrow raised. "Yes. I made four pictures with Gordon Quinn. We had a wonderful working relationship."

"Now, Miss Carver," Roger said slyly. "Don't be coy. I noticed you didn't mention anything in your book about your long relationship with Gordon. Everyone knew about it, so I find it interesting that you didn't write about it."

"I did write about my *friendship* with Gordon," Kath said calmly. "Right there in Chapter Nine. We made four movies together over the years and we were friends. Other than that, there's nothing more to say."

"Are you telling me that all those tabloids and Hollywood gossip magazines got it wrong? You two were the biggest topic of conversation for years. 'Married Gordon Quinn living with single actress Kathleen Carver.' Why would they make up such a story?" Roger asked.

"Tabloids and movie magazines, and even the evening news make up stories all the time, as you well know, Mr. Connally," Kath said steadily. "How would I know why."

Kath watched as Roger's face turned red. He looked like he was choking on something. *He's probably choking on his own lies,* she thought.

"I think we're done for today," Roger said, setting his notes on the table beside him. "I'll see you tomorrow, Miss Carver." He stood and left the set.

Kath sighed. As much as she enjoyed sparring with Mr. Slick, it did tire her out.

"This week just keeps getting longer," Carolyn said, coming up beside Kath's chair. "I thought we'd be done today, but Roger seems to want details on everything."

"Yes, well, he'll only get what I wrote in the book—nothing more." Kath slowly stood up and let the blood rush to her legs before attempting to walk. "Did he question you about Gordon when he interviewed you?"

Carolyn smiled. "Oh, yes. And I'm positive he questioned Uncle Danny as well. I didn't say anything, but I can't promise Danny didn't."

Kath rolled her eyes. "Danny didn't know anything about my life then, so who knows what he made up." The two walked toward the room where they'd locked up their purses and coats. "Let's go home, dear. I'm beat."

Later that evening, Kath stood at the large living room windows, looking out over the brightly lit Los Angeles skyline. It was beautiful at night, lights shining in the inky sky. But Hollywood was ugly in the daytime with the smog, littered sidewalks, and "working women" on the street corners. Hollywood was all smoke and mirrors and was only beautiful to the rich, who were able to hide behind gates in mansions that kept them safe from the rest of the town. And Kath knew many of Hollywood's seedy secrets. She'd been here long enough.

Turning, Kath stared at the old chair in the corner that still had the imprint of the last owner who'd loved it so well.

"Gordon, old boy. They're still trying to dig up our secrets after all these decades. But trust me. I won't give them up. What we had was between you and me—and always will be."

Sitting down on the sofa that faced the chair, Kath lifted a cup of tea to her lips and sipped slowly. Carolyn had gone up to her bedroom already, leaving Kath alone with her thoughts and memories. Memories that could comfort or hurt, depending on which ones she thought of.

That first day in January of 1951 when the entire cast of *The Night Sky* had gathered for a table read of the script had been incredible. The cast included Gordon Quinn, Peter Lawford, Grace Kelly, and a young man who was just making a splash in Hollywood, Anthony Crane. Scotty was their director, and Kath was thankful for that. She felt comfortable around him, which was something she didn't feel around Gordon Quinn.

1951

Kath found her spot at the large table after being introduced to all the actors in the picture. She knew Grace from her days at the Barbizon and also from a few of the parties Kath and Rock had attended. Peter Lawford, too, was a person she'd met several times out and about. The young man, Anthony, she'd never met before, but he seemed to have a gentle personality and was thrilled to be in this movie. Gordon Quinn, however, was all business and didn't have time for niceties—he wanted to get to work.

Kath watched Gordon as he stood across the room talking to Scotty. Gordon was all of five feet, ten inches tall, and was stocky with broad shoulders. His hair was thick and sandy blond, and his eyes were a deep blue. He was ten years older than Kath—thirty-five—yet his face looked older. There was a sadness and wisdom about him that gave him the appearance that he'd lived much longer and knew too much.

Coming around the table, Gordon acknowledged Kath with a nod as he sat beside her. Kath didn't mind. Men in Hollywood didn't fawn over women like her—women who wore trousers, smoked, and didn't smile at everyone to be pleasant. Grace, though, sitting across the table from him, received a big smile.

They started to read the script. Since Gordon and Kath were the lead characters, they did most of the talking. It wasn't until they were halfway through the script that Kath finally understood the allure of the man sitting beside her. He'd read a joke from the script and turned and grinned at her while speaking. His smile and bright, mischievous eyes took her off guard. This was the face that the movie-paying public fell in love with. The smile took ten years off his face, and his eyes practically twinkled.

"Your line now," Gordon said in his regular gruff voice.

Kath shook herself out of her trance. She'd been staring at Gordon outright, surprised at how his smile could shake her to her core. "Oh, sorry," she said softly, embarrassed. Then she took up where he'd left off, trying to pull herself together.

After the table read, the rest of the cast left the room except for Kath and Grace, who hung back, both lighting a cigarette.

"Well, that wasn't too bad, was it?" Kath said aloud. She felt comfortable around Grace despite her being a gorgeous blonde with a perfect figure. Kath remembered her from the Barbizon days, sometimes dancing down the hallway, topless, just to shock the other girls. Kath had always thought she was funny rather than a beauty queen.

Grace chuckled. "He got to you, didn't he? Gordon seems so average until he turns those blue eyes on you. They take your breath away."

Kath wanted to deny it, but she couldn't after her flub earlier. "I hadn't expected it," she said, taking a long draw from her cigarette. "He totally took me by surprise."

"That's what he does," Grace said. "Say, if you ever want to get together for a drink or lunch, let me know. There are so few 'normal' women in this industry. I have a feeling you and I might have more in common than we think."

Kath was surprised by her offer of friendship. Most of the beautiful women didn't pay much attention to her. In this business, the press pitted you against the other actresses, and that became real life. But she felt the same as Grace—they might have a lot in common.

As filming began for *The Night Sky*, Kath's respect grew for Gordon Quinn. Like her, he was always on time and ready to work. He knew his lines and hers backward and forward. He kept her on her toes, which she liked. She hated carrying the leading man, as she'd done before. It was fun sparring with this talented actor to show who could outact who.

Kath invited Grace over to her house often on a Saturday night or Sunday afternoon. They would lounge by Scotty's pool if there wasn't an all-male party going on or sit out on her porch and share stories about the business. Unlike Kath, Grace had put up with many touchy-feely men on her way up the ladder. But she'd used the class and grace she'd been raised with to deter the men.

"What happened to your friend, Jane?" Grace asked one afternoon as they both sipped iced tea in lounge chairs. "Didn't she live with you?"

"She married an executive from MGM," Kath told her. "They're very happy, living in a cute house in the valley. She's expecting their first child."

"Really?" Grace looked stunned. "Not to be rude, but did you know that the rumor was you and her were a couple?"

Kath laughed out loud. "Oh, yes. We knew. Why do you think I never had to worry about the casting couch? We were only friends. I like men. I dated Howard Hughes for a while."

"I thought that was just a rumor," Grace said, laughing.

"See. Nothing in Hollywood is real."

As they worked on the movie, Kath hoped Gordon would warm up to her. He was always cordial but cold. She'd see him off with the crew, telling jokes that made everyone laugh, but he never spoke to her more than a word or two when he had to. She asked Scotty if he thought Gordon didn't like her.

"He likes you just fine," Scotty told her. "He's just not the type of man to show it."

"But he's joking with the crew all the time," Kath said.

"He tells dirty jokes. He'd never say those things around a woman. He's a very old-fashioned man," Scotty told her.

Kath didn't take his ignoring her personally after that. They did their scenes—kissing scenes and fighting scenes—as if they were truly a couple, both at the top of their acting skills. Even Grace mentioned it when they had lunch in the commissary one day.

"You two are on fire when you have intimate scenes," Grace told her. "It looks like you're really a couple."

"It's supposed to look that way," Kath said offhandedly.

Grace shook her head. "No. You both have a chemistry you just don't see every day. Like Bacall had with Bogart or Gable and Lombard. Believe me, you'll be amazed when you see the two of you on screen."

And Kath was amazed. When she went to the premiere, Kath was stunned by their chemistry on screen. The four main actors had appeared at the premiere after Gordon had been forced to go—he hated publicity—and photos were taken of him and Kath together before the movie started. Once the film became a success, those photos were in every gossip magazine with captions like, *"They are on fire together,"* or *"Hollywood's new power couple."* Kath understood it was just the studio's publicity department pushing the movie, but Gordon was enraged. He had a wife and two young children at home and didn't want anyone to think he was having an affair with Kath.

Kath just took it all in stride.

Weeks later, with no project yet assigned to her, Kath had grown bored. She went down to one of Scotty's Saturday night parties and mingled with the guests. She was surprised to see her brother, Graham, there but knew he'd been invited to many parties after the first one he'd attended. She told him to stay at her place that night and not drive home, but he only grinned.

"If I don't go home with someone else," Graham said.

Kath sighed. He was twenty-two, and she couldn't boss him around.

Walking inside the house, Kath said hello to Rock, always a mainstay at Scotty's parties, and Cary Grant. She wandered around a bit, sipped a glass of wine, and then stopped short. Sitting in the corner with his signature bourbon and water was Gordon Quinn. He looked up from his drink, looking both forlorn and tired. But his eyes still sparkled with mischief.

She stared at him, wondering if she should approach him or walk away. He stared right back. Sighing, Kath walked up to him. "Hello, Gordon. I'm surprised to see you here."

He just looked at her, then tipped his glass and drained it. "Scotty and I are friends. Have been for years," Gordon said. "I'm more surprised to see you here."

Kath pulled a ladder-back chair over and sat down. She'd worn a simple black dress that was right below her knees, and she sat, smoothing the skirt down. "If you and Scotty are such good friends, he must have mentioned I live in one of his guest houses."

"Ah," Gordon said. He lifted his empty glass in the air, and a waiter came immediately with a fresh drink. "We don't talk about personal matters, Scotty and me. So, how long have you lived here?"

"In the guest house," she reiterated. "I moved in about a year ago. It's safe and quite convenient."

Gordon nodded. "I've been known to stay in one of Scotty's guest houses a time or two." He lifted his glass and drank it down in one gulp.

Kath was about to stand and leave when Gordon flashed her one of his warm smiles.

"We made a good movie, you and I," he said. "At least, that's what people are telling me."

She nodded. "Yes. I think we did make a good movie."

"We were so convincing on screen, my wife thought we were having an affair. It's taken a lot of convincing—and a diamond necklace—to make her believe otherwise."

Kath winced. "I had no idea she was the jealous type. You've been making movies for a long time. Isn't she used to it by now?"

Gordon snorted. "Women never get used to their husbands kissing other women on the big screen. You'll find out when you get married someday."

Kath chuckled. "I don't plan on getting married, ever. I don't need a man to tell me how to run my life."

His brows rose. "Hm. I thought all women wanted to be married. Well, good for you." Gordon stood, swaying a bit on his feet. "I hope we work together again soon. It was fun."

"Me, too," Kath said, surprised. He hadn't seemed to enjoy working with her the first time.

Gordon walked toward the front door. Kath was worried he would drive down the winding Bel Air road inebriated. She followed him.

"Do you have a ride home?" she asked. She'd be willing to drive him herself if it got him home safely.

Gordon turned, frowned, then seemed to recognize her again. "No. This is one of those times I'm staying in Scotty's guest house." He walked away and out the door.

Kath sighed. She was relieved he'd be staying in the other guest house and not driving home. As she turned and headed out the patio door to go to her own house, she noticed her brother was huddled with a group of young men, talking animatedly. She had no more control over him than she did over Gordon, so she let him be.

As Kath climbed the steps up to her house, she smiled. She would enjoy working with Gordon again. They played off each other well. Maybe she could get to know him better if they did another picture. Perhaps they could be friends.

Maybe.

CHAPTER ELEVEN

1951

Later that year, Kath got her wish and was scheduled to co-star with Gordon Quinn in another picture. Unfortunately, it kept getting rescheduled because of the shakeup at MGM. Louie B. Mayer resigned in August, and the new order was still getting their bearings. But once the script was approved and the cast was chosen, their second movie was underway.

This time, the movie was a romantic comedy with Gordon and Kath as the main characters. Working together again, Kath felt differently about Gordon. He was nicer to her and joked with her like they were old friends. His usually serious demeanor had vanished, and he seemed happy and enjoyed the filming. He was still professional and always knew his lines, but he wasn't as critical of her as he'd been before. With Gordon's new attitude, Kath felt more comfortable and enjoyed the work.

Their characters' names were Harvey and Alice. As they filmed, they jokingly began calling each other by those names, and their nicknames stuck.

Halfway through the movie, the director became ill, so

they took a long weekend off. Kath invited Gordon to join her and her family at the beach house, expecting him to decline.

Gordon stared at her for a moment and turned serious, making Kath laugh. "I didn't mean a tawdry weekend in Malibu with just me. My parents and possibly my brothers and sisters will be there too. We try to go there on long weekends."

Gordon relaxed and chuckled. "I thought you were trying to seduce me, Alice," he said.

She shook her head. "That would be difficult to do with a crowd around, Harvey."

He took her up on her offer, and they drove together in her car to Malibu.

"Mom, Dad! I brought a guest," Kath hollered when she entered through the door Friday morning.

Her mother was in the kitchen and came out wiping her hands on an apron. "Well, how nice," Catherine said. "Welcome to our home, Mr. Quinn," she said, offering her hand to shake.

"Thank you." He shook her hand. "But please, call me Gordon."

"And you can call me Catherine." She turned to Kath. "Why don't you give Gordon Graham's old room. Daniel stole Kat's empty room a while back."

"Where is everyone?" Kath asked.

"Your dad is out in the water, of course, and only Daniel and Lillian are here. Kat is home with Grant, and Graham rarely comes out here anymore," Catherine said.

Kath watched her mother as she mentioned Graham. Her eyes had turned sad, saying his name. "Okay. Come on, Gordon. I'll show you to your room."

Later, when Kath introduced Gordon to her father, the two men hit it off immediately. Gordon wasn't a swimmer, so he sat on the beach in shorts and a shirt and watched as Kath and her father raced in the water. Kath often swam in Scotty's pool late at night to relax after a long day of working, so she was in excellent shape. Gordon cheered them both on, deciding not to pick sides.

Later, Kath left her father and Gordon to talk on the front porch while she helped her mother make dinner.

"He seems like a nice man," Catherine said, watching Kath as she snapped green beans and tossed them into boiling water. "Not as old as Howard was, so that's good."

Kath shook her head. "We're just friends, making a picture together. Gordon is already married and has two young children."

"Really?" Catherine said. She put the roast and potatoes in the oven. "Then why is he spending his weekend with you?"

Kath stopped and thought about that. Why was he here instead of with his wife? He never talked about his family. And from what she knew, Gordon had his own apartment near the studio and sometimes stayed at the other guest house at Scotty's.

"He's been working long days and needed a break," Kath finally said, even though it was a lie. "I guess he thought this might be fun."

Her mother placed a hand on Kath's arm. "Be careful, dear. Don't let him break your heart."

"We're just friends," Kath insisted. She wondered what her mother thought she'd seen that made her believe otherwise. She decided to change the subject. "Mom. Why doesn't Graham come here anymore?"

Catherine sighed. "That's something you'll have to ask your father."

"Mom? What is it?" she persisted.

"Do you see much of him?" Catherine asked. "The few times I've spoken to Gray on the phone, he's mentioned staying a night or two at your house. Is he okay?"

"He's fine, Mom," Kath said, confused. Graham had always been a good kid and close to their parents. Why didn't he see them anymore? "He comes to parties at Scott's house and I have him stay with me so he doesn't drive those dark roads at night. He seems to enjoy his job, and he's had a couple of bit parts in movies, which tickles him. But why don't you ever see him?"

"Ask your father, dear," was all Catherine said before leaving the kitchen to set the table.

Danny came home from a friend's house in time for dinner and Lillian did also. Danny was now eighteen, and Lillian was twenty. Unfortunately, neither one had grown up very much, despite Lilly being engaged to her soon-to-be minister boyfriend.

"Another boyfriend?" Danny said aloud when he was introduced to Gordon. "What happened to Howard?"

Kath seethed. "Gordon is a friend. We're making a picture together," she told Danny through gritted teeth.

Danny just grinned and walked away.

"Eugene says that movie stars lead ungodly lives," Lilly said primly. "Look at all those sordid stories in the papers about celebrities. It's horrible."

Kath couldn't believe what Lilly had just said. "How many movie stars does your fiancé know personally?"

Lilly tossed her head. "You don't have to know them personally to know they're bad."

Kath wanted to strangle her. But Gordon seemed to take it

all in stride. He chuckled at what Lilly had said but remained quiet. Luckily, Kath's father spoke up.

"We are never rude to our guests, Lillian," he said sternly. "No matter what Eugene thinks. I respect his opinion, and I also expect you to respect our guests."

Lilly quieted down, but Kath could tell she was livid.

After dinner, Kath offered a bourbon and water to Gordon and he took it out to the front porch while she helped her mother clear the table. First, though, she pulled her father aside.

"Dad? Why doesn't Graham come here anymore? And why did he leave the Toluca Lake house? It seems like it would be closer for him to work than the small apartment he rents."

Crandell looked uncomfortable. "Graham is nearly twenty-three years old, and he's earning a living. Why shouldn't he have his own place?"

Kath frowned. "What's going on, Dad? When I asked Mom, she said I had to ask you."

"Graham has made his own life choices, and I don't necessarily agree with some of them. It's best if he and I have some distance between us," Crandell said.

"What do you mean by 'life choices?'"

Crandell cleared his throat. "I'd prefer not to talk about this. Besides, you would agree with your brother anyway since he's like your friend Rock."

"What do you mean by that?" Kath asked, confused.

"You know perfectly well what I'm saying," Crandell said. "I'm not going to spell it out."

Kath did know what her father was saying, but she was so taken aback by his attitude she couldn't stop grilling him. "Dad. You and Mom have always been proud of your liberal point of view and your acceptance of people from all walks of life. How can you judge your own son so harshly?"

Crandell turned an angry face to Kath. "Being liberal is one thing. But having your own flesh and blood—your son—go in unacceptable circles like Graham has chosen, well, that's quite another thing. Wait until you have children, Kath. Then you'll have the right to come back and judge me." He turned and walked away.

Kath had never seen her father so angry. She could hardly believe that he'd be as unbending as that about his own son. Did she not know her father at all?

Later that evening, she joined Gordon on the front porch with a glass of wine after refreshing his bourbon. She was still so shaken up about her father's narrow-minded views that she needed to calm down.

"You rarely drink," Gordon said. "Do you want to talk about it?"

Kath smiled. Gordon never asked anyone about their feelings, and she certainly wasn't going to dump her family's problems on him tonight. "Just family stuff," she said. "And I'm sorry about my sister and her big mouth. She's been judging everyone long before she decided to marry a minister."

Gordon chuckled. "She's not that far off the mark, though, is she? Celebrities tend to be an odd bunch. I've never understood why, either. I guess when you spend your life creating make-believe characters, you become a little off-kilter."

Kath laughed. "Is that a warning? Because I think I've always been a bit odd. What about you? Are you off-kilter?"

His face grew solemn. "Yes, I am. I have trouble facing reality. Most of the time, I ignore it."

Kath suddenly felt sorry she'd asked. She sat on the wicker sofa next to him. "I'm sorry. I didn't mean to make you sad."

Gordon shook his head. "I'm not sad. Didn't you notice that I'm serious all the time? Everyone is always telling me to lighten up, but that's hard when you're carrying so much weight on your back."

"Do you want to talk about it?" Kath asked softly. "Because I'm here if you do."

Their eyes met, and for an instant, Kath thought Gordon was going to kiss her. Instead, he gave her a little smile and sat back against the sofa. "It's just family stuff," he said. "I wouldn't want to bore you."

Kath didn't want to pry, so she remained silent and they both enjoyed listening to the waves crash against the shore.

Soon, the weekend at the beach was forgotten as Kath and Gordon returned to work. There were long hours on the set, then when the picture was finished, they spent two days taking publicity photos for the poster and to promote the film.

"Well, it's been fun, Alice," Gordon said before they parted ways on the studio lot. "Maybe we'll be able to make another picture together again."

"You make it sound like our friendship is over," Kath said. "You know where I live, and you're always welcome to spend time at the Malibu house. You know, we can be friends."

Gordon nodded. "Maybe we can," he said. Then he left.

The studio had fantastic feedback about *The Coocoo's Call* from the test audiences. They knew they were going to have a hit on their hands. They set up a dazzling premiere and told Kath and Gordon they had to attend—no excuses, or they'd be fined. Kath had no problem attending, but Gordon was furious.

"They only want us at the premiere together so the gossips will talk," Gordon said one night to Kath on the phone. He called her sometimes, but he always called her Alice, and she called him Harvey. The last thing they needed was for gossip columnist Hedda Hopper to start writing about their friendship and turning it into a scandal.

"We can arrive in two different cars and only walk the carpet together," Kath suggested. "I'll bring my brother, Graham, along as my escort. We have nothing to hide."

Gordon agreed, and that night, Kath waited at her house for a phone call from Gordon saying he was on his way to the theater. Helen Rose, the costume designer at MGM, had created a gorgeous cream satin dress for Kath with a matching long cape and hood that draped beautifully around her head. Graham was thrilled to be asked to the premiere and was there in his tuxedo, as was a public relations executive from the studio.

Gordon's call never came.

"We have to go now," the PR man finally said when they'd waited as long as they could. "Maybe Gordon will be at the theater and just forgot to call."

But Gordon wasn't there, and there was no word from him.

Kath walked the red carpet on her brother's arm. She smiled for the cameras as if she didn't have a care in the world, but she was worried about Gordon. As Kath and Graham sat in the back of the theater, watching the picture, all she could think of was getting home and calling Gordon to make sure he was okay.

She didn't have to call. When she arrived at her door, there was Gordon, clutching a bottle of bourbon, sitting on her front steps. His tuxedo was rumpled, and his bowtie hung loosely around his neck.

Graham had planned to stay the night at Kath's house, so

he helped Kath lift Gordon up and walk him into the living room, where he dropped onto the sofa. Kath pried the bottle out of Gordon's hand and set it out of his reach.

"Will you make a pot of coffee before you go to bed?" Kath asked her brother. He nodded and headed for the kitchen.

Kath discarded her cape and sat on the sofa beside Gordon, who watched her with glassy eyes.

"You look like a princess with that cape," Gordon slurred. "A stately, beautiful princess."

Kath smoothed his thick hair out of his eyes. "I was worried about you," she said softly. "Why did you miss the premiere?"

Gordon reached for the bottle, couldn't find it, and dropped his hand to his side again. "My wife had a terrible fit about it. She didn't want me to walk the red carpet with you," he said unsteadily. "She called me at my apartment and screamed and screamed. I grabbed a bottle and, well, lost myself in it." He slumped over and dropped his head in Kath's lap.

Graham entered the room with a coffee pot and two mugs. His brows shot up at seeing the two together.

"I think he's passed out," Kath said. "Considering the bottle is almost empty, it doesn't surprise me."

"Should we try to get him upstairs into one of the beds?" Graham asked.

Kath shook her head. "No. We'll leave him here on the sofa. You go on up and get some sleep. Thanks for helping."

Graham walked behind the sofa and placed a soft kiss on Kath's cheek. "Goodnight," he said, then went upstairs.

For a long time after Graham left, Kath sat on the sofa with Gordon's head in her lap, slowly brushing her hand over his hair. She knew nothing about Gordon's marriage, only the rumors she'd heard around the studio. He lived in a small apartment near the studio even though his contract was for one million dollars a year. His wife and kids lived in a large home in Beverly Hills. Tonight, she realized that everything Gordon had went to his family—everything but his presence. For whatever reason, his wife didn't want him around—or the other way around—but they weren't legally separated, either. But no matter what the circumstances were with his family, Kath knew that tonight, when she should have been angry at him for not attending the premiere with her, instead, she felt her heart going out to him. She was falling in love with Gordon Quinn.

CHAPTER TWELVE

1952

After that night in early December, when Kath had found Gordon on her doorstep, he'd continued to stay at her house. She had three bedrooms, and he occupied one of them. They'd never planned it; it just happened, and Kath was fine with it. They lived their separate lives each day but spent each evening eating dinner at home and talking. Much to Kath's surprise, Gordon, when sober, was very good at talking.

Another surprise to Kath was her deep desire to take care of Gordon. Despite him being a rather tough, independent man, he also had a vulnerable side that attracted her. He craved being cared for—maybe even loved—and she wanted to give him that. Kath had never felt genuine love for any other man she'd ever dated, but this time, she knew it was real.

Of course, she never said that to Gordon. But she knew he appreciated her taking care of him, and in return, he was kinder to her than to anyone else.

Lillian married Eugene Reynolds in January in a lovely church wedding paid for by Kath's father. Kath attended with

Graham, who hadn't been invited, but she brought him as her plus one. Despite Lillian giving her the cold shoulder for bringing Graham, Kath still enjoyed being there with her family. She noticed, though, that her father didn't acknowledge Graham either, and that upset her. Her brother was one of the kindest, sweetest people she knew. Just because his lifestyle wasn't of their choosing didn't mean they should disown him.

That year, Kath's contract with MGM had been renewed, and to her delight and surprise, she'd been offered $2,000 a week for the next two years. It wasn't the largest contract on the lot by far, but it was a significant increase, and she knew if she was careful and saved her money, she would be well off.

Kath was also very busy that year making movies. In February, she co-starred with Fernando Lamas in a suspense thriller, and in May, she and Van Johnson co-starred in a light romantic comedy. Each movie did well at the box office, but the chemistry with the other male co-stars was never the same as what she had with Gordon.

In July, the head of production pulled Gordon from a film he was rehearsing and placed him and Kath in a legal drama. Gordon was furious about switching films, but after he read the script, he had to agree it was better than the one he was supposed to do.

"They're only doing this because our last film together made a pile of money," Gordon told Kath as they sat at the kitchen table and ate a roast and potato dinner.

Kath shrugged and smiled. "Does it matter why they did it? We get to work together, and that's fine with me. Plus, Scotty's directing. It's the perfect combination."

Gordon smiled at her. "It is," he agreed.

Since living with Kath, Gordon drank less and was calmer

and happier. Their relationship has been strictly platonic so far, and she was okay with that. Even though she cared deeply for him, she didn't want to push him into anything serious. And as far as everyone in Hollywood knew, Gordon was renting the other guest house on the property, so there was no gossip about them living together.

During this time, Marilyn Monroe was staying at Scotty's other guest house but she'd be the last person to tattle on them. She craved privacy as much as they did. Kath would only see her as they both were leaving or returning home and wave at each other. Otherwise, she barely noticed the young starlet at all.

Gordon and Kath started rehearsals for their new movie, *The Clock's Ticking*, and their characters bonded immediately. When filming began, they usually stayed right on script, but occasionally, one of them would change a line, and the other was able to continue as if nothing had happened. They knew each other that well, and enjoyed the back and forth in the movie where one minute they were on opposite sides of the case, and the other they were kissing. They were unlike any other couple currently on screen together, and Scotty knew they had another hit on their hands.

One night, after a long day of filming, Kath and Gordon returned home in separate cars. They never drove together to give away their living situation.

"Do you want to rehearse tomorrow's scenes?" Kath asked him. They usually did before eating dinner and heading off to bed.

"No," Gordon said. He walked up to Kath and embraced her, kissing her passionately. After a moment, she pulled away and looked into his gorgeous blue eyes. "Was that our rehearsal?" she asked breathlessly.

He smiled. "No. I was hoping you wanted to kiss me as much as I wanted to kiss you."

"I did," she said, and they kissed again. This was no chaste stage kiss; this was true passion.

Gordon took her by the hand and led her upstairs, and Kath followed willingly. At the door to her bedroom, he stopped and turned to her. "You can call it off right now, and I won't blame you a bit," he said. "You know I'm married—for whatever that's worth—and I'll never be able to divorce her. But she and I have no physical relationship. I can't promise you marriage or forever, but I can love you for as long as you'll have me."

Kath took a breath. No one had ever vowed their love for her before. She knew in her heart that she loved Gordon, but to hear him express it to her was more than she'd ever expected.

"I love you, Gordon. No matter what happens."

He smiled at her, and they entered her room with both understanding how the other felt.

Kath never regretted that night or the many nights to follow. She was deeply in love.

After the filming ended, Kath and Gordon both took a week off and spent it at the beach house. It was September, and the weather was perfect for long walks and swimming in the ocean. If either of them had any doubt about their relationship, it was gone by the time they returned to the guest house and started work again. Their week together, where they could simply be two people in love, not Hollywood's hottest on-screen couple, cemented their relationship.

As usual, Kath and Gordon went their separate ways most days, and they reunited in the evenings. By October, Kath hadn't yet been scheduled for a movie, so she spent her days visiting family and friends. She stopped by Jane and Kirt's valley home to visit her best friend and see her one-year-old namesake. In August 1951, little Kathleen Jane Williams was born, and Kath was her godmother. She adored the little curly-headed girl with the large brown eyes.

"I'm sorry I missed little Kathleen's birthday," Kath said as she and Jane settled into her lovely sunken living room. Their house was gorgeous, with five bedrooms, four bathrooms, a living room, a family room, and a to-die-for kitchen. "But these should make up for it."

Kath had brought along an armful of presents and enjoyed watching the toddler's expression as she helped her open them.

"You're a busy woman from what I read in the movie magazines," Jane said, grinning at her. "How do you date so many men and keep one in your house as well?"

Kath laughed. "All lies, I assure you. Although Gordon and I have become close. But that information is just between us."

"I figured you'd fall for him. The silent brooding type. But I'm happy for you," Jane said.

"Thanks. I'm not sure where it will lead, but I'm not expecting anything from him either. He says he can't divorce his wife, so I'll have to accept that. I never wanted to get married anyway."

"Marriage isn't so bad," Jane said, smiling. "I'm enjoying it more than I thought I would. And having little Kathleen has been such a pleasure. I highly recommend marriage and children."

Kath laughed. "It suits you, and believe me, I never thought it would. You and I are so much alike. But I'm glad you found a great man and love your life."

"I do love my life. But the question is, do you love yours?"

Jane asked seriously.

That question followed Kath all the way home.

The next day, she dropped by Kat's house. She hadn't seen her in quite a while and was excited to talk to her without family around. Kat and Grant had bought a house in the hills with the help of Grant's parents, and as Kath pulled up their driveway, she felt a twinge of jealousy. Grant had worked his way up in the accounting offices at Paramount Studios. While he made good money, he'd never have been able to afford this house without his parents' generosity.

"Oh, I'm so glad you're here!" Kat said, hugging Kath closely. "I get so bored being at home alone all day." Even though she and Grant had been married for two years, they hadn't yet been blessed with children.

"I wish I could see you more," Kath said. "The studio has kept me busy."

"That's a good thing," Kat said. She led Kath out to a table by the pool underneath a large umbrella. It was a beautiful California day, not too warm with a nice breeze. "You wouldn't want it any other way, would you?"

Kath sat and poured herself a glass of iced tea from the pitcher on the table. "No. I love making films. Hey! Why don't you come to work for me and be my assistant? Then you won't be bored."

Kat laughed. "No, thank you. I know you. You'd run me ragged, and nothing would ever be perfect enough. Hire Graham instead. He'd love hanging out there at the studio all day."

"He already works at Warner Brothers," Kath said. "And he loves it. They use him all the time as an extra or for small parts. He's so handsome, he should be a movie star."

Kat nodded. "I feel bad about the way Dad treats him. Have you noticed he's never at family gatherings anymore? It really hurts Graham and Mom, too."

"Yes, I have noticed. And I talked to Dad about it, but he's unwavering. It makes my blood boil. Gray is such a sweetheart, and everyone adores him. Dad's just being a jerk," Kath said.

"Well, Lilly isn't much better. Now that she's a minister's wife, she condemns everyone," Kat said. "She's especially hard on you and Graham. It really aggravates Mom."

Kath frowned. "Why is she condemning me? Just because I'm in movies?"

"She thinks you're carrying on with a married man. Haven't you read the movie magazines lately? You and Gordon Quinn are all over them."

Kath rolled her eyes. "They have nothing on us. The studio's publicity department makes it all up and sends it to the magazines to sell movies. Gordon and I have a new movie coming out, so they'll try to link us together with a scandal so everyone will go watch the movie."

"That's terrible," Kat said, looking stunned. "But you two are good friends, aren't you?"

Kath nodded. "We are. But we've worked together on two movies, so of course we're friends." She hated lying to Kat, but she wasn't ready to share the fact that she and Gordon were more than friends.

She enjoyed her visit with Kat and was in a good mood while driving home. Kath tried not to think about the nagging question Jane had asked her the day before. *Do you love your life?* Kath did love her life. She loved making movies and earning good money, which gave her freedom. But she always felt like something was missing. She loved Gordon, but they really had no future together. Was she okay with that?

When she arrived home, Gordon was already in his favorite chair that Kath had found at a lovely little furniture store on Sunset. It fit his body perfectly, and he could sit back, put his feet on the footstool, and read his favorite novels. He had a drink in one hand and a pipe in the other when she walked through the door. She could instantly smell the black cherry tobacco, a scent she loved.

"How was your day of filming?" she asked, coming up beside him and giving him a peck on the cheek.

"Not as good as I would have liked," he grumbled. "Where were you?"

Kath took off her blazer and placed it over the back of the dining room chair. It was unusually hot inside the house despite the windows being open. "I went to visit my sister, Kat. She sure has the life. A lovely home up in the hills with a pool, and she doesn't have to work." Kath sat on the sofa and stretched out her legs. As usual, she was wearing trousers and loafers, her favorite clothing.

"So, is that what you want? A cozy little marriage where your husband pays all the bills and buys you everything you want?" Gordon asked sharply.

Kath's brows rose. "No. I didn't say that. I merely said that was what Kat has. I love working."

"Well, you don't have a choice, do you? Especially since you're shacking up with a married man."

Kath stood, her anger rising. "I'm not going to sit here and fight with you. If you had a bad day, I'm sorry. But I won't let you take it out on me." She stormed into the kitchen and began banging pots and pans around, although she wasn't even sure what she was going to cook. Hot tears stung her eyes. How could he be so sweet and then so cruel?

"Why am I cooking him dinner?" she said aloud. "Screw him!" Kath hurried out of the kitchen and up the stairs without looking his way.

Up in her room, Kath threw herself on her bed. Tears ran down her cheeks despite her trying to hold them back. They'd been getting along so well, and his drinking had practically stopped. No wonder his wife didn't want him around—his drinking caused him to become a jerk.

Kath sat on her bed for a long time, wondering if she should tell him to leave. They had no future together, and she refused to put up with his bad behavior just because his day was terrible. He could go live in the other guest house. Marilyn had moved out, and it was empty.

Heavy footsteps sounded on the staircase, and there was a knock on her door. "What?" she called out.

"Can I come in?" Gordon asked sheepishly.

"Will you be nice?" she shot back.

Gordon opened the door and came inside, balancing a tray with two plates and two glasses of milk. "I thought you might be hungry," he said. He set the tray on the bed, and Kath glanced at it.

"What is it?"

"Peanut butter and jelly sandwiches," Gordon said. He was still tipsy but was trying hard not to show it.

Kath stared at the sandwiches, then back at him and smiled. "You made a sandwich for me?"

He nodded solemnly. "I know I was being a jerk. I'm sorry."

Tears filled Kath's eyes.

Gordon frowned. "Why are you crying? I thought this would make you happy."

"It does make me happy," she said. "These are happy tears."

Gordon shook his head as he sat on the bed beside her. "Women! I'll never understand."

Kath laughed and picked up her sandwich. After taking a bite, she said, "I was just thinking of kicking you out."

"Really? You want me to leave?"

"We'll see how I feel after this sandwich," she said.

They ate in silence and drank their milk. Finally, Kath asked, "Why were you in such a bad mood?"

Gordon breathed in deeply and let out a sigh. The food had sobered him. "Ellie called me today—a lot! She called me on set and kept interrupting filming. She's going berserk over all the magazine articles suggesting you and I are a couple."

"Oh." Kath thought a moment. Ellie. She'd never asked what his wife's name was because it was easier not knowing. "I'm sorry. She must know by now that those are just planted by the studio to sell movie tickets."

"She does know that, and it never bothered her before. But for some reason, this time is different," Gordon said. "We have an understanding, her and I. We don't ask what the other is doing or who they are seeing. She likes that she's married to a celebrity because it makes all her friends jealous. But when the publicity starts to look real, then it makes her angry. She doesn't want her friends to think I'm stepping out on her." He snorted. "As if she doesn't have a male friend to keep her company."

This was the most Gordon had ever said about his wife, and Kath wanted to know more. "Why doesn't she divorce you? She'd still have the house and money for the children. She could be a martyr then."

Gordon shook his head. "She'll never let me divorce her. She likes the status my name gives her. When she walks into the swanky department stores, the saleswomen practically bow to her. It's the same when she goes to get her hair done. She likes the attention and won't give that up."

"Hm," Kath said. "Meanwhile, she's living in luxury while you rent a place and own very little."

He smiled over at her, that gorgeous smile that had drawn her to him. "I don't need anything more than I have right here."

Kath's heart melted. She knew then she'd never kick him out because she loved him too deeply. *God help me,* she thought.

CHAPTER THIRTEEN

TODAY

Kath once again sat across from Mr. Slick, waiting to see what new story he'd conjure up. These interviews were lasting too long, and they'd only covered a small part of her life. Originally, they'd told her they'd be filming for three days. But from what she could tell, they had many days left, and it was getting on her nerves.

Kath reached into her blazer pocket and pulled out a cigarette and lighter. Before the man-boy could reach her to tell her not to smoke, Roger was there and lit the cigarette for her.

"Thank you," she said, slightly surprised. "I see chivalry isn't completely dead."

Roger chuckled as he sat in the chair opposite her. "My mother taught me well. I'll let you finish that before we start filming."

Carolyn rushed over with an ashtray and set it on the table. "Didn't you have one already today?" She stared hard at her aunt.

"Yes. One with my coffee this morning. But I'm allowed two," Kath said.

Carolyn shook her head and walked back to her seat.

"Are they afraid smoking will kill you?" Roger asked with a grin.

Kath laughed. "It's a little late for that, isn't it? At ninety-eight, I'm going to die soon anyway. I might as well enjoy what life I have left."

Roger chuckled along. "I want to assure you, Miss Carver, that I'm not trying to upset you with these interviews. You and I are on the same team. I'm just trying to do my job and draw out the interesting stories of your life. Please don't think I'm trying to sabotage you. In the future, if a subject is off limits, just tell me to move on."

Kath thought about that for a moment. Same team? Hardly. He was looking for the juicy tidbits of her life. But it would be nice to get along with him if they still had a few more days of filming. "Agreed," she said. "I will talk about only what is in the book. Everything else is off limits."

Roger smiled. "Great. I'll stick to the book."

After inhaling her last puff and breathing it out, Kath stubbed out the cigarette in the ashtray. She had no illusions that Mr. Slick would keep to his agreement.

"Okay, everyone. Let's start," Roger said.

The stage manager counted down, and the cameras began rolling.

"Miss Carver," Roger began, smiling widely at her. "Let's shift gears here and talk about your brother, Graham. He was younger than you, but you two were close, weren't you?"

Kath glared at Roger. She was foiled by her own words. Graham had been in her book, so she couldn't tell him to skip it. She took a breath and said steadily. "Yes. Graham was three years younger than me, and we were close. He, Katrina, and I would roam the neighborhood together as children, finding all sorts of mischief to get into."

"That must have been fun," Roger said. "And when you were older, after establishing yourself as a movie star, did the two of you still do things together?"

Kath knew exactly where he was heading and she didn't like it one bit. It was bad enough writing about what happened to Graham, but talking about it with this slithering snake made her skin crawl.

"Graham stayed with me often at my house," she said. "He worked as a stagehand at Warner Brothers, and they frequently used him as an extra in films. He was quite handsome and looked wonderful on the big screen."

"It sounds like you were very proud of your brother," Roger said. "What happened that night in August must have devastated you."

"It did," Kath said, feeling her heart break all over again. "It definitely did."

1955

Scotty was throwing one of his famous parties celebrating the end of filming Gordon and Kath's third film together. Practically all of Hollywood was there, including Kath's brother Graham, who'd come along with an up-and-coming male actor who Kath recognized but didn't know personally. She did know that her brother and the actor were very close, and their relationship had made him very happy these past few months.

Mayhem was happening out at the pool, with males and females alike undressing and jumping into the water. This happened often—too often for Kath's liking—so she usually stayed inside the house with the celebrities who didn't want a scandal tied to their names.

Tony Curtis stood with his wife, Janet Leigh, beside the piano while Dean Martin sang an upbeat song. Cary Grant sauntered over to congratulate Kath on her new film, and she asked him how Howard Hughes was. She knew they were good friends.

"He's busy as always," Cary said. "But I've noticed his behavior has become worse these past couple of years. He's always washing his hands, and sometimes he eats only one thing for every meal. He goes through some strange phases, and then off he goes, creating a new company. He's quite the man," Cary told her, looking amused.

She nodded. "Yes, he is. I hope his behavior doesn't get worse. He's almost too intelligent for his own good."

Cary agreed. "So, where's your co-star? I haven't seen him yet tonight."

"Sitting in his favorite corner," Kath said. "He's not one for schmoozing."

Cary laughed. "That's the truth. I'll go over and say hello."

Kath wandered around a bit more, greeting some of the actors she knew. She made her way to Scotty's new addition—another large living room with one wall of windows—and stared out at the craziness by the pool. As she looked around, her attention went to two men who looked to be fighting. Not throwing punches, but their arms were waving, and they were yelling at each other. Finally, the one man stormed away, and when the other man turned around, she realized it was Graham.

Worried about her brother, Kath hurried down the stairs and to the pool area. He was still standing in the same spot when she approached him. "Gray? Are you okay? I saw you fighting with someone."

Graham looked up at her with glassy eyes. "He left me. He said that now that he's becoming well-known, he can't be seen with me or any other men, or it will ruin his career."

Kath wrapped her arms around him. "I'm so sorry, sweetie," she said soothingly. "This town can be so horrible."

Graham pulled back. "I don't understand. We've been careful not to be seen together. Just like Rock and Scotty and the countless others here. Why does he think we can't have a relationship?"

"The rag sheets make everyone nervous. And he's new to all this. Maybe if you give him some time, he'll try to make it work," Kath said. She'd known several men who were run out of Hollywood from rumors alone, so she understood why Graham's male friend was so scared.

Graham shook his head. Kath was worried about him. His hair was mussed because he kept running his hand through it, and his suit looked rumbled. Typically, Graham was very fastidious about his appearance.

"Why don't you come up to my house with me?" Kath asked. "We can have coffee and talk, or you can get some sleep." She linked arms with him and guided him up the hill to the house, leaving no room for argument.

Kath led Graham into the kitchen, and he sat at the small table. She quickly doffed her heels and slipped on a pair of loafers that were by the back door. She looked silly in her red sequined dress and loafers, but she didn't care. She just wanted to make sure Graham was okay.

Putting on a pot of coffee, she set a tin of ginger snaps in front of Graham—his favorite—and took down two coffee cups to place on the counter. In the past year, she'd hired a cook and maid to care for their small home. She and Gordon now had dinner waiting for them when they returned home from the studio, and their cook also made treats, like the cookies. It was an extra expense but well worth it to Kath.

She returned to the table to sit down across from her brother. "I know it's hard, sweetie. But if this man really cares about you, he'll come back," Kath said.

Graham snorted. "Hard? What would you know about that? You can do whatever you want, and you're still America's sweetheart." He stood and began pacing in the small space. "Everyone knows you live with a married man, and yet they all choose to ignore it. But for me, it's different. Men like me aren't free to be who we are. Even our own father has banished me from the family, but you can bring Gordon to the house and they all accept him."

Kath understood that Graham was blowing off steam, but his words still hurt. "You're right," she said, despite being stung by his words. "And it makes me angry how Dad has treated you. He has always been a liberal thinker, except now about you. It's wrong. I'm sorry."

All the anger left Graham, and he dropped into his seat again, looking deflated. "I'm sorry. I didn't mean to take it out on you. It's not your fault; it's mine. But I can't help being who I am."

"Oh, Graham, I know that. It's who you are. And I love you for who you are. Never forget that," she told him. She stood and took the pot of coffee off the stove. "You're tired, dear. Why don't you go up to the guest bedroom and get a good night's sleep."

Gordon walked into the kitchen then, surprised to see the

two in there. "I thought I heard voices," he said. "I just came in for some water before heading to bed."

Kath noticed Gordon wasn't as drunk as she'd thought and was thankful for that. He usually used parties as an excuse to get blasted, but tonight, he looked sober.

Graham stood. "I'm going home," he said, rushing out of the room. Kath ran after him and tried to stop him.

"Please. Don't drive tonight. Stay here," she pleaded.

Graham turned around and faced her. "Maybe he went back to my apartment. I need to go home. Thanks for being so kind and putting up with me." He hugged her tightly and kissed her on the cheek. "I love you, Kath. You know you're my favorite sister. Always have been."

Tears filled Kath's eyes. "I love you, too. Please, be careful."

Graham smiled his gorgeous smile and turned to leave.

Gordon walked into the living room with his glass of water and came up beside Kath. "Is he okay driving?" he asked as they watched him get into his roadster. He'd parked near their house because the road had been filled with cars.

"I hope so," Kath said. Gordon placed his arm around her and kissed her on the same cheek as Graham had.

Gordon went to sit in his favorite chair, and Kath walked outside to the patio. She could still hear the party going strong, the laughter, the music, and splashing from the pool. She watched Graham's taillights curve down her side of the driveway and then out the big gate. Aside from the party, the night was quiet, and the sky was clear. Stars twinkled above. Gordon walked outside and placed one of Kath's blazers over her shoulders.

At that moment, they both heard it. The squealing of tires in the distance and the sound of metal crashing. Kath turned to Gordon. "Graham!" She took off running down the driveway with Gordon right behind her.

The twisty roads were dark, but Kath saw taillights in the distance. She ran toward them, praying it wasn't Graham, praying he was okay if it was. Footsteps ran behind her, more than just Gordon's. By the time she reached the car, she knew immediately it was Graham's. The distinctive blue color gave it away.

"Graham!" she yelled, her breathing heavy from exertion. There were two men already at the car, looking inside. "Graham!" She reached the men as Gordon came up behind her. "Help him out!" she screamed.

Both men stood there, shaking their heads. "We've called for help," one man said. "We heard the crash and came outside. There's no way to get him out."

"What's wrong with you?" she screeched. "Get him out!" Kath ran to the driver's side, and that was when she saw it. The car had hit a huge oak tree, and the entire front end was smashed up into the front seat.

"Kath!" Gordon said, reaching her. "Nothing can be done." He tried to wrap his arms around her, but she rushed forward and fell on her knees. She could see through the broken window. Graham sat, crushed behind the steering wheel, his body crooked, his head tilted sideways. His unseeing eyes stared back at her.

Kath screamed.

Days later, when the police had finished investigating the crash, they ruled it an accident. Graham had simply missed a curve and plowed into the huge tree. However, they noted no tire marks on the road to show that Graham had tried to stop. Rumors spread that Graham may have hit the tree on purpose.

Many people from the party had seen him fighting with his male friend. Perhaps Graham had given up on life.

Kath, however, knew she'd heard the tires screeching on the pavement before the crash. Gordon had heard it, too. But there were tire marks on the opposite side of the road. Maybe another driver had slammed on their brakes upon seeing Graham's car rushing around the curve too fast. Whatever happened, no one came forward to say they'd witnessed it.

Kath had been the last one to talk to Graham before he'd left. She didn't believe he'd taken his own life. But the rumor mill wouldn't stop no matter how many times she told people it was just an accident. So, she gave up. That was when her hatred of the press began. They wouldn't listen no matter what, and they made up stories to sell papers and magazines. Awful stories. Stories that hurt families. She never trusted the press again with anything more than a grain of the truth.

All Kath knew was she'd lost her beloved brother—and that was enough to break her heart.

TODAY

"Miss Carver?" Roger said gently.

Kath shook herself out of her reverie and stared at him. "What was the question?" she asked.

"I was asking you about the night your brother Graham died. You were there, weren't you? You were having a party at your house, I believe."

"No," she said. "The party was at Scotty's house next door. I attended for a while, then Graham and I returned to my house for coffee."

"How did he seem?" Roger asked. "Was he too inebriated to drive? Was he depressed? Your brother, Daniel, said he'd had a fight with someone—possibly his lover—and was upset."

Anger rose inside of Kath. "Danny wasn't there," she said sharply. "He has no idea what happened that night. He's just repeating the rumors that flew around after the crash. No one knew anything."

"Can you tell us what happened?" Roger asked.

Kath took a breath and glanced over at Carolyn, who encouraged her with a smile. Then she returned her gaze to Mr. Slick. "I asked Graham to stay the night, but he wanted to go back to his place. I do believe he was too drunk to drive, but there was no stopping him. It was an accident, pure and simple. The roads were dark in those days and it's curvy that far up in the hills. He simply didn't see a curve and hit a tree. End of story."

"So, you don't believe he tried to kill himself?" Roger pushed.

"No. I don't believe it. He was looking forward to the future and was happy when he left. The police ruled it as an accident, and that's exactly what it was." Kath stared hard at Roger.

Roger nodded. He obviously knew he wouldn't get any more out of her.

Relaxing a bit, Kath sat back and waited for the next question.

"You were good friends with the director, Scott Cooledge," Roger began. "So good, in fact, that you rented one of his guest houses on his property. I believe Gordon Quinn rented the other house there as well."

Kath bristled. *Here we go again!* "Many stars and up-and-coming actors rented from Scott. He was a generous man and liked to help those just starting in the industry."

"I see," Roger said, glancing at his notes. "Rumor has it Scott had many wild parties at his home. Especially his Sunday afternoon parties. I suppose you had a front-row seat for those, with your house next to his."

Kath's eyes narrowed. "Scotty liked having get-togethers. There's nothing wrong with that."

Roger chuckled. "I hear these were more than just 'get-togethers.' I hear that most of the guests were men who liked to swim in the pool wearing nothing at all."

"Were you at these parties, Mr. Connally?" Kath asked.

"Oh, uh, no. Of course not. They were before my time," Roger said, practically stuttering.

"Then who are you to say what took place?" Kath asked.

"Well, Miss Carver. I've done my research. A couple of other actor's biographies mentioned these all-male parties."

Kath shrugged. "I would never negate someone else's experience. If they say they were there, then maybe they were. I did not attend all of Scotty's parties, so it wasn't my experience."

"Come now, Miss Carver. You must have seen some of what went on at Scott's house," Roger said.

"What Scotty did on his own property was no business of mine. And I've never said a derogatory thing about Scotty. He was a well-beloved director and friend."

"So, if you knew him so well, can you tell us if the rumors that he was gay are true?" Roger asked.

Kath was ready to walk out; she was that angry. "I have no idea what Scotty's sexuality was. That was his business, not mine. And I didn't write any of this in my book, so the subject is now closed."

Roger moved uneasily in his chair. He slowly sipped his

coffee and returned his attention to Kath with a fake smile. "Let's move on. In late 1956 to early 1957, while at the top of your career, you took several months off and went to France with your sister Katrina and her husband. I believe your niece, Carolyn, was born while you were there. What made you leave and take so much time off?"

Kath took another deep breath. When was this interview ever going to end?

Chapter Fourteen

1956

"I'm pregnant," Kath told Gordon. It was September, and they'd just finished dinner and were having one last drink out on the patio. Kath was drinking water.

Gordon stared at her. "How?"

"I think you know how," she said.

He frowned. "We were using birth control."

"No, *we* weren't using birth control. *I* was using it. And no birth control is one hundred percent foolproof."

Gordon stood and walked to the end of the deck. He looked tired. Kath knew his latest film had taken a toll on him, and she felt bad, but she was also exhausted. She'd finished her latest film last month even though she'd been sick throughout the filming. She'd thought she had some sort of flu and soldiered on. Then, she'd felt better, but something hadn't felt right, so she went to her personal doctor. That's when Kath learned she was carrying Gordon's baby.

"How far along are you?" he asked, still looking out over the city.

"Roughly four months. Since I'm tall and slender, the doctor said the pregnancy won't show for a while," Kath said. Except for a tiny bulge on her stomach, there was no sign she was expecting.

He turned around. "How could you not know you're pregnant for four months? It's too late to take care of it now."

Kath backed up in her chair, feeling physically assaulted by his words. "I was busy working. I had other things to do besides count the days between my periods," she shot back. "Besides. I've never been regular, so I thought nothing of my missing a couple of months."

Gordon walked back to his seat and sat. His anger had quickly abated. "I can't have any more children," he said softly.

Kath moved closer to him. "Why not? Why can't we have a child? We'll keep it quiet. No one knows for certain whether we live together or have a relationship. It's all speculation and rumor. I can keep out of the spotlight for a while—maybe say I have exhaustion or something—and have the baby. We could do this." Kath had already thought about it, and she wanted Gordon's baby. She knew he'd never leave his wife, but at least she'd have his child.

"You're not being reasonable," Gordon said. "People will know. We both will lose our contracts and our careers. Look what happened to Ingrid Bergman. She was ostracized for having an affair that resulted in a pregnancy. Do you want the same thing to happen to you?"

"Bergman's career is slowly coming back. And what happened to her won't happen to me. We can plan this out carefully."

Gordon shook his head. "No. I'm sorry, Kath. I can't raise a child with you. I love you. I really do. And I can see us spending the rest of our lives together. But not with a child. I already support my wife and kids, and I can't afford to lose my career. I'm sorry." He stood and walked inside.

Kath sat there a long time looking out at the city lights. She knew Gordon was right—she'd lose everything she'd built here in Hollywood if the world learned she was pregnant from her affair with a married man. Kath had never planned on getting married or having children, but once she'd learned of this child, she'd suddenly wanted it more than anything. But did she want a child enough to lose her entire future?

That night, Gordon slept in the guest room and left Kath alone. She didn't care, really. She had to think of what she wanted with or without him. She understood Gordon's fear of being found out. He was right—he couldn't lose his career because of their relationship. She didn't want to do that to him. But it made her sad, too. A little part of her had hoped they could have made it work. By morning, though, she realized that they couldn't. This town was small and had big ears. It would be impossible to keep a baby a secret.

That day, she called Cary Grant and asked him for Howard Hughes' phone number. Howard moved around often, and it was hard keeping track of him, but Cary was his good friend, and he had the number. She called Howard and told him her circumstances. He was more than happy to help.

Then, she went to see her sister, Kat, at her beautiful house. They were still childless, and Kat had suffered two terrible miscarriages over the years. Kath knew that if anyone wanted a child badly, it was Kat and Grant.

"I want to give you my baby," Kath announced to her sister.

Kat was dumbfounded. "What? You're pregnant?"

"Yes." They were sitting outside by the pool underneath an

umbrella to protect them from the harsh California sun and drinking iced tea. "And it's obvious I can't keep the baby, so I want you and Grant to have it."

"What about Gordon? What does he think of this?" Kat asked.

"Gordon doesn't want to be involved. This is my decision to make," Kath said. She knew it sounded harsh, but that was the reality of it. "If you and Grant truly want a child, we can make this work."

Tears filled Kat's eyes. She was still as cute and petite as ever, and it hurt Kath to see her sister upset.

"I do want a child more than anything," Kat said, wiping her eyes. "But I don't want you to do anything you'll regret. If you give us the child, would you want him or her to know you're their mother?"

Kath shook her head. "No. I won't be involved other than to be the child's favorite aunt." She smiled. "This will be your child. One hundred percent. No one can ever know about my pregnancy or my giving the child to you."

"How can we do that here? Even if you hide the entire time, someone will learn what's going on," Kat said.

"I have a plan. It will mean you and I going away to France for a few months, but I think the plan might work. No one will suspect the child is mine. The moment it's born, your name will be on the birth certificate, along with Grant as the father. No adoption. No paperwork. The child will simply be yours."

Kat finally agreed on one condition. "You have up until after the child's birth to change your mind. If you decide to keep the child, then so be it. I won't take your child away unless you're certain you want that."

Kath nodded. "I'll agree to that, but I already know I can't keep the child. At least I will be in its life as its aunt. That's enough for me."

A plan was put into motion. Kath told the studio she was suffering from exhaustion and needed a few months off. They didn't argue with her—if a female actress needed time off, the head executive figured it was for an unplanned pregnancy and didn't want to get in the way.

"Just make sure whatever you do, it's discreet," the head of MGM told her kindly. "We'll look forward to your return."

Kath told her parents and siblings she was going on an extended vacation to France and bringing Kat along. Her father and mother thought that would be nice for Kat since she'd been so sad since her last miscarriage the year before.

Grant was hesitant at first but then agreed. "You're giving up a lot for us," he told Kath. "Are you absolutely sure?"

"As sure as I've ever been. I'll lose everything if I keep the child, and so will Gordon. It's what has to be done."

In early October, Kath and Katrina boarded the RMS Queen Elizabeth in New York City to take them across the Atlantic to Cherbourg, France. Grant stayed in Los Angeles because he had to work but planned on coming in late January for the birth of the child.

Kath was sick on the first day of their seven-day cruise across the ocean, but soon, her stomach calmed enough for her to eat in the luxurious dining room. Word by then had spread that the famous movie star, Kathleen Carver, was on board and she and Kat were invited to sit at the captain's table for dinner. Luckily for Kath, she was barely showing, and her evening gowns still fit. But her goal of quietly slipping away from America wasn't going exactly as planned.

For the first time in years, Kath and Kat spent night and day with each other. It felt like they were teenagers again, having sleepovers. They had their hair and nails done in the ship's salon and gorged on delicious meals and heavenly desserts. They giggled about the overly rich passengers who wore diamonds and furs and walked tiny, fluffy dogs around the deck. Kath couldn't imagine flaunting her wealth that way. She supposed Gordon's simple way of living had rubbed off on her, and she was glad about that. The men and women trying to impress everyone were ridiculous.

Seven days later, they departed the ship at Cherbourg, and there, waiting for them, was a black limousine ordered by Howard Hughes to drive them to his chateau.

"My goodness, this is the life," Kat said, resting her head on the black leather seat. Kath sat across from her in the other seat. There was a bucket of ice with a bottle of white wine cooling in it, but neither woman touched it. Kath couldn't because of her condition, and Kat wasn't much of a drinker.

"Howard does know how to pamper a woman," Kath said. She felt tired after the long cruise and couldn't wait to lie down in a bed that didn't sway back and forth.

"Do you miss dating him?" Kat asked. "He was very kind to you, even though he had some odd habits."

"We're still good friends," Kath said. "I don't believe I was ever madly in love with Howard or he with me. We had a lot of fun, though. I'm grateful he could help us when I really needed it."

The driver drove them north of Le Harve to a quiet place on the English Channel. There, on a hill overlooking the water, was a beautiful stone chateau that looked bigger than any Hollywood mansion Kath had ever seen. They passed through a black iron gate connected to an eight-foot stone wall and drove by luscious gardens to a curved driveway up to the front door. The place was three stories high, and the wooden arched door was beautifully carved. It opened, and a middle-aged gentleman and woman stepped out to greet them.

"Welcome, welcome," the portly woman with gray hair pulled back in a bun said in a French accent. "I am Lucette, and this is my husband, Pascal. We will be caring for you during your visit."

Kath smiled and extended her hand. "Thank you, Lucette. I'm Kath, and this is my sister, Katrina. But you can call her Kat. We all do."

"Oui, oui," the woman said, a smile on her round face. "S'il vous plait, follow me, and I will show you your rooms."

Pascal, the gentleman, helped the driver bring in the luggage. Kath reached inside her handbag to tip the driver, but he waved it away. "Mr. Hughes has generously paid me." He bowed and left.

Kath and Kat both glanced around the lovely home. The entryway was large, with a fireplace on the other end and gorgeous marble floors. To the right was a big living area, again with a stone fireplace. To the left was a staircase that led to the upper floor. They followed Lucette up the polished wooden staircase, admiring the beautiful floral wallpaper and the crystal chandelier that hung over the entryway. At the top of the stairs, Lucette turned right and showed first Kath and then Kat their rooms.

Both women stepped into Kath's room first and nearly squealed with delight. The room was large, with a beautifully carved tray ceiling, a crystal chandelier, and soft pink wallpaper covered with flowers. The four-poster white French provincial bed was spectacular, with a soft pink satin bedspread and matching nightstands on each side.

"The washroom is attached through that door," Lucette said. "Towels are in the armoire. Please let me know if you need anything at all."

Kath followed to see Kat's room, and it was just as luxurious. After Pascal delivered their luggage to their rooms, they thanked the couple and waited for them to leave before letting out the squeals they were holding in.

"I've been in some of Hollywood's most elaborate mansions, but nothing compares to this place," Kath said. "Howard has certainly outdone himself."

Kat agreed. "I've never felt so pampered."

The women settled in and explored the large house before going to the kitchen, where Lucette was preparing their supper. The kitchen was old-world charm meets new-world function. A huge brick fireplace stood on one wall—big enough to step inside—and the ceiling had wooden beams across it. The floor was red tile, and a large butcher-block island sat in the middle.

"This kitchen is amazing," Kath told Lucette, who smiled and nodded.

"Mr. Hughes spares no expense but enjoys keeping the old with the new," Lucette said proudly.

They ate a dinner of pasta and tomato sauce with warm bread and rich, creamy butter in the large dining room off the kitchen.

"Between the ship's food and now this, I'm going to get fat," Kat said, laughing.

Kath snorted. "I'm going to get fat, so please join me." She laughed, and Kat did, also. If one had to banish oneself to nowhere, this was the place to be.

"I may never want to leave," Kat said after dinner, reclining on a sofa in the living room in front of the roaring fire. Being so close to the water caused the nights to become damp and cold.

"I may never be able to leave if my secret gets out," Kath said.

"Do you think Howard's staff will keep your secret?" Kat asked, suddenly nervous.

"Howard will pay them well to stay silent, I'm sure," Kath said. "He seems to keep his secrets safe from the world."

"You're so lucky to have someone like him to depend on," Kat said. "I wish Gordon had been more sensitive to your predicament."

Kath wished that, too. Before she'd left, she'd snidely told him he should go home and spend time with his children. He'd looked physically ill when she'd said it. She was sure he understood he was turning away his own flesh and blood, but he refused to budge. She should hate him, but it was hard. She loved him too much, even after how he'd treated the situation.

"He's stuck in a corner, I'm afraid," she told Kat. "And he had made it clear from the beginning there'd be no marriage or children between us. I'm the one who broke the rules."

"I'm sorry, Kath," Kat said. "Maybe you should find someone who is available and leave Gordon behind."

Kath smiled. "Oh, but if it were that easy."

The two women settled into their days at the chateau, enjoying the beautiful home, the delicious food that Lucette prepared, and walking the grounds near the channel on the days it didn't rain. They spent evenings inside by the fire, reading books from Howard's extensive library. Kath was surprised at how relaxed she felt. Normally, she wanted to be busy and active all the time. But here, time stood still, and she enjoyed breathing in the fresh air and luxuriating in the gorgeous views.

There was a small village nearby where Lucette and Pascal could buy all the necessities they needed for cooking and maintaining the house. Because Howard was a car collector, there was a selection in the garage, and sometimes Kat and Kath would drive around the countryside. Only Kat could go to the village and wander around because Kath would be recognized immediately. Even in a small area like this, people would recognize her face.

As the weeks went by, Kath wondered what Gordon was doing. Was he making a new film? Had he moved back home for the time being, or had he stayed at her house? She'd sent him a letter telling him she'd arrived safely and giving him the address, yet she hadn't heard from him. Maybe this had been the one thing that would tear them apart. And if that was the case, she didn't quite know how she felt about it.

At this point in her life, the only important thing was giving her sister the greatest gift she could—her baby.

Chapter Fifteen

Today

Roger stared intently at Kath, waiting for her answer. Kath took a deep breath, then let it out slowly. She sipped her water. Finally, she turned to Roger.

"I had been working on one film after another for nearly ten years. I was exhausted. My doctor said I needed to take a vacation and rest. So that's what I did. And I brought my sister, Katrina, along for company."

"And you stayed in Paris?" Roger asked.

Kath had never stated they stayed in Paris in her book. "As you well know, I wrote that we stayed in a lovely chateau north of Paris on the English Channel. It was gorgeous and relaxing."

"You also wrote that the chateau was owned by Howard Hughes. Did he spend time with you there?" Roger asked.

"No," Kath said sharply. "Howard offered his chateau to me to use as long as I wanted. I don't even know where he was living at that time, but it wasn't in France."

"I see," Roger said, smirking as he looked down at his notes. "So, was it before you left for France or after you arrived there that your sister, Katrina, discovered she was expecting a child?"

"It was after we'd arrived at the chateau that she realized she was pregnant. My sister had suffered from several miscarriages prior to that pregnancy, so she was fearful she'd lose this child too." Kath smiled over at Carolyn. "Thankfully, she was able to rest there and have the baby."

"And that baby is your niece and assistant, Carolyn Kathleen Kirby Gibson?" Roger said.

"Yes."

"How exciting that you were there when your niece was born," Roger said. "And you wrote that Katrina's husband, Grant, also came in time for the baby's arrival."

"Yes, he did," Kath said. She was growing tired and wanted the day of interviewing to be finished.

"Some people, as in the Hollywood gossips, found it convenient that you and your sister were in Europe on vacation when your niece was born. And as Carolyn grew, she looked more like you than her mother. What did you think of that speculation?" Roger's brows rose.

"I think it was exactly that," Kath said, wishing she could tell him to go screw himself. "Speculation."

Roger smiled slyly. "I figured you'd say that."

1957

Kath felt like a whale. It was a week after the new year, and she was due very soon. When she'd started showing to the point where it was obvious she was pregnant, Lucette had been a little surprised but made no mention of it. Instead, the dutiful housekeeper and cook brought the local midwife to the house and introduced her to Kath.

"Madame Arvella has delivered every baby in the area for several years," Lucette told Kath. "When the time comes, she can deliver yours."

Madame Arvella shook her hand and then asked to measure the baby and feel her belly to see how the pregnancy was progressing. Once she was finished, she nodded and said, "Bon, bon. Le bébé progresse bien."

"What did she say?" Kath asked.

"The baby is progressing well," Lucette said. She smiled. "You are sure to have a big, healthy baby."

Kath thanked the woman and had Kat place a fifty-dollar bill in her hand. "To assure she will return when I need her," Kath told Kat.

After the woman left, Kath spoke to Lucette. "Will Madame Arvella keep this pregnancy a secret?"

Lucette nodded. "Oui, Madame. Monsieur Hughes has already paid for her silence."

"Merci," Kath told the housekeeper. She was thankful to have Howard on her side.

When Grant arrived the last week of January, after two long flights and the drive from Paris, he was shocked to see how big Kath was. He couldn't help but laugh.

"Hey! I'm carrying your baby in here. Don't laugh," she said, unable to keep a straight face. She and Kat laughed along. It was true. Kath was huge.

Later, after a delicious dinner, Grant handed Kath an envelope.

"Gordon came to see me and gave this to me. He said he wanted to write to you or telegram you, but he didn't dare. The press is already making a big deal about your absence, and they'd find out where you are."

Kath set the envelope down to open later when she was alone in her bedroom. Gordon had been right not to contact her. The press would have somehow found her.

Later, when she opened the letter, tears filled her eyes. *I'm sorry*, it read. *I'm so, so sorry.* It wasn't much, but she knew it came from his heart. She loved him. It didn't matter that they fought sometimes or that he wouldn't divorce his wife. She knew that deep down, he loved her too.

The next day, they braved the chilly weather and walked along the path by the channel.

"Did Mom and Dad believe our story about Kat's pregnancy?" Kath asked Grant.

"I think so. They agreed that once Kat was here and had learned she was pregnant, she shouldn't take a plane or ship home," Grant said. "They know how important this baby is to her and me."

"Good," Kath said. "It looks like we might just get away with this."

"How will we get our names on the baby's birth certificate instead of yours?" Grant asked. "Won't the midwife have to sign it?"

Kath chuckled. "Howard has taken care of everything. He paid the midwife handsomely to say nothing. After the baby is born, you will have to go to the U.S. Consulate in Paris and request paperwork for the baby. They will never know that you are not the baby's parents."

"You're right, Kath. It looks like we will get away with this," Grant said. "Do you have any reservations about giving us this child?"

"No. None. I love my career, and although I'll love this

child, I know I wouldn't be able to give it the loving home it deserves. You two can do that. I'm satisfied with my decision."

A week later, with the help of Madame Arvella, Kath gave birth to an eight-pound, eight-ounce healthy baby girl. She let Kat and Grant hold the baby first and throughout those first few days to bond with her. Then, she finally held the little princess in her arms.

"You're beautiful. Much more than your mother. You'll grow up loved and protected, strong and opinionated, just like your grandmother and Auntie Kath." Tears streamed down her face as she stared into the little girl's blue eyes. "And I will love you forever," she whispered.

Two weeks later, Kath, along with Mr. and Mrs. Grant Kirby and their newborn daughter, Carolyn Kathleen Kirby, boarded the RMS Queen Mary to take them back across the ocean.

"Back to reality," Kath said to her sister. "Are you happy?"

Kat was beaming as she held little Carolyn in her arms, snuggled in a soft blanket. "Happier than I've ever been. Thank you, Kath. Thank you for this wonderful gift."

The sisters hugged, and later, alone in her cabin, Kath allowed herself to cry.

TODAY

"I think I've had enough for the day," Kath said, waving her niece over to help her out of the chair.

"Of course," Roger said, standing. "Cut," he called to the cameramen, then turned back to Kath. "Will you feel well enough to return tomorrow, or would you like a long weekend off?"

"I'd like to wait until Monday," Kath said. "When do you think we'll be finished? This is getting to be too much."

"Maybe Tuesday of next week?" Roger said. "We still have over half of your book to get through."

Kath sighed as her niece placed a lightweight jacket over her shoulders. "Fine. I hope we can finish soon. This has been much more than I was told it would be."

Roger nodded. "We'll do our best to finish soon. Have a nice weekend, Miss Carver." He smiled at her and walked off the set.

"Ugh. I like him less every day," Kath told Carolyn. Her niece laughed as she led Kath to the small room where they kept their stuff.

"Do you want to go to the beach for the weekend?" Carolyn asked her.

"Yes. But we'll go tomorrow. I'm too tired today for the long drive."

The next afternoon, Carolyn packed their bags, and they drove the hour to Malibu. The closer they got to the house, the more relaxed Kath felt. The Malibu house was her safe space. It was the place she felt the most at home in, despite Daniel living there full-time.

They arrived and settled in, putting their luggage upstairs and placing the groceries they'd purchased in the kitchen. Kath walked out to the front porch and sat on the wicker sofa, enjoying the salty breeze through the open windows. Years ago, she'd paid for central air conditioning to be connected to the natural gas furnace she'd had installed when her parents were growing older. But Kath had insisted on no air conditioning on the front porch. She preferred the breeze from the ocean, no matter how cold or warm it was.

Daniel returned from a walk on the beach and sat down in a chair near Kath. "It's a warm one out there today," he said.

"Yes, it is," she agreed. "Remember when it didn't bother us how warm or cool it was? When you're kids, you don't feel it. You just enjoy being outside and having fun."

Daniel nodded. "True. And we did have a lot of fun here. Although, everything was a competition. You and Graham loved being competitive. Kat, Lilly, and me, not so much."

Kath turned and looked at her brother. "I don't remember you complaining about competing. Although, you were a lot younger than the rest of us. Maybe that's why you didn't like it."

"Dad thought everything was a competition. You either won or lost at sports, games, and even life. In his mind, we all lost at life, except maybe for you."

Kath snorted. "Dad hated that I became an actress. He was only impressed when he realized I was succeeding and making good money. Before that, he was ready to cut me off."

Daniel's brows rose. "Really? I didn't know that."

"You didn't know a lot of things," Kath said sharply. "You were too young, and then you were off doing your own thing."

Daniel shrugged. "You don't know that much about me, either."

"I know that you talked to Roger about Graham after I specifically told you not to," Kath said. "He's our brother, for Pete's sake. Why would you say he committed suicide that night? It's an awful thing to say, especially when you weren't there."

Daniel sighed. "No one knows for sure that it was an accident. Everyone had their own theories."

Kath sat forward in her chair. "I knew what happened. I

was there. He'd had too much to drink, and he wouldn't listen to me. The road was curvy and dark. It was an accident."

"Yet others at the party said they'd seen him arguing with his boyfriend, and he was depressed," Daniel told her. "Plus, Dad all but disinherited him from the family for being gay. So, Graham had a lot of reasons to end his life."

Kath's heart pounded. "He did not kill himself. He also didn't dwell on how Dad treated him for who he was. He wanted to go home to see if his friend would show up. That's why he didn't stay at my place. He was hopeful, and when you're hopeful, you don't ram your car straight into a tree on purpose." She sat back, exhausted. All she'd done lately was spar with people. Kath was surprised she hadn't had a heart attack yet.

"If that's true, then I'm sorry I said anything to that interviewer. But he probably would have added it into the documentary anyway," Daniel said. "It was big news back then with a hint of scandal. *'Famous actress' brother dies in questionable accident after drunken Hollywood party.'* You saw the headlines. It didn't matter what anyone said; the papers wanted a scandal."

"Which is precisely why I don't want to talk about it now," Kath said. "It's the past, and there's no sense in maligning the dead."

"That's what these documentaries do. They dredge up past scandals so people will watch. Everyone wants to hear the *real* story," Daniel said.

"Well, they aren't going to hear it from me," Kath told him. "They only got what I wanted to tell them, and that's it. There's only so much of yourself you can give away, and my life isn't available for public consumption."

"Your life has always been out there for public consumption,"

Daniel said, laughing. "Even after all these years, they're still hungry for your story." He stood and slowly walked to the doorway. "I'm taking a long nap. You should, too."

Kath had to admit that a nap sounded good. She usually didn't sleep well at night. But here at the beach, she could open her bedroom window and relax to the sound of the waves. That helped.

Kath stood and made her way to the back staircase. She was careful with each step, not wanting to trip and fall. As a young woman, she'd run up and down these stairs with ease. Now, they could be the death of her if she fell. Growing old was hard—but being ancient was horrible.

Up in her room, Kath opened the window a little and then lay down on her bed. As usual, her thoughts went to all the people who were now gone. Family, friends, and the few special people in her life like Scotty, Rock, and most of all, Gordon.

Chapter Sixteen

1957

When Kath returned to her house, Gordon wasn't there. His clothes were gone from the guest room closet, and his personal items were no longer in the bathroom. Gordon was gone. But she didn't have to look too far for him because he'd moved into Scotty's other guest house.

Kath went down to the main house and found Scotty talking with an architect about adding another room to his house.

"Don't you have enough space for one person?" Kath asked, laughing as she hugged him.

"One can never have enough space," Scotty said.

After the architect left, the two sat on the upper terrace with ice-cold drinks.

"How is he?" Kath asked softly. She didn't have to tell him who because Scotty already knew.

"Gordon's not doing well. He's been drinking heavier than usual and was put on a leave of absence from the studio," Scotty said. "It's like he fell to pieces after you left. And Bogart's death was another heavy blow to him. You know those two were always tight. Gordon visited Bogie often in the last couple of months before his death, and each time, he'd come home and binge like crazy."

Kath had heard about Bogart's death while in France. The news had spread all over the world. She and Gordon had visited Bogart often during the first stage of his cancer diagnosis. Bogart, Gordon, Spencer Tracy, and a revolving cast of celebrities would meet for drinks and lunch at Romanoff's nearly every day when they weren't working. She knew his death would tear Gordon apart.

"Whatever happened between you two, I hope you forgive him," Scotty said seriously. "He's going to drink himself to death otherwise."

Kath shook her head sadly. "I don't know if what happened can be so easily forgiven."

In the days that followed, Kath never once saw Gordon enter or leave the other guest house. She told the studio she was back and ready to work. They had withheld her salary while she was gone, and her bank account was getting smaller. They sent her a few scripts, and one stood out more than the rest. It was a legal drama that pitted a female lawyer against an older male lawyer. Kath thought it was the perfect script for her and Gordon, so she took it to Scotty.

"I don't know if we can dry Gordon out enough to make a picture," Scotty told her. "But you're right—this is the perfect part for him."

"Will you direct it?" Kath asked. "I think if you ask him to do this movie, he'll make the effort."

"First, I have to tell the head of production that I want to direct the picture. If I get the go-ahead, then we can see if

Gordon will do it," Scotty said.

The studio loved the idea of pairing Kath with Gordon again and having Scotty direct. Scotty approached Gordon about the picture, and after reading the script, he agreed. It wasn't until he was drying out that he learned he'd be playing opposite Kath.

Gordon stormed over to Kath's house and banged on the door. When she answered it, she saw a fury in his eyes she'd never seen before.

"What's going on?" she asked, backing up into the living room. The fire in his eyes scared her.

"Did you set this film up? Is this a pity project to get me working again?" he roared.

Kath remained composed even though she felt like fleeing. "No. It was Scotty's idea and a damn good one at that. The script is good, and it's perfect for us."

All the fire in Gordon extinguished. He dropped down on the sofa and ran his hands through his hair. Kath noticed how thin he'd become while she'd been away.

"Why would you want to work with me after what happened?" Gordon asked, his voice now small and timid. "You should hate me."

Kath went to him, kneeling in front of him and taking his hands in hers as she'd done so many times before. Why did she always feel she had to save him? And why was it so easy to love a man this difficult? She looked up into his sad eyes. "We make a good team, and audiences love it when we're in a movie together. This is about making high-quality pictures. It has nothing to do with us. It's about work."

He stared at her with those blue eyes that melted her heart every time. He didn't ask her about the baby or her time away.

He didn't ask her how she felt or if she was okay. What he did do was reach out and pull her to him, hugging her tightly. "I'm sorry. I wish I was a stronger man. I'm so sorry."

Tears filled her eyes at his words. She knew he could never offer her more than his love for as long as they were together. But maybe that was enough.

Gordon had his drinking under control by the time they began shooting the picture titled *Guilt*. It always amazed Kath how Gordon could just stop a bad habit cold turkey.

At this point in time, MGM was known as the studio that made musicals and little else. The studio heads hoped that this new Carver-Quinn movie would bring them back as a studio that made serious films.

Kath and Gordon still lived separately while working on the film, and they hadn't rekindled their relationship. But being together in nearly every take—fighting one moment and kissing another—made it hard for Kath to have only a working relationship with Gordon. She hopelessly loved him, and by the end of the picture, he moved back in with her and they never spoke about France or the baby.

Guilt was released in early 1958 with the entire publicity department behind it. Kath and Gordon walked the red carpet together at the premiere, which brought cheers from the crowd. Gordon's wife had made a fuss, but he ignored her this time. This was his job. He told her if she wanted to live like a queen, she had to put up with the publicity.

The film drew rave reviews from critics for both the story and acting. Even Scotty was getting great reviews for his directing. It was a huge success for them all, especially the studio, and Kath couldn't have been happier. Still, despite the hit, the studio continued its cuts of contract actors and new films.

Kath made two more films that year, which weren't as important or impressive as *Guilt*. The studio had let their best contract actors go over the past few years including Clark Gable and Spencer Tracy. Gordon Quinn and Kath were two of the very few contract players left. When the Oscars came along in early 1959, Kath, Gordon, and Scotty were all nominated for Academy Awards. Kath won best actress, but neither Gordon nor Scotty won their categories. Instead of feeling elated as she'd once thought she would by winning such a prestigious award, she felt empty. Her castmates should have won too because the film was that good. She swore she'd never attend the Academy Awards again after that. It was much ado about nothing.

Right after winning her Oscar, Kath and Gordon were let go from their MGM contracts. It seemed ridiculous considering their great success that year, but the studio was bleeding money and had to cut back somewhere. It was the end of an era.

TODAY

Kath was once again in the bland studio awaiting Roger's next question.

"You won your first best actress Oscar in 1959 for the movie *Guilt,* which you made with Gordon Quinn," Roger stated. "How did that feel?"

Kath wanted to roll her eyes but resisted the urge. "I was honored to receive an Oscar for that film. It was one of the best films I ever made. But I did feel that Gordon Quinn and Scott Coolidge, our director, were cheated that year. The picture wouldn't have been as spectacular without them."

"That's very kind of you to give credit to your co-star and director," Roger said, smiling. "But I'm sure you deserved that Oscar all on your own."

Kath studied Roger. Today, he wore a dove gray suit with a white shirt and royal blue tie. He looked ridiculous. His tie should have been a deep gray, not blue. Of course, that was just her opinion. "Have you ever watched the film *Guilt*?"

Roger sat back and cleared his throat. "Um, no. I don't believe I've had the pleasure. I suppose it's one I could rent or stream on Netflix."

"Well, if you watched it, you'd understand why I felt the way I did. Gordon Quinn gave one of his greatest performances in that film. He deserved the Oscar."

"Yes. Well, one could say you're biased, don't you think?" Roger said, chuckling.

Kath knew he was attempting to be funny, but she didn't think he was. She only glared at him.

"Well." Roger quickly looked down at his cards again. "You said in your book that 1959 was a year of ups and downs. Both you and Gordon Quinn were let go from your contracts with MGM not long after you won the Oscar. That must have been devasting."

"It seemed that way at first," Kath said. "But we both knew the studio was bleeding money and couldn't afford contract players anymore. They'd let go of all their big stars, and we were two of the very last. But then, all the studios were chang-ing. Gone were the days of making hundreds of films a year. The new order was actors were free to move from studio to studio and studios only made a few pictures a year. Luckily for me, the offers kept coming in, and I had my choice of scripts instead of being told what movies to make. I hired an agent, and I worked steadily for years."

"And Gordon Quinn? Was it the same for him?" Roger raised an eyebrow.

"How should I know?" she shot back. "I was too busy with my career to keep tabs on everyone else." Kath knew he was trying to trip her up again about their relationship, but she couldn't be tricked so easily.

"You made a few films between 1959 and 1962, but that year was a hard one for you," Roger said, trying to look serious and sympathetic all at once. Instead, Kath thought he looked constipated.

"Yes," Kath said. "That year was a difficult one personally. I almost lost someone close to me, and the entire world was stunned by the loss of one of our own."

1962

Kath's phone startled her awake in the middle of the night. It was early February, and she'd worked a long day on her current film and was exhausted.

"Answer the damn phone!" Gordon bellowed, half awake beside her. Kath finally got her bearings and lifted the receiver.

"Hello?"

"Kath? I'm so sorry to wake you, but it's about Dad," a frazzled Kat said from the other end of the line.

Kath sat straight up and turned on the lamp on the nightstand. "What's happened?"

"He was rushed to the hospital. Mama just called me. Grant and I are going to run there now to see what happened,"

Kat hurriedly told her.

"Tell me which hospital, and I'll meet you there," Kath said. After Kat told her where to go, Kath hung up the phone and quickly dressed in yesterday's slacks and shirt.

By now, Gordon was wide awake. "Would you like me to go with you?" he asked, looking concerned.

Kath stopped a moment, touched by his offer. "I would. But you can't risk being seen with me in the middle of the night. Besides, you have to be at work early tomorrow, so you should get some sleep."

"You have work tomorrow, too," Gordon said.

"I'll call in sick. My father comes first." Kath grabbed her bag and car keys and gave Gordon a peck on the cheek.

"Be careful driving," Gordon said. "I'm sure your father will be okay. He's only sixty-two. He's the healthiest man I know."

"I hope he'll be okay too." Kath rushed out the door to her car.

The drive seemed to take forever, even though the roads were empty and the hospital wasn't far away. At times like these, Kath wished she had a normal relationship so she'd have someone at her side. But as long as her heart belonged to Gordon, that would never happen.

Kath arrived at the same time as Kat and Grant. They entered the quiet hospital, and Kath asked the receptionist what room her father was in.

"Visiting hours don't start until eight a.m.," the young girl said. "You'll have to come back later."

Kath's eyes turned to slits. She wasn't going to waste time on this nonsense. "My father, Crandell Carver, was rushed here a little while ago. I need to see him now."

The woman stared at Kath, and suddenly her eyes lit up. "Carver? You're Kathleen Carver, aren't you?" She looked at Kath, starstruck. "Oh, yes, Miss Carver. I'll check and find his room for you."

Finally, they were told to go to the third floor to room 303. On the elevator ride up, Grant chuckled. "Must be nice to get movie star privileges."

"It doesn't hurt," Kath said, grinning.

They found their father's room, but he wasn't in the bed. Their mother, however, was sitting in a chair.

"Mom!" Kath rushed to her mother and hugged her. Catherine hugged her back tightly as if hanging on for dear life.

"I'm so glad you're all here," Catherine said after hugging Kat, too. "I was so scared when your father fell in the living room. The doctor said he might have had a minor heart attack. They're taking X-rays now."

"A heart attack? Dad?" Kath was shocked. "But he's so active and healthy."

Catherine nodded. "I know. It's a shock. But we're hoping there are no lasting effects from it."

When Crandell returned to the room, being wheeled in by a nurse, he looked tired but otherwise fine. "You girls didn't have to come here in the middle of the night," he said. The nurse helped him into bed despite his protests that he could do it himself.

"Of course, we had to come," Kath insisted. "For you and for Mom."

Crandell gave her a wan smile. "Well, I'm glad you did, then," he said. "But I'm fine. Just a minor blip. I'm as healthy as I've ever been."

Kath crossed her arms. "You can't be that healthy if you

had a heart attack, Dad. Do the doctors know what caused it yet?"

"No," Crandell said. "And I don't care anyway. I live a healthy lifestyle, eating right and getting plenty of exercise, so there's nothing else I can do."

The nurse came in and shooed them out. "Your father needs his sleep," she told them. "Come back during visiting hours."

"That means you, too, Catherine," Crandell said. "Go home and get some sleep. Hopefully, I will be able to leave this place tomorrow."

They all hugged Crandell goodbye, and Kath offered to drive her mother home. Once they were in the Toluca Lake house, Catherine fell apart.

"What will I do if something happens to your father?" she said, tears spilling down her cheeks. "He's my everything. I'd be lost without him."

Kath was surprised to hear her mother so distraught. She'd always thought of her mother as the strong parent. Catherine was independent and never leaned on anyone. But here she was, falling to pieces over the thought of her father dying.

"It'll be okay, Mom," Kath said soothingly. "Dad is fine, and I'm sure you both will live long, long lives."

"You don't know that," Catherine said. "We're getting older. Either of us could die at any time."

"You're just tired, Mom. Get some sleep, and things will look better in the morning, I promise." Kath walked her mother up to her bedroom and stayed with her until she was in bed. "I'll stay the night in my old room. If you need me, just call for me, okay?"

Her mother nodded, her eyelids already drooping. Kath figured the trip to the hospital in the middle of the night must have taken a toll on her mother.

As Kath lay in her childhood bed, her thoughts kept returning to her father's heart attack. Her parents were physically active and involved in many organizations. Kath had never thought of either one of them dying. Yet, her father could have died tonight. It felt odd coming to terms with the fact that her parents were growing old and might not have many years left. That meant she was growing older, too. That brought on a whole new set of depressing thoughts. She was in her thirties now. Did she like the life she was leading? Was she satisfied with the choices she'd made so far? Did she regret giving up her daughter?

It was too much to contemplate in the early morning hours after having been up all night. Kath brushed her thoughts away. She'd worry about her father first and herself another time. Before going to bed, she called the studio to tell them she couldn't come in that day because of a family emergency, and then Kath laid down again and tried to sleep.

Chapter Seventeen

1962

"An enlarged heart," Crandell said in disbelief. "I can't even fathom my having such a thing." He was home from the hospital and the entire family had come over for Sunday dinner to see him. Gordon had accompanied Kath for support.

"So, what did the cardiologist say you should do?" Kath asked. She wasn't one to dwell on problems, only solutions.

Lilly glared at Kath. She'd already made it known that she disapproved of Gordon's presence because he was an adulterer. She'd said it out loud for all to hear, and Crandell had sharply told her and her husband Eugene to keep their opinions to themselves.

"Dad will have to rest and take it easy from now on," Lilly said directly to Kath. "And the last thing he needs is any kind of stress or aggravation."

Kath rolled her eyes. "Then maybe you shouldn't visit, so he'll stay calm."

"Girls!" Catherine said as if they were still children and needed to be corrected. "No fighting at the table."

Kath didn't care if she was too old to do it; she stuck her tongue out at the self-righteous Lilly.

Crandell shook his head and suppressed a grin at Kath's antics. "The doctor said I'll need to be on medication for my high blood pressure and take an aspirin every day. That's it. He did say that my activity level should be moderate—in other words, don't overdo it. But don't think I can't still beat you all in a swimming contest."

Kath, Kat, and Daniel laughed, but Lilly pursed her lips.

"Dad. You have to take your health seriously. We want you around for the grandchildren for as long as possible," Lilly said.

Kath stared over at the smaller table her mother had set up as a children's table. Lilly's two children, Jonathan, age eight, and Lauren, age five, sat next to Kat's daughter Carolyn, also five years old. Kath's gaze stayed the longest on Carolyn. She was a beautiful little girl with wavy auburn hair and Gordon's large, blue eyes. Kath wondered if Gordon was curious at all about his daughter, who sat only a few feet away from him. He hadn't even glanced in her direction all evening.

"Of course, we want Dad around for a long time," Daniel finally said. "But we also don't want him to be bored to death doing nothing." Daniel was now in his late twenties and was a tall, blond, and blue-eyed man. He carried himself like he was the king of England, but in reality, he'd hopped jobs endlessly around Hollywood before landing at the post office last year.

For once, Kath agreed with her younger brother. "Keeping active helps people stay young. Of course, Dad will keep doing as he's always done."

"Don't any of you worry," Crandell said. "I will definitely be around and able to keep teaching the younger generation how to swim, play volleyball, and cheat at chess like Kath has always done." He laughed.

"Cheat? Me?" Kath grinned at her father. "It's impossible to cheat at chess."

Gordon spoke up for the first time all evening. "Somehow, you manage, though."

This caused fits of laughter all around. Kath didn't mind being the butt of the joke—she was just happy to see her father looking cheerful again.

"She's pretty, isn't she?" Gordon said to Kath on the drive home after dinner. He had his eyes glued on the road as he drove, so Kath couldn't see the emotion on his face. But Kath knew him better than he thought.

"Carolyn is beautiful. She has her mother's hair and her father's eyes. I hope she grows up to have her father's intelligence as well," Kath said.

Gordon didn't respond. He reached over and took Kath's hand in his. Kath hoped he wouldn't see the tears that had sprung up in her eyes beneath her sunglasses.

* * *

As the year progressed, Kath stayed busy making movies, but each one was less popular than the last. She had chosen dramas because she wanted to be considered a serious actress, but the audiences weren't showing up. Kath constantly scoured the scripts sent to her in the hope of finding the perfect part to keep her star rising.

While her career was lagging, Gordon was enjoying an upswing in his career. Ever since he was nominated for *Guilt,* the scripts he was offered were brilliant, and he chose well. Two of his newest films were the highest-grossing pictures he'd ever made. Kath was thrilled for him. It wasn't long ago that Hollywood had almost given up on him. But no longer being tied down by one studio seemed to work well for Gordon. Now, she had to find a way to make it work for her.

Surprisingly, a script found her from an unlikely source.

Kath walked into her living room with a new script in hand one evening and curled up on the sofa to read it. Gordon was also reading a new script while relaxing in his favorite reading chair in the corner. He glanced up at her as she settled in.

"New script?" he asked, taking a puff of his pipe. He was trying to quit smoking cigarettes and was told a pipe would be better for him.

"Yes," Kath said, smiling up at him. "Howard sent it to me. It's for a play, not a movie, though."

Gordon frowned. "Howard Hughes? Why on earth would he send you a play?"

"Of course, Howard Hughes. He called me the other day and asked me why I was making such terrible films." Kath laughed. "I was insulted at first but then had to agree with him. They aren't as good as some of my earlier ones."

"And?" Gordon said impatiently.

"He said he had a play he'd bought a while ago that he thought would be perfect for me. If I decide to do it, he'd fund the play and give me half the profits. Then, if the play is a hit, I can sell the script to a studio with the condition I play the leading lady."

"And what makes him think it will be a hit?" Gordon asked. He was chewing on the end of his pipe, a habit that annoyed Kath.

"Because Howard has a knack for these things. I trust his judgment," Kath said.

Gordon stared at her for a moment. "You trust the judgment of a man who's slowly losing his mind?"

Kath bristled. "Howard isn't losing his mind," she snapped. "I'll be the first to admit he has odd habits and goes on strange binges, but he knows show business, and I trust him."

He glared at her, then shrugged. "It's your career."

"Yes, it is." Kath opened the script and began reading despite being furious. She knew Gordon was just jealous of Howard, and that's why he wasn't being supportive. But what was there to be jealous of? Howard was a friend and nothing more.

Kath loved the script. She called Howard that next week and told him she'd like to do the play. He said he'd have contacts in New York begin work on it, and they'd get to rehearsals as soon as possible. Howard had contacts with the best directors, casting agents, and designers in the business, and he'd call in whatever favors he needed to make this play a success. Kath trusted him implicitly.

"Will you be coming to New York, too?" she asked Howard hopefully.

"I can do everything from here," Howard said, not telling her where "here" was. Kath knew he used to live at the Beverly Hills Hotel, and even though he owned houses, he moved around a lot. With a plan in motion to return to the theater, Kath was excited.

As Kath made plans to rent a friend's apartment in New York and move there for her upcoming play, tragedy struck Hollywood. Early on August 5th, she and Gordon awoke to the news of Marilyn Monroe's death. Both of them had known Marilyn since the young woman had started in show business, and they were saddened by her sudden death.

That day, Kath's phone rang constantly. Friends called, crying about Marilyn's passing. Rock was in tears over her loss, and her friend Jane was in shock.

"She was so sweet and so talented," Jane told Kath. "Why on earth would she kill herself? It makes no sense."

Kath agreed. She'd gotten to know Marilyn quite well when she and Rock and the young starlet had made *Grab a Good Girl*. Yes, in the later years, everyone knew Marilyn had problems with drugs, but Kath would never have guessed she'd die this way.

Newspapers were filled with the day-to-day details of her death to the point where Kath stopped reading them. It was all too sad.

Marilyn's funeral was a small one and even though Kath and Gordon had wanted to attend, very few people were invited. Kath understood. Marilyn's ex-husband, Joe Dimaggio, hadn't wanted the funeral to be a star-studded event. Despite that, onlookers swarmed as close to the memorial as possible, and the media strained to take photos and video of it all. It sickened Kath that the press wouldn't leave the poor woman alone, even in death.

Kath happily left Hollywood to begin rehearsals for her play in New York in early September. She hated leaving Gordon behind, but he was busy making a movie, and it wouldn't have looked proper for him to follow her to New York anyway. So, with great excitement and a little anxiety, Kath looked forward to a new phase of her life.

The play, *My Turn*, was about two women who, after years of marriage, divorce their husbands and start a clothing design business together. It was a modern topic that Kath knew women could relate to, and she loved the snappy dialogue and the feel-good ending. She had hoped they could get Lauren Bacall to play the other female role, but unfortunately, she was busy. Instead, they found a successful theater actor, Allison Holmes. Allison was nearly as tall as Kath, but she had short blond hair and brilliant blue eyes. Her figure was curvy—the exact opposite of Kath's long and lean shape—and she had the absolute best personality that meshed with Kath's. Allison was witty and sharp and loved sarcasm, but she wasn't mean. Kath liked her immediately, and once rehearsals started, the two became fast friends.

The director Howard had chosen was Clyde Drummond, a veteran of the theater. His appearance was the opposite of his personality. When Kath first met him, she thought he was a stagehand. He was short with dark, shaggy hair and wore thick black-rimmed glasses over his dark eyes. His suits looked like they were two sizes too big for him. But once she started working with him, she realized he was an actor's director. He knew how to mold, bend, and even shape a performance without upsetting an actor in the least. He got the best out of the two women and the entire cast.

In between wardrobe fittings and rehearsals, Kath and Ali went everywhere together. They frequented the five-star restaurants, went to other plays, and sat in coffee houses talking for hours. Eventually, the press started following the two, taking photos and shouting questions, but they ignored them and went about their business.

Jane called Kath one morning. "They're doing it again," Jane told her, laughter in her voice. "The gossip columnists claim you left Gordon for a new fling in New York City—the woman you're co-starring with."

Kath never read the movie magazines anymore, so she had

no idea what rumors were circulating. "What is wrong with them? First, they insist I'm in love with you, then Gordon, now Allison? That doesn't even make sense!" She laughed despite how annoying it was.

"Well, I'm jealous you've found a new woman friend," Jane said. "Is she replacing me?"

Kath knew she was teasing her. "Never! You are my one true friend for life. But we've had a great time rehearsing and carousing around New York together. I really needed this break from Hollywood. Everything here is so different. And actors take acting seriously—it's not just about fame, awards, and movie ticket sales. Although, if this play bombs, it will be about money."

"It won't bomb," Jane told her. "But if it does, Howard can afford it."

Kath knew that was true, but she really hoped to have success with it. This play would make an excellent movie and would be perfect for today's audiences. It could revive her career and make her relevant again.

On opening night, Kath received a huge bouquet of yellow roses from Gordon, wishing her success. Her heart went out to him—she did miss the grouchy curmudgeon. She called him before heading to the theater and was happy when he answered the phone.

"Someone sent me an outrageous bouquet of roses," she told him. "And I just love them."

"Well, hopefully, they weren't from one of your many girl-friends," he teased. "Seriously, though, I'm rooting for you. I may not have wanted you to leave, but I do want you to succeed."

"Thanks, dear," Kath said, tears filling her eyes. "I have

a lot riding on this, so I hope it does well. Knowing you're behind me makes me very happy."

Kath headed to the theater, nervous about more than just the play. Her parents had come across the country to see the play, which made her doubly anxious. They had stayed in a hotel near the theater because they didn't want their presence in the apartment to make her more nervous. For the first time ever, her parents would see her live on stage, and the thought of that was daunting.

Then give a damn good performance! the voice inside her head told her. Well, she'd certainly try.

Another beautiful bouquet of roses awaited Kath in her dressing room at the theater. Howard had sent them wishing her luck. Kath dressed and tried to get into her character's mindset while waiting for the five-minute call. Once it came, she stepped out of her room and walked past all the backstage equipment to the wings where she'd enter. Ali was there, dressed and ready, and the two hugged but didn't say a word. They were both transforming into their characters and didn't want to break the trance.

The curtains opened, and Kath walked onstage to applause and, hopefully, to a successful play.

Chapter Eighteen

Today

"You found yourself onstage in New York at the end of 1962. That must have been exciting," Roger said. "Tell us how you felt about it."

Kath felt dazed, jumping from one timeline to another in her life. "Yes. The play *My Turn*. Howard Hughes had bought the play and told me it was time I got back to my roots on the stage to boost my career. As always, he was right. Howard had a knack for knowing what the public wanted, whether in entertainment or products, and he was rarely wrong."

"So, the play was a success?" Roger asked, beaming slyly like he knew the answer.

Of course, he knows the answer. It's right there in the book, Kath thought. "Yes. It was a huge success. After a year on Broadway, I sold the screen rights to 20th Century Fox on the condition that I play the lead role. I tried to convince them to hire Allison Holmes for the other female role, but they refused. She was fine with not making the movie, but I wasn't. She had been perfect for that part. But I did get Scotty to direct, and that made me happy."

"Speaking of Allison Holmes," Roger interrupted, raising an eyebrow. "Weren't there rumors about you and her while you were in New York?"

Kath sighed. "There have always been rumors about my personal life and I've never paid attention to any of it. I know the truth. I don't have to explain myself to anyone."

Roger sat up straighter. "Yes, of course. It's your personal life. But that's why we're here, isn't it? To talk about your life and your career. Even if some of the topics are uncomfortable."

"My life and my career," Kath said slowly. "That is what we're talking about. Stick to what I wrote in the book, and we'll get along just fine." She sat back and crossed her arms.

"Well, okay," Roger said, staring at his notes. "You spoke about your friendship with Howard Hughes quite often, and he was the person who bought the play for you. Did the two of you see each other while you were in New York doing the play?"

Not this again, Kath thought. "No. He set up the play for me and then gave me full reign of it. He even signed over the rights to me. Howard didn't need the money—he liked helping a friend. I have always been thankful for his friendship."

"How was Mr. Hughes' behavior in 1962? Was he sinking into insanity by then?" Roger asked.

Anger erupted in Kath. "What is wrong with you? We've had this discussion before. If all you're going to do is malign the people I knew, then I'm finished with this interview." She stood, and Carolyn was quickly at her side to steady her.

Roger stood, too, a deep crease between his eyes. "Please, Miss Carver. I didn't mean any offense by that question. We all know that he slowly sank into insanity. I'm just asking if you knew how his mental health was at that time."

"Howard Hughes was never insane!" Kath yelled. "He had a variety of issues but never insanity. He was a great man, and someone like you would never understand that!"

"Aunt Kath, please calm down," Carolyn said softly. "This interview is going to kill you."

"I'm so sorry," Roger said, trying to sound calm. "Please. We'll change the subject. Let's take a ten-minute break and start over. I didn't mean to upset you, Miss Carver."

"You damn well did mean to upset me," Kath said, but she allowed Carolyn to help her sit again. "Or else you wouldn't make false accusations and pry where you're not welcome."

"I apologize," Roger said, not looking sorry at all. "We'll take a break and start again. I promise to do better." He turned and left the sound stage.

"I loathe that evil little man," Kath said through gritted teeth.

Carolyn laughed. "I agree with you on that. He's a slimeball."

Kath turned to her niece. "Yes. That's the word. Slimeball." Then she relaxed and laughed, too.

Mr. Slimeball reappeared a few minutes later, looking calmer and refreshed. "Are we able to work a little longer today?" he asked Kath as if she were a senile old lady.

"I'm not sure about *we*, but *I'm* ready to work some more," she said tightly.

"Wonderful. Let's move on." He turned toward the stage manager and waited for the countdown, then began. "Miss Carver. You made the movie version of *My Turn* in early 1964. We all know it was a smash hit that year. What happened with your career after that?"

Kath took a breath. She was getting so tired of this. "My career took off. I was being offered every great role that came along—so many that I had a difficult time choosing which to pick. It was the highlight of my career." *Unfortunately,* Kath thought, *it was the worst years for Gordon.*

1965

Kath's career skyrocketed after the release of her movie *My Turn*. The fact that she had also sold the movie rights to the studio and was a producer on the project was significant for a woman in Hollywood. She was nominated for an Oscar and so was Scotty as the director. When they both won, everyone involved in the picture was ecstatic. It escalated Kath's career and everyone wanted her in their pictures, magazines, and even on television talk shows. But Kath, being the private person she was, only wanted to make movies and do none of the rest.

That year, Kath made a successful suspense movie with Cary Grant and a drama with her old friend, Anthony Crane. She was choosing her films carefully. She didn't want to choose something that would cause the public to turn on her again. Her image was all she had, and she was very protective of it.

Unfortunately, as her star rose again, Gordon's was fading fast. After a few successful films back in '62-'63, he was no longer offered good scripts. The film industry was changing. Madcap comedies and musicals were all the rage, as well as "artistic" films that Gordon didn't find interesting. The less he worked, the more he drank.

"What's wrong with Hollywood these days?" Gordon complained to Kath one evening at their house. They sat in the living room, him in his favorite chair and Kath on the sofa. "All the movies seem cheap—like B movies used to be. Where are the dramas and suspense movies? Even the comedies are more like slapstick than being smart and funny."

Kath didn't want to remind him that she was finding good scripts. But maybe the studios weren't offering the better ones to Gordon. She had no idea why. He was such a talented actor with a list of strong roles behind him.

"I asked Spencer at lunch the other day why he was doing those awful films," Gordon continued. "I'd been offered his part first in that ridiculous movie, *It's a Mad, Mad, Mad, Mad, World*, but I turned it down. And then the talented Spencer Tracy accepted the role." Gordon shook his head. "He told me he's had to change with the times like everyone else, or else he wouldn't be able to pay his bills. He also said he wasn't above doing comedy, but I reminded him that movie wasn't his type of comedy—it was slapstick. He just shrugged and said, 'It made a lot of money.'"

Kath knew the movie was one of the highest grossing films of the 1963-1964 season, and the critics had loved it. But she didn't say that to Gordon, who was just blowing off steam.

"Movies have changed," Kath said gently. "People have changed too. If we don't keep up with the times, our careers will be over."

"I don't see you making these stupid films," Gordon said, drinking down a large gulp of bourbon. "You're still getting good scripts that do well at the box office. I was sent a script for a television movie. Can you imagine that? Television! I'm a serious actor. I'd never lower myself for that medium."

Kath shrugged. "Television is the future, too, dear. It's not going away. And they will need good movies to keep the public's interest. Lucille Ball has done quite well on television. And several of our contemporaries have done serious work on the CBS Playhouse 90 shows. So, I wouldn't mark it off entirely."

Gordon stared hard at her. "Would you do television?"

"I guess I'd say never say never," Kath said.

Gordon stood and made himself another drink. He'd gained weight since he wasn't working, and the alcohol wasn't helping. "It's easy for you to say because your career is booming right now. Wait until you fall flat on your face again."

Kath winced. She hated it when Gordon was drunk and angry at the world. "You could try returning to the theater, like I did, to revive your career. They're making amazing plays on Broadway these days."

"I'm too old for the theater," he mumbled as he sat back in his chair.

Kath chuckled. "Too old? You're only forty-nine. You're in your prime for male roles. It's women who are tossed aside at your age."

"Theater is a lot of work. It takes high energy. You have abundant energy, but I don't."

"I've always had a lot of nervous energy, that's for sure," Kath agreed. "Maybe we should look for a script we could do together. Our movies as a team always did well at the box office."

"No!" Gordon said sharply. "I don't need your charity. If I revive my career, I'll do it myself."

Stubborn old cuss, Kath thought. "We should go to the beach house this weekend," she suggested. "You always feel better after spending a few days there. And the weather has been beautiful. I'm sure Dad and Mom would enjoy the company."

The next day, a sober Gordon agreed that a weekend at

the beach might lift his spirits. On Friday, they packed a few clothes and headed to Malibu. As the car drove over the hill and the ocean spread out before them, Kath could already feel the tension leaving her body.

"I do love it here," Gordon said as he lifted the suitcases from the trunk.

Crandell and Catherine were already there and greeted them at the door. Crandell was suntanned and bright-eyed, even if he looked a bit too thin. Catherine looked tired but happy to have family at the house.

"Finally. Someone to have swimming races with," Crandell said as he hugged Kath. "And you, Gordon. You can join us for a game of volleyball."

Gordon snorted. "I plan to lay in a beach chair all weekend and sleep to the sound of the waves. No overexertion for this old man."

"Old man?" Crandell said. "Ridiculous. I'm ancient compared to you, and I'm still in top form."

"Dear," Catherine said softly. "You promised you'd take it easy this weekend. Please don't overdo it and wear yourself out."

"Oh, I'll be fine," Crandell said with a grin. "Get your swimsuit on, Kath, and we'll go for a swim before dinner."

After a quick swim with her father, Kath joined her mother and their cook in the kitchen to help make dinner. Their cook, a lovely Japanese woman named Mio Saitō, had begun working for them after Mrs. Cray retired in 1960. Mio was an excellent cook and a welcome member of their family.

"I wish your father would slow down," Catherine confided to Kath as they cut up vegetables that Mio would sauté. "He worries me. Even though he's retired, he continues to fill his days and never takes a break to rest."

"I'm sure he likes to stay busy," Kath said, chopping carrots. "What about you, Mom? Are you still attending your meetings and women's organizations?"

Catherine sighed. "I've resigned from a few of the groups. I'm spending more time helping at our local soup kitchen and trying to get a food bank set up in the area. There is such a great need for these places around the Los Angeles area."

"That's wonderful," Kath said, amazed at her mother's continued work with those less fortunate. "I'd be happy to donate to both causes."

Catherine smiled. "I'd appreciate that, dear."

Gordon had fallen asleep on the lounge chair on the porch after dinner, and Kath didn't have the heart to wake him up. She gently placed a blanket over him and let him sleep. He usually had trouble sleeping, so it was good to see he was resting peacefully. On her way to bed, she saw her father was still up, reading a book in the living room. She sat in a chair near his.

"How have you been feeling, Dad?" she asked.

"I've been fine," he said. "And I'm not just saying that. I'm doing fine. I'm taking my medications and following the cardiologist's instructions."

"That's good to hear," Kath said. "Mom seems overly tired."

"Your mom does too much, volunteering her time everywhere. She tells me to slow down, but she doesn't do it herself." He chuckled. "I guess we're just from a generation that likes to stay busy."

"I'm that way too," Kath said. "If I'm not working, it drives me crazy."

"See," Crandell said with a smile. "It runs in the blood." He studied her for a moment. "How is Gordon doing? He looks tired."

"It's been a hard couple of years for him," Kath said. "He has to continue to work to support his kids, but he hates the scripts he's been given. And when he's upset, he drinks. It takes a lot out of him."

Crandell nodded. "It's none of my business, dear, but don't you think your life would be easier if you found someone who isn't already attached? Someone you could see freely and not have to hide. All the secrecy must take a toll on you and Gordon."

"I love him, Dad," Kath said softly. "You know me. I've always been selfish and done what I've wanted. But with Gordon, I'm different. I actually want to be with him and take care of him. He's such a sad, lonely soul. He needs me."

"But what do you need, Kath? Who takes care of you?" Crandell asked.

Kath smiled wanly. "I can take care of myself. I always have. I always will."

They had a wonderful weekend with her parents, and Gordon looked rested by the time they left on Sunday night. Kath liked seeing him happy and carefree. He was always so serious that it was a nice change. She hoped his career would take a turn for the better soon. Work always made him happy.

On the ride home, Kath thought about her father's words. Would life be easier if she found someone else to share it with? Definitely. But since she and Gordon had been together, she'd never even looked at another man. No one else compared to him. He was smart, talented, and interested in life. He could be funny and have a good time when he was in a good mood. He could also become morose and depressed at times. But despite it all, she loved him, and nothing would ever change that.

Chapter Nineteen

TODAY

After a long day with Mr. Slick, Kath and Carolyn returned to her Bel Air home. Kath relaxed while Carolyn made an easy dinner of baked chicken and salad, and they sat at the kitchen table to eat.

"The publisher called me today while you were being interviewed," Carolyn said between bites of her salad. "They're hoping you'd be willing to do an appearance or two when the book releases."

Kath stopped eating and stared at Carolyn. "Good God! They aren't expecting me to sit and sign books at some stuffy bookstore, are they?"

"I think they were hoping you'd do a signing, but I told them that would be difficult with your arthritis. So, they suggested you might consider initialing books or doing selfies with readers. I guess most readers today want a picture more than an autograph."

Kath sighed. "Isn't it enough that I'm doing these interviews for the documentary? How much more do they want from me?"

"I could tell them no," Carolyn said. "The book will sell well whether or not you make appearances. They just hoped you would."

Kath returned to eating her meal. This was why she'd never done interviews or press of any kind throughout the years. She hated talking about herself and having photos taken. Especially now that she was older. It was like everyone wanted to take a piece of your soul. Just because a person made movies didn't mean they should be available for public consumption.

After a while, Kath sighed. "I guess we should do at least one. I could try initialing books, but there should be a limit. If I only do photos with readers, they may not buy the book, and isn't that the purpose of the whole thing?"

Carolyn smiled. "Yes, it is. I'll arrange something. People will line up for miles just to meet you, you know."

Kath shook her head. "I don't know why. I'm just an old lady who used to be famous."

"Ha!" Carolyn said. "You're an icon. There is no 'used to' for you."

"When does this blasted book come out?" Kath asked.

"Early September. And the documentary will show in early October," Carolyn told her.

"I'll be so happy when this is all over. You know how much I hate crowds," Kath said, pushing her plate aside.

"I know, Aunt Kath. But it's all part of the process."

Later, as Kath lay in bed, she thought about doing appearances for the book and her stomach turned. Everyone thought she was tough as nails, and when it came to business, she was. But appearing in crowds or discussing her personal life scared her to death. She had hated it when the press chased after her for a picture or story, and had really hated that she could never go places without it being reported on. Now, no one cared about her, but when the book came out, that would all change. It wouldn't be above the press, or paparazzi, as they were now called, to chase down an old lady to see if they could squeeze one more story from her.

"Parasites! Every one of them," Kath said aloud. Hadn't they killed enough people? They harassed poor Marilyn into an early grave and chased down that lovely princess, Diana, to her death. And what about the horrible things the press had said about Elvis Presley those last months before he died. "Fat and Forty," were the headlines. The list of casualties went on and on.

Sure, Kath thought, the press could blame all those deaths on addiction or driving too fast or crazy behavior. But the truth was, when you continually push people into corners until they have to become hermits in their own life, they snap. Kath had always tried to protect herself so she wouldn't become one of those casualties.

Unable to sleep, Kath sat up in bed and looked out over the lights of Hollywood. She remembered how many times she couldn't be with Gordon—important times—because the press would be all over them. Yes, it was her own fault for being involved with a married man, but still, who cared? Why would it be news? Everyday people were able to live their lives incognito, so why not them?

But there was the one time when she'd thrown caution to the wind and went to be with Gordon no matter what the consequences. Because when someone you loved needed you, that's what you did.

1967

Kath's work schedule had been crazy for the past couple of years and she didn't see it slowing down anytime soon. She had projects booked one right after the other. Not that she was complaining. Being this busy as an actress was unheard of and she wanted to ride the wave as long as possible. She wished she could say the same for Gordon.

Although Gordon had made a couple of movies over the past two years, his heart wasn't in it. He hated the movies being made these days. He would have preferred to do a detective movie or political intrigue, but he wasn't sought out for those roles. Younger, good-looking actors were given those leads. He was now considered the second or third character in a movie. It was a long fall for someone of his caliber.

Kath returned from a two-week filming on location in Italy and walked into her house, excited to see Gordon. She'd worried about his being alone and hadn't heard a word from him. But when she searched the house after dropping her suitcase in the entryway, he was nowhere to be found.

Kath headed down the stone steps to Scotty's house. She thought that Gordon was there, having an afternoon drink with the director or playing a game of chess. Seeing the glass patio door open, she entered, half expecting to find Gordon sprawled out on the sofa, napping. Instead, she found a ruffled-looking Scotty.

"Oh, Kath. I'm so glad you're home," Scotty said, hugging her tightly.

"Thanks, dear," she said, feeling confused. Scotty was a toucher, but this was more than she was used to. "Do you know where Gordon is?"

Scotty's forehead creased with worry. "I was told not to say anything to you, but now that you're home, I don't see why I shouldn't," he said.

"Scotty! Tell me. What's happened?" Kath was growing scared.

"It's Gordon. After you left, I didn't see him around the house that first week. I thought he was either working or holing up in the house. So, I left him alone. Then, last Sunday afternoon, he came over to ask me if I had any bourbon. I figured he'd run out. He looked terrible. His eyes were red-rimmed, and his face was pale. It looked as if he hadn't shaved or showered for days. I asked if I could get him coffee instead or if he'd like to join me for lunch, but all he wanted was bourbon. So, I reluctantly went to the bar to get him a bottle. He followed me inside, then I saw his eyes roll back in his head and he dropped to the floor."

"Oh, my God!" Kath felt sick. "Where is he?"

Scotty raised his hands as if to soothe her. "He's fine. He's in the hospital. He passed out from alcohol poisoning, and they had to pump his stomach. They also think Gordon had a minor heart attack. They won't let him leave the hospital until he dries out, and the doctors suggested he go somewhere safe to rest and relax under a doctor's care for a while."

Kath was devastated. She fell onto the sofa, and Scotty ran to get her a glass of water.

"It's all my fault," she said after taking a sip. "I shouldn't have left him alone. He hasn't been doing well for a while, and he can be so obstinate."

Scotty sat down beside her. "Stop that. It's not your fault. Gordon is a grown man, and quite frankly, he's had a drinking problem for years. Just because he stops long enough to make a movie doesn't mean he's kicked the habit. He starts right up again. Only he is to blame."

Kath understood that on some level, but she still couldn't help but feel guilty. She knew he was having a hard time mentally, but she'd left anyway. It had been a selfish move on her part.

"I need to see him," she told Scotty.

Scotty shook his head. "There's no way you can walk into that hospital without the press being all over you. It would be a disaster."

"You could go with me, and we could say we're just two good friends of his coming to see him," Kath said.

Scotty sighed. "Kath. You know as well as I do that if you're seen visiting him, it will prove that you and Gordon are a couple. The press will never let it go. You know Gordon doesn't want that."

Tears filled her eyes. "But I'm the only one who cares about him. His wife only wants his money. She probably hasn't even been there. So what if everyone finds out. At least it will finally be out in the open, and Gordon and I won't have to sneak around anymore."

"Kath. Is that really what you want to do while Gordon is in such a delicate state?" Scotty asked gently. "He almost died. He needs our support, but he also needs to stay calm to get well. You can't want to disrupt everything right now."

"You're right, of course," Kath said, dropping her head on Scotty's shoulder. He put his arm around her. "But I just have to see him."

Scotty patted her arm. "I'll see if I can find a way to sneak you in."

"Thank you, Scotty. You're a true friend," Kath said.

The next day, Scotty paid off a hospital security guard to let him and Kath in through the service entrance. Kath wore a blond wig and sunglasses and hoped no one would recognize her. Scotty went to the nurse's station alone to check in to see Gordon, and then he and Kath entered the private room. Luckily, no other visitors or nurses were there.

Kath rushed to Gordon's side. He was lying in bed, looking pale and shaky. His usually bright blue eyes were dull, and he looked like he'd aged ten years.

"Darling, I'm here. It's me, Kath."

Gordon stared at her, confused, then gave her a smile. "You're a blonde," he said. "I like it."

She laughed and sat on a chair by the bed, pulling it close. She reached for his hand. "I'm so sorry I wasn't here for you," she said softly. "I wish I'd been there when you needed me."

He squeezed her hand. "No, dear. It's all my fault. I'm so sorry. I'm so, so sorry." Tears filled his eyes, and Kath moved even closer and laid her head down beside Gordon.

"They want me to go to a hospital to dry out," Gordon said, sounding like a scared child. "I can stop on my own. I don't need to go."

Kath looked up and watched Scotty slip out of the room. She appreciated that he gave them their privacy. "What does your family think?" she asked. "I'm afraid I have no say in this, but your wife and children may." Kath didn't know his wife, Ellie, or either of his children. She did know that his son, Connor, was in his last year of law school, and his daughter, Lisa, was getting married.

"I don't care what they think," Gordan said. "I only care what you think."

Kath watched him and saw he was sweating and shaking. She had heard that people who were drying out had these symptoms, and it could be dangerous if they didn't have medical supervision.

"I want you to do this safely," she finally said. "I think you should go someplace to rest and get healthy again." Tears filled her eyes. "I don't want to lose you, Gordon. I love you so much."

Gordon Quinn, her strong, stoic leading man, her lover, and her life companion lay there crying. Kath had never seen him so vulnerable in the sixteen years they'd been together. It broke her heart to see him in such pain, but it would tear her apart if he died of alcoholism.

"Okay. I'll do it for you," he whispered.

Relief flooded over Kath. All she wanted was for him to get well so they could continue to enjoy life together.

The next few weeks were difficult. The newspapers and movie magazines were filled with stories about Gordon disappearing from the local hospital and not being seen anywhere. Had he died, and no one had reported it? Had he been sent to a mental hospital? Or was he hiding out with his long-time mistress, Kathleen Carver? Kath read the articles with disgust. When newspapers didn't have facts, they made them up.

It was also difficult for Kath because she couldn't visit Gordon at the new hospital. It was nestled on the coast in northern California with a beautiful campus and great care for those who could afford it. There was a swimming pool, exercise room, private golf course, and tennis courts so patients could get plenty of exercise and fresh air. Gordon wrote her notes that Scotty delivered so no one would raid her mailbox. He said he was feeling better than he had in years—both mentally and physically—and he didn't miss the bourbon at all. Gordon couldn't wait to return to his real life and be with her. Kath couldn't wait, either.

In the meantime, Kath finished filming the movie that had been shot partially in Italy. She had another one lined up in one month and was busy learning her lines. She also spent time at the beach house visiting her parents and playing with ten-year-old Carolyn. They swam together, body-surfed the waves, and built sandcastles by the waterside until their skin turned golden brown and the sun highlighted their auburn hair. Kath loved the time she spent with her niece, but it was never nearly enough.

"You two look like mother and daughter," Crandell said offhandedly one afternoon as Kath and Caro, the nickname they called her, came running in from the beach. His words stopped Kath dead in her tracks, but Caro didn't think twice about it. People were always saying that Caro looked exactly like a younger version of her aunt.

Recovering from being startled, Kath said to her dad, "Strong family genes, I suppose," and continued through the front porch into the kitchen. Her heart had nearly stopped at her father's words. He was a bright man, and it wouldn't take much for him to figure out the truth.

When Gordon was well enough to leave the hospital, Kath suggested they spend the first weekend together at the beach. She had started her new film but had Friday through Sunday off. She thought the easy-going lifestyle at the beach house would be the perfect way for Gordon to transition back into regular life.

The first day there, Gordon and Kath took a long walk along the coastline and talked openly like they hadn't in a long time. Gordon was hopeful for the future. He was reading a few new scripts, and he'd made a few life-altering decisions.

"I told Ellie we have to sell that big mansion, and I'll buy her a nice, smaller place in Beverly Hills," Gordon said. "She was angry, but I stayed firm. Both children are now out on their own, and she doesn't need that sprawling mansion anymore. And quite frankly, I can't afford it."

"That'll take a lot of stress off of you," Kath said. Secretly, she had hoped Gordon would tell his wife he wanted a divorce, too, but he made no mention of it. Kath didn't want to add any stress to his life, so she stayed quiet about it.

"I would also love it if you and I spent more time together and worked less," Gordon said, wrapping his arm around her still slender waist. "Maybe we can go on vacation once or twice a year. How does the Bahamas sound? Or Europe? I'd love to explore the English countryside."

Kath smiled. "I'd love that too, but what about the press? We'd be recognized everywhere we go."

Gordon shrugged. "Maybe that doesn't matter anymore."

This surprised Kath. Gordon had always been so careful.

After dinner with her parents, Gordon went out to the porch to enjoy the cool breeze while Kath helped Mio and her mother with the dishes.

"Gordon seems to be in high spirits," Catherine said. At sixty-three, her mother still looked lovely. Her high cheekbones were as prominent as ever, and her brown hair, pulled into a bun had strands of silver running through it. Like Kath, she had a slender figure because she kept moving. But her brown eyes looked tired. Kath knew her mother worried about all her children even though they were grown and on their own.

"Yes, he's feeling wonderful. I'm glad he decided to spend a few weeks at the hospital. It was so good for him," Kath said as she stacked dishes into the cupboard.

"I think it was," Catherine said. "Sometimes, it's regenerative to start over fresh again."

Kath agreed. It was like Gordon was given a second chance at a new life, and he seemed to be taking advantage of it.

Later, Kath found Gordon fast asleep on the porch. It was a warm night with a cool breeze, so she covered him up so as not to disturb him and headed upstairs to her own room to sleep. Sometime after midnight, Gordon slipped into bed with her and curled up around her.

"You're chilly," Kath said, half awake.

"Don't worry. I'll warm you up," he said, a smile in his voice.

Kath couldn't remember when she'd felt this happy.

Chapter Twenty

Today

Once again, Kath found herself facing Mr. Slick as they filmed more of the interview. She was growing tired of talking about herself and playing cat-and-mouse games with Roger. They had just come to an impasse again when he alluded to the fact that Carolyn looked just like her. Now, he'd finally moved on.

"You had several good years of films in the late 1960's and were nominated for more Oscars," Roger said. He was stumbling over his words because of their tussle earlier.

"Yes, I did. My audience was no longer everyone's grandmothers; it included daughters and granddaughters as well. Every age seemed to enjoy the pictures," Kath said.

"Why do you think that is?" Roger asked.

Kath shrugged. "Good scripts, possibly. And interesting stories people could relate to. I think also it's because I came across as the everyday woman—not voluptuous and sexy, pretty, but not Hollywood pretty. So, I suppose movie goers felt more of a connection to me than, say, Elizabeth Taylor. Obviously, Liz was extremely famous, but she was unattainable. I looked like someone you could be friends with."

Roger chuckled. "I never saw you as the girl next door type. I always felt you were a sophisticated woman, possibly from the east with an education."

"Well, then. The joke's on you. I grew up in California and went to college out east. I basically am the girl next door," Kath said.

"Yes. One who lived an extraordinary life, I'd say," Roger added.

Kath wondered where he was heading with this now. "Yes. I've had a very extraordinary life. I've been thankful that my career allowed me to travel and enjoy the finer things in life. But, I also worked very hard for it."

"Speaking of traveling," Roger said. "You took a couple of significant vacations in the late 1960s. Surprisingly, Gordon Quinn was also at those places at the very same time."

Kath didn't blink an eye. "I have no idea where Gordon traveled to. His vacation time was his own. I, on the other hand, enjoyed a wonderful trip to London with my younger sister Katrina and her gorgeous daughter, Carolyn." Kath smiled over at Carolyn, who sat off in the wings.

"You also went to the Bahamas on vacation," Roger said. "You even shared pictures of the beach on Paradise Island in your book. Did you know Gordon was seen there that year, too?"

"Well, good for him. It was a beautiful place back then and not the crowded island it is today. Howard Hughes offered the ninth floor of The Britannia Beach Hotel to me. He had rented it out for quite some time while he considered purchasing property in the Bahamas. It was a relaxing place to go."

"Howard seems to pop up regularly in your life," Roger

said, his eyebrows raised. "Yet by some accounts, he was nearly comatose by then."

Kath laughed. "Howard was never comatose. But yes, he offered me his rooms and I took advantage of it. He wasn't there, but I was, and so was my friend, Jane, her two children, and her husband. We had a lovely holiday."

"I see," Roger said. "And what about Gordon Quinn?"

Kath shrugged. "I have no idea where he stayed or if he was even there. Do you have any photos of us together there?"

"Well, no. But rumor has it…"

"Rumor? You're speculating again, Roger. Stick to the facts," Kath said. She knew there were no photos or proof of any vacations with Gordon. At least not for public consumption.

1968

London in September was perfect, as far as Kath was concerned. The weather was just cool enough to wear comfortable trousers and sweaters and perfect for hiking around the English countryside and touring old castles.

Kath, Katrina, and eleven-year-old Carolyn had taken the RMS Queen Elizabeth on her last voyage to England, enjoying the lazy days on the luxury liner. Gordon, however, waited a week and then flew to London. They met in their suite of rooms at The Savoy Hotel in the heart of London.

"You made it," Gordon said excitedly when Kath entered the room.

"We made it," she said, laughing. "Finally. A vacation together."

Kath had booked a suite with three bedrooms that boasted

a large living room. Katrina and Carolyn each had their own bedroom, and while they were there, Kath and Gordon were in the third room. But they didn't plan on staying in downtown London long. Renting a car, Kath and Gordon took off for a week of sightseeing in the English countryside while Katrina and Carolyn did their own sightseeing.

"I can't believe we're doing this," Gordon said, smiling as he drove the convertible along the quiet country road. "I never thought we'd be able to pull it off."

Kath sat beside him, a scarf around her hair and large sunglasses protecting her eyes from the cool wind. "We haven't gotten away with it yet," she said. "But we're going to try."

They traveled the back roads north of London and stayed in small-town inns, many of which were pubs. No one recognized them. They stopped at castles for tours and walked around Stonehenge, marveling at the large stone columns. Kath felt happy and carefree for the first time in years as they made their way up north then turned and headed down to Bath before returning to the Savoy. Never had she and Gordon enjoyed their time together more.

A year later, they took advantage of Howard Hughes' offer of his rooms at the Britannia Beach Hotel on Paradise Island in the Bahamas. They had their choice of rooms, as all nine upstairs suites were rented by Hughes. Kath had invited Jane and her family to come along so no one would suspect she was there with Gordon. Gordon flew in by himself and Kath snuck him up to the room. They spent a delightful week on the quiet beach, unnoticed by the other guests, as well as in the casinos. Kath wasn't much of a gambler, but Gordon liked to play cards, so they were never seen together. It was a fabulous, relaxing trip—one they'd never forget.

Once home, though, they were back to their work schedules and the stress of everyday life. Gordon wasn't offered as many scripts as in the past, but Kath was still busy. She didn't love all the movies she made, but she knew she had to make money while she could, and she was saving it in case the jobs stopped coming. Now, at age forty-three, Kath knew her days as a film star were numbered. Soon, she'd be offered the mother, then the grandmother parts, and then they'd dwindle to nothing. She worked hard to keep herself relevant and even considered returning to the theater to try challenging roles that would stretch her acting abilities.

Gordon, however, didn't want to do theater. He also knew his days were numbered, and he was once again falling into a deep depression. He'd managed to talk his wife into selling the mansion and buying a smaller home in the Hollywood hills, which took some pressure off him. But he was still paying her bills while she played cards with her friends and spent days at the beauty parlor and spa. Slowly, the extra money leftover from selling the mansion was being whittled away with his wife's expenses.

"Divorce her," Kath said one evening as Gordon poured himself another bourbon and water. He'd returned to drinking, although so far, he hadn't overdone it. "Make a settlement and be done with it. It's obvious she doesn't love you or care if you two are together."

Gordon shook his head. "I can't. She'd consider it the ultimate betrayal if I did."

Kath was dumbfounded. "And living with another woman for eighteen years isn't?"

Gordon frowned. "She knows nothing about you. She thinks I live here alone, renting from Scotty. Ellie never did enjoy being a 'wife.' But she adores being able to say she's married to a movie star."

"Ridiculous!" Kath said. "How can she be that stupid?"

"Kath!" Gordon's face grew red with anger. "Enough about her. You knew what you were getting into when we started this."

Kath had known, and it usually didn't bother her. But seeing Gordon so stressed because of his obligation to a wife who didn't even love him drove her crazy. Life was tearing Gordon apart. He looked pale and tired—an exact contrast to how happy and carefree he'd been when they'd traveled the past two years. But she let the subject drop so as not to upset him further.

In late 1969, Kath was offered an opportunity to play Mary, Queen of Scots in a made-for-television movie. She pondered this offer seriously. The historical figure, Mary Stuart, had been played by several actresses through the years. Katharine Hepburn had played her in 1936. Even though the thought of playing Mary intrigued Kath, she was intimidated by it. She also worried that a movie made for television wouldn't be as well made as a motion picture.

"Why are you worried?" Gordon asked her one evening, looking up from his book while sitting in his favorite chair. "You can run circles around any actress who's played Mary Stuart."

Kath smiled at him. "You have to say that. But millions of people watching it on television won't necessarily agree with you."

"Then don't do it." Gordon took a puff from his pipe. Kath loved the smell of his black cherry tobacco.

"It's not that simple," Kath said. "I need to work, and this is a great opportunity to be seen. But if the production isn't good, it'll look cheap."

Gordon frowned at her. "You have plenty of money. It's not like you live a high lifestyle. Why do you need to work?"

Kath sighed. "I've been helping father and mother with their living expenses. Dad had a good retirement and savings when he retired a few years ago, but between medical expenses and the cost of both houses, they've nearly gone through it all."

"Then they should sell the beach house," Gordon proclaimed.

"But I love the beach house," Kath said. "I've suggested that I buy it, and everyone could still use it, but dad won't agree. And they don't want to sell the Toluca Lake home, either. So, for now, I'll have to help them with their expenses."

"It doesn't seem fair," Gordon grumbled. "Everyone uses the beach house. Everyone should help with the expenses."

Kath chucked. "Yeah. Try getting Daniel to pay his fair share. I'm sure Kat would, but I'm not going to ask her. Carolyn is getting older, and they'll soon be paying her college tuition, and then maybe for a wedding." The idea of Caro getting married someday touched Kath's heart. She hoped, in some small way, she'd be able to be a part of her special day.

Gordon became silent at the mention of Carolyn. They had never discussed her except for the one time he'd commented on how beautiful she was. Kath knew that, for Gordon, if you didn't talk about something, it didn't exist.

Kath ended up making the television movie and was pleased with how it turned out. It aired a few months later, and she received many notes and letters saying how much her friends and fans enjoyed it. Afterward, her agent sent her several more scripts for television, but she hoped to get some for actual motion pictures. In late 1970, an amazing script came her way.

"Australia," Kath told Scotty as they sat together on his back terrace drinking iced tea. At least she was drinking iced tea. Scotty's was spiked.

"Australia?" Scotty said, his eyes growing wide. "Are they actually going there to film or finding a location here?"

"We'd be going there for about three months. Oh, Scotty. The script is perfect, and the cast so far is fabulous. It's going to be one of those epic movies—like *Gone with the Wind*. And the director, James Justin, is a cross between John Ford and John Huston. He knows how to work on location and loves every minute of it." She pushed the script across the table for Scotty to look over. "They also have Walter Bergan as the leading man. He's a combination of Bogie and Spencer Tracy. It's such a perfect set-up."

Kath was so excited about this new movie. She hadn't accepted it yet because she feared leaving Gordon for so long. But to say no would be career suicide. At forty-four years old, Kath couldn't give up an opportunity like this one.

Scotty scanned through the pages. "The dialog is snappy and snarky—I love it! It's so perfect for you, Kath." He set the script down. "So, what's stopping you? This is a movie of a lifetime."

"Gordon," Kath said softly. "He hasn't been well, and he's drinking too much again. I've tried talking him into going to the hospital up north again, but he refuses. He says he's just tired. I'm so afraid he's going to drink himself to death."

Scotty shook his head. Over the years, they'd all grown older, but Scotty had aged like fine wine. His now silver hair was still thick and wavy and even the lines on his face made him more handsome. Kath supposed that dating younger men helped keep him young, too.

"Gordon has to take care of himself, Kath," Scotty said. "You can't give up prime scripts because he needs looking after. Let me talk to him. I'm not working much these days. Maybe he and I can keep busy while you're gone, and I can get him out of his doldrums."

Kath knew Scotty was right. She couldn't give up this opportunity because of Gordon. She loved him dearly, but she wouldn't let him drag her down with him. She needed to work, and this kind of project came once in a lifetime. With that in mind, she accepted.

"Of course, they want you to play this part," Gordon said one evening after reading the script and drinking too much bourbon. "It's about an old widow cattle rancher in the early 1900s. You'd fit that part perfectly." He eyed Kath, who sat across the room from him.

"Sometimes you can be downright mean," she said, returning her eyes to her book.

"Well, it's the truth, isn't it? You're no spring chicken, and neither is the character. The script describes her as thin, plain-faced, with graying hair. That's you to a tee."

"They chose me because I can act the hell out of that part," she said.

"Seems like a helluva long way to go to play an old lady when you could stay here and find a lot of movies to play a washed-up widow in," Gordon said.

Kath stood and stormed past him, grabbing the script from his hands and heading into the kitchen. Tears burned her eyes. She knew he was being mean because he didn't want her to leave. Still, he could cut her to her core sometimes.

A few minutes later, Gordon entered the kitchen looking

more sober than before. He sat in the kitchen chair across from her. "You are perfect for that part," he said, this time his tone kinder. "You're tough as nails, yet you have a soft underbelly. That's what makes the audience love you. You can give it back as good as it's given to you, but you're vulnerable, too. Of course, you should play that role. I'm just jealous, so don't listen to me. And I'll miss you."

Kath wiped her eyes and studied him. Gordon looked defeated. He understood his drinking kept him from being offered great parts in films, yet he drank anyway. "Come with me," she said, practically pleading. "It will be a great adventure."

He shook his head. "I can't do that. Tongues will wag."

"Who's going to know? Who's going to tell? You like the director—you've made two films together, and you used to go hunting together. You can be a guest on the set. Everyone will be thrilled to have you there."

"No, Kath. I can't go. This is your picture. We've never intruded on each other's work before, and we never will," Gordon said.

Kath sighed. "I don't want to leave you. But I want to do this."

"Then you have to do it." Gordon stood and left the room.

"Then I will," Kath said softly to herself.

Chapter Twenty-One

1971

It took time for the director and crew to scout out locations in Australia and set up accommodations for the cast and crew. While she waited, Kath studied the script, had wardrobe fittings, and took speech lessons to learn the Australian accent. She also spent time at the beach house with her parents and visited Kat and Caro often. She'd only be gone for three months at the end of the year, but it meant leaving over the holidays and missing family gatherings.

In that time, Kath also begged Gordon to go into a hospital to dry out. She hated seeing what his drinking was doing to him, and even friends of his who stopped by to visit looked shocked at his appearance. He'd lost weight, which meant his skin drooped from his face and neck. His once distinctive blue eyes were now dull, and he was losing his hair. Gordon looked much older than his fifty-five years, and even when he was offered a script to read, once the casting director saw him, they politely declined. In his condition, he'd be a liability to a studio, not an asset.

Still, Gordon refused to seek out help. In his earlier years, he could stop drinking cold turkey while he shot a film, but now, even when he tried to quit, it didn't last. He either didn't have the will to quit, or he was too far gone.

They were filming during the summer season in Australia, so the entire crew and cast were leaving in early November and staying through January. Their destination was Brisbane, and then they'd be driving to an actual cattle station north of there. The owners were allowing them to use their home and land for filming and would stay at their son's house miles away. They were also being highly compensated for it.

Their flight from Los Angeles was at night, with a stop in the Hawaiian Islands and then on to Brisbane. A studio car would drive Kath to LAX. She finished packing and placed her bags just outside the door.

Gordon watched her from his chair, a drink in hand.

"Promise me you'll take care of yourself," Kath said, going to him and kneeling beside his chair. "Scotty's cook is going to bring you lunch and dinner. And Scotty invited you to come over anytime you want to."

"I don't need a babysitter," he grumbled. But to Kath, he looked like he did.

"I'll miss you," Kath said. "I'll send you letters via Scotty. Write to me, too, okay?"

Gordon looked at her with watery eyes. "Don't go. Please? I need you here."

Kath's heart broke. She knew Gordon had swallowed his pride to ask her to stay. "I wish I could, but I have a contract. They're expecting me. I promise the time will go by quickly, and before you know it, I'll be here to annoy you again." She tried to smile but was afraid it looked more like a grimace.

Gordon reached for her hands. "Stay. Please. I'll do anything for you if you just stay."

Kath stood and turned away, swiping at her tears. This was tearing her up inside.

"Anything, Kath. Just ask," Gordon said.

Kath turned. "Will you divorce your wife so we can finally be together properly?"

He sat there a beat, almost as if considering it. But then he dropped his eyes. "You know that's the one thing I can't do."

"I know," Kath said gently. "I really have to go." She drew closer and leaned over to kiss his cheek. "I'll see you in three months. I love you, Gordon. Take care of yourself." Not wanting to fall apart in front of him, she rushed out the door and to the waiting car.

It took the entire ride to LAX for Kath to compose herself. She wished now that she hadn't taken the part. Gordon had looked so lost and sad. But she had her career to think of, and she'd really wanted to play this character.

Unfortunately for Kath, her career was the only stable thing in her life. And also the one thing that took her away from those she loved.

Finally, she arrived at the airport, and the driver carried her bags inside. Most of the cast was already there as well as the young woman, Alma Winters, who would be Kath's assistant and dresser for the movie. The clothing designer, Selma Darnell, was the only other woman who'd be on set. Aside from the three of them, there were multiple men in the cast and crew.

The flight was long and tedious. Their layover in Hawaii was only an hour long, and then they were back on the plane and on their way to Brisbane. Kath and Alma played gin rummy for a large portion of the flight before finally falling asleep. Kath found that she liked Alma despite her being only twenty-four. She was cute and bubbly but seemed smart and quick to catch on. Kath thought they would get on together nicely.

Kath also found she liked Walter Bergan, her leading man for the film. She'd never worked with him before or even met him, but she'd seen his work. He had the good looks and humor of Spencer Tracy with the rough edges like Bogie. He was her age, and she felt lucky to be in a film with this accomplished leading man.

The director, James Justin, was a completely different story. Kath had worked with him on one film and knew to expect the unexpected from him. He was brilliant, but he could also get distracted and run off and do something crazy in-between filming. Like John Huston, James had no timeline in his head. If he woke up feeling like going on a hunt or fishing, that's what he did. And he'd drag the male cast and crew with him. Kath wasn't sure what there was to hunt in the Outback, but she hoped James would stick to the script and not get distracted so they could finish on time.

Although, the fact that James had brought his rifle along didn't bode well.

After very little sleep overnight on the plane, the group arrived in Brisbane around noon the next day. The cast and crew were immediately put into several Jeep 4x4s along with their luggage, and the caravan made the hot, bumpy trip north-east for over five hours. Once they arrived at the small town of Roma, Kath hoped they were done. But after a quick stop for more supplies, they were off north for another hour until they finally stopped at their filming location.

Kath unfolded herself from the front seat of the Jeep as

Alma squeezed out of the back. They both stood there, looking out over the vast landscape, transfixed.

"It's breathtaking," Kath said to no one in particular.

James, the director, came to stand next to her. "It's absolutely perfect," he said, smiling at her.

A large, ranch-style house sat in the shade of several trees. The owners had rented it to them, along with the property, for the three months they'd be filming. It had a porch that wrapped around the entire house with chairs and rockers on it.

"You three ladies will have the house to yourself," James said. "The rest of the crew will be in tents.

Kath usually didn't expect special treatment on a movie set, but she gratefully accepted the use of the house over a tent. She, Alma, and Selma picked up some of their bags and headed inside. The living room was large, with a stone fireplace and big, comfortable leather sofas and chairs. Then there was the dining room with a long table and the kitchen. Everything was wide open, like the landscape outside. Past the kitchen were three bedrooms. Each woman chose one. Surprised there was electricity, Kath clicked the switch on the bedroom wall. Nothing happened.

"Maybe they use a generator," Selma suggested. "I'll ask one of the crew to check."

Since it was growing late, the day was cooling down, so Kath didn't think they'd need to use the bedroom fans overhead or the ones in the main living room. But if they wanted water, she supposed they'd need the generator running so the pump would work.

Walking back outside to get the rest of her luggage, Kath was amazed at how fast the crew worked to put up the tents. She took the rest of her personal luggage in and left the big trunks filled with her movie wardrobe for someone else to carry. Then she headed outside again to ask James, who was directing the tent set-up, what she should do to help.

James laughed. "I appreciate you wanting to pitch in, but you're the star. We can't let you get hurt helping with the set-up. So, relax and enjoy the show."

Kath hated not being busy, so she went to the biggest tent that had been set up as a mess hall. She helped the two cooks and the young man who was their dishwasher unpack boxes and set up their makeshift kitchen. At first, Gerard, the main cook, refused her help, but she continued helping anyway, which eventually put a smile on his face. She assumed he wasn't used to the movie stars helping out.

As night fell, the mosquitos came out, and Kath headed inside. The generator was working, so she had electricity and running water, thank goodness. She ran around the house closing the windows to keep the bugs out and turned on the overhead fans.

"Nice set-up, ladies," Walter said, stepping inside the house. "Somehow, they managed to set up running water for us outside, too, but this is much nicer."

Kath felt guilty having the entire house for just the three of them. She'd grown up in a house full of people, so she felt they had plenty of room here. "I could bunk with Alma so you can have one of the rooms in here," she offered. Alma nodded, unfazed by having to share her room.

Walter shook his head. "Thank you, ladies, but no. I'd be the laughingstock of the men out there if I didn't sleep in a tent like them." He winked. "But then again, they'd be jealous as hell if I bunked with three lovely ladies." He smiled, tipped his brown leather outback hat—which Kath assumed was a part of his wardrobe—and headed outside.

Kath slept like the dead that night after the long flight and drive. She was up with the sun, though, bathed and dressed in cotton slacks and a long-sleeved cotton shirt in time to enjoy the delicious breakfast the cooks had made.

"Sit over here, Kath," James called. His table had the main crew and cast—Walter, the camera men, the cinematographer, and others— and he was handing out a schedule. "We're going to get acclimated to how the sun hits the land during the day today and begin picking out a few locations for the first scenes. Tomorrow, we start filming," James said. "I'll give you the scene cues each day for the next day. Here's the sheet with what we hope to film tomorrow so you can study your lines and be ready."

"Very organized. I like it," Kath said approvingly. "Can I have a copy for our wardrobe lady, too? She'll need to prepare the clothes for each scene."

James tapped his forefinger on the side of his head. "Smart thinking. Thanks for reminding me." He handed her another sheet.

"Where are you getting copies from?" she asked. They were in the middle of nowhere.

"I have an entire tent just for an office," James said. "We even have a mimeograph machine." He laughed, showing straight, white teeth.

Kath was happy to see that James really knew what he was doing.

The rest of the day, Kath and Alma explored their surroundings. They made sure to wear tall boots, long sleeves, and hats to protect them from the sun. And Kath brought her camera along to take pictures. She knew this was a trip of a lifetime, and she wanted to make sure she had memories of it to look back on.

The next day started early in the morning. They were filming the scene where Kath's character's husband died, leaving her to run the cattle station alone. Middle aged and without children to help her, the woman was desperate for help. But when Walter's character comes to her house to offer his services as a ranch foreman, Kath's character is reluctant. The man is known to be a drunk and has been kicked off other cattle stations for his rough behavior. But she's also desperate. So, she hires him, and they start their adventure of running the cattle station together.

By the end of the day, Kath was hot, sweaty, dirty, and worn out. But it had been a good day of shooting. She'd had to change her costume twice—she had two sets of each costume—because of the sweat under her arms and down her back. This kept Alma and Selma busy. They'd take one costume and place it under the fans in the house to dry out while Kath wore the other. It wasn't perfect, but it worked.

Kath was also pleased with the immediate chemistry she and Walter had. They both understood their characters well, which helped, but they seemed to understand each other too. They played the snappy dialogue off each other perfectly. It reminded Kath of the movies she'd made with Gordon. Such great chemistry.

They filmed every day, despite the weather. If it rained, they filmed. They slid in the mud and dried out in the heat and kept on going. James said the change in weather made the film authentic, and he loved every moment of the good and bad weather.

If Kath was off for the day because they were filming other

scenes, she'd tail along with the cook and the crew responsible for replenishing supplies. They'd go to Roma, and Kath would wander the town and buy trinkets to send to friends and family and send off her letters to Scotty's house for Gordon.

Every night before going to bed, she'd write a letter by candlelight to Gordon, telling him about her experiences that day. The generator was off at night to save fuel, and everything was quiet except for the sounds of night creatures filling the air. The owls, cicadas, frogs, and crickets made music all night long. Even after a month of living there, Kath hadn't heard back from Gordon, but she wasn't worried. She knew he wasn't much of a writer, and he was probably spending his days having lunch with old friends and playing chess with Scotty.

A week before Christmas, Kath returned to the house all wet and dirty from a scene where she and Walter were trying to save a steer from a muddy pond. It hadn't been the easiest scene, but James assured them it had turned out well.

Alma had wrapped a clean towel around Kath, so she wouldn't be chilled, and after taking off her muddy boots outside, Kath entered to see the head cook, Gerard, in the kitchen warming up food.

"You and Walter missed chow time, so I brought your plates of food to heat up," Gerard said. "It looks like you had a long day."

"We did have a long, dirty day. Thank you so much for thinking of us. I'll have Alma find Walter to tell him to come over and eat."

"Not necessary. I'll drop by his tent and tell him. Have a nice evening," Gerard said, then headed out the door.

"A bath and food," Kath said. "In that order."

Selma came to help her undress so she could clean the

garments for the next day. "A package came for you today. I placed it on the dining room table," Selma told her.

Kath was excited to see what it was but desperately needed to wash the mud off herself. After a bath and washing her hair, she dressed in an old pair of trousers and a sweater and went out to the kitchen. Walter was already eating his dinner, along with Alma, at the table.

"I hope you don't mind us starting before you," Walter said. "But I was starving."

Kath smiled. "Not at all. Eat up. We both worked hard today." Before getting her plate, Kath glanced at the package on the table. The return address was Scotty's house. She picked it up and took it to her room for later, then sat and ate with Alma and Walter.

Once alone in her bedroom, Kath quickly sat on her bed and opened the package. Inside was a small notecard and velvet box. Opening the box first, she gasped. Inside lay a lovely diamond pendant in a gold setting, hanging from a thick gold chain. Gordon rarely bought her jewelry—she could count on one hand the pieces he'd bought her. A birthstone necklace once for her birthday and a small emerald ring encircled with tiny diamonds for Christmas. They were lovely pieces that she could wear daily because they weren't gaudy. So, this beautiful diamond pendant was a big surprise to her.

She opened the small card, and tears filled her eyes. *I miss you dearly,* it read. *Know that I love you always. Gordon.*

Kath cried over the heartfelt note. The diamond was beautiful, but his words meant much more. She was happy she hadn't opened the gift in front of everyone this evening because it would have been hard to explain. How would anyone understand that the man she loved with all her heart—and had loved for twenty years—was a married man? No one would under-stand. Sometimes, she didn't understand. And even though rumors abound about them in the early years, and sometimes still today, Kath never wanted to give them fuel for the fire. Her relationship with Gordon was hers only. It wasn't for the rumor mill.

They worked until the day before Christmas Eve, then took two days off. The cooks made a delicious turkey dinner along with shrimp and lobster because seafood was so abun-dant during the Australian summer season. They also added all the trimmings and even managed to make pumpkin pie. Of course, they had to use the kitchen in the house to make many of the dishes because their make-shift tent kitchen wouldn't have been able to handle it all. But everyone enjoyed the deli-cious food and lazed around afterward while Christmas records were played.

Kath missed spending the holidays with Gordon and Scotty, but Scotty had written to tell her Gordon would be at his wife's house with his family this year. She was thankful for that. She knew he'd have a good time with his grown children.

Christmas Day, James gathered as many of the crew as he could to go for a hunt in the fields. By law, they could only hunt certain nuisance animals and only on the property they were staying on. The list was pretty long—bison, wild pigs, fallow deer, hog deer, fox—and many more. James hoped to find a wild bison so they could have a huge barbeque but said he'd be just as happy with some wild pigs.

Kath wasn't one for killing animals and declined their offer to join them. The group returned later that evening, dirty, tired, and empty-handed, which made Kath chuckle.

They began filming again the day after Christmas. Everyone

was getting tired of being on location and wanted to finish as soon as possible. Kath agreed. Even though she was enjoying the adventure, she was ready to go home.

The third day after Christmas, Gerard brought Kath a telegram he'd picked up for her from town. To Kath, telegrams only meant bad news. She went into the house before opening it. Her heart stopped when she read it.

GORDON QUINN DIED PEACEFULLY AT HIS HOME ON CHRISTMAS MORNING. STOP. MY HEART BREAKS FOR YOU. STOP. SCOTTY

Kath stared at the words, unable to comprehend them. Gone? Gordon was gone? How? He'd just sent her a present. He was only fifty-five years old. What happened?

"Kath? Are you alright?" Selma asked, coming inside to check on her.

Kath dropped the telegram to the floor and sat hard on one of the dining room chairs. Selma picked up the telegram and gasped.

"Oh, Kath. I'm so sorry." Selma said, coming to her side. Even though Kath had tried to keep her relationship with Gordon secret from the public, all the Hollywood insiders knew about it, and no one ever told the press. It was the way of Hollywood—I'll keep your secret if you keep mine.

Kath stared at Selma. "I don't know what to think. I don't know what to do."

"I'll tell James you won't be working the rest of the day," Selma said. She headed to the door, then turned around. "Do you mind if I tell him about Mr. Quinn? Half the people working here have worked with him at one point in their careers."

Kath just sat there, staring at the wall. Finally, she waved her hand. "It will be worldwide news by now anyway. Yes, tell him," she said.

By the time James came in to see Kath, she'd moved to her bedroom to sit in the rocking chair in the corner. The slow, steady rocking soothed her.

"Kath?" James called out, then found her in the bedroom. "I'm so sorry, dear," he said. "We're all devastated by his passing. What can I do for you? Do you want to fly out for the funeral?"

Kath's eyes grew wide. Funeral? Would they have had his funeral already? There was no way she'd ever be welcomed at such a devastating family event. Going to Gordon's funeral—even if other celebrities went—would place a spotlight on her, proving that the rumors for twenty years were true.

Slowly, she shook her head. "I won't be welcomed there," she said. "Even Gordon would agree it would be best to keep working."

James frowned. "You don't mean that, do you? You two have worked together for years. You did four very famous movies together. You have every right to be at that funeral."

"I don't belong there," Kath said. "I was lucky enough to have him in my life. Let them have him in death."

James nodded and left, and Kath dropped onto the bed and cried.

Chapter Twenty-Two

1972

In the end, Kath and the entire cast and crew decided not to stop production to attend Gordon's funeral. Many felt a great loss for the renowned actor's passing at such a young age. Walter, especially, had lost a good friend. But they all agreed that finishing the picture as soon as possible was important so they could go home.

Kath, Alma, and Selma left on the last day of January 1972. The rest of the crew stayed a little longer with James to get a few more location and scenery shots. All Kath wanted was to go home to grieve Gordon in peace. Instead, after hours on the flight home, she stepped off the plane at LAX to a media frenzy. Somehow, the media had learned she was coming home, and everyone wanted the first photo of the bereaved mistress.

As cameras flashed in her face and photographers blocked her way, Kath, Selma, and Alma held onto each other tightly so they wouldn't be separated. Finally, security came and pushed the leeches away and escorted the three women to their waiting car. Their luggage, however, was left in the baggage area, and they didn't dare go after it.

Kath was the first person to be dropped off at home. She hugged the women goodbye with promises they'd all get together again when the madness was over. Once inside, Kath immediately called the airport to have her luggage delivered to the house and asked for Selma's and Alma's luggage to be delivered to them. Then she collapsed onto the sofa. As she sat there, feeling shell-shocked from what happened at the airport, she realized she was staring at Gordon's favorite chair, and she broke out into tears.

Once again, the dam opened. The loss she was able to soldier through for the past month was now a fresh wound. She'd never see Gordon again.

Scotty knocked softly on her door and then stepped inside. He wrapped his arms around her as she cried, and his own tears mixed with hers. They both had lost an important person in their lives. Kath was thankful to have someone who truly understood her relationship with Gordon. He knew it was more than an affair. Theirs had been a real relationship with its ups and downs, loving each other no matter what happened.

"I'm so sorry, Kath. I was in shock when I sent the telegram, but I knew you'd want to know before it became worldwide news," Scotty said as they both wiped their tears.

"I was at the end of the world. I never would have known if you hadn't contacted me," Kath said. "But I also knew I couldn't fly home for his funeral. Attending it would have been the wrong thing to do."

Scotty grimaced. "He loved you more than that wife of his, believe me. You deserved to be there, not her. She only wanted him to support her. Well, now we'll see how she does without his paychecks being given to her."

"Scotty. This isn't the time to talk badly about Gordon's wife. She lost her husband, even though their relationship wasn't good. And his children lost their father. It doesn't matter that they're grown. It'll be difficult for them."

"I know," Scotty said, looking worn. "And you're right. Attending the funeral would have made it an even bigger media circus. You should have seen the big display Ellie put on for the cameras. She invited every movie star on the planet and allowed the press to take photographs. It was awful."

"Gordon would have hated it," Kath said softly. "He was always so low-key. He liked his privacy."

"Exactly," Scotty said. He looked into Kath's eyes. "Be prepared to be swamped by the press wherever you go over the next few weeks. The tabloids are brimming with stories about you and Gordon, and they're all trying to get at you. I've had to chase off men with cameras who were trespassing on my property. And I hired two security guards to watch the house and grounds day and night. These people are relentless."

Kath shook her head. "It's all so terrible. Gordon's gone. I wish they'd just let him rest in peace."

"Dear. Why don't you move into my house for a while so you're not alone. I'd feel better if you did," Scotty said. "All the memories of Gordon in here will be difficult to bear."

"Thank you, Scotty, but I want to stay here," Kath told her friend. "The memories are what make me feel sane. I like knowing he was once here, and we were happy."

Scotty nodded. "Can I get you anything?" He stood to leave.

Kath looked up at him. "Should I have stayed? Gordon pleaded with me to stay. It's as if he knew something wasn't right. At least I would have been here to care for him. Maybe he'd still be alive if I hadn't left." A sob escaped her lips as she choked on the words.

Scotty sat beside her again and hugged her closely. "Gordon was so proud that you went. He told me so during one of our many dinners together. He said he'd begged you to stay, but you said you had to leave. And he said you were right. He wouldn't have wanted you to stay and baby him, Kath. He was proud of the work you were doing. He loved you more than anything."

The tears continued to fall as those words fell over Kath. And Scotty held her until she was all cried out—at least for that night. There would be so many more nights of tears to come.

* * *

After hiding in her house for weeks and receiving calls and visits from a multitude of friends to share in her grief, Kath began to make some changes. She called Alma Winters and offered her a full-time position as her live-in assistant. The young woman was thrilled and accepted. Kath had grown to like Alma immensely during their time in Australia and knew she'd work out well.

Then Kath called her agent and told him she was ready to work again. He immediately sent a messenger over with a pile of scripts that had been sent her way. The press for her upcoming movie with Walter Bergan and all the tabloid coverage over Gordon's death had put her in the public's eye again. Television talk-show hosts were keen to book her, and every newspaper in town also wanted an interview. Kath declined them all but happily began reading the scripts.

Alma moved into the guest room at the house that next

week, and they soon began going over schedules and correspondence. Kath had received thousands of letters from friends, family, and fans acknowledging her loss. She could hardly believe that so many people cared enough to send their condolences. A few of the letters were mean and nasty, telling her she deserved to lose him and she was going to hell. But most of the letters were kind and sympathetic. Despite everything Kath and Gordon had done to keep their relationship secret, the public still thought they knew the truth. So, Kath had Alma answer each letter personally, and she signed them. It was the least she could do for those who'd been kind enough to write.

Every day without Gordon seemed unbearable. But Kath knew she had to keep moving. Gordon would want her to. So, she was determined to work and do the best she could. For Gordon.

TODAY

Kath stared at Roger, alias Mr. Slick, waiting for him to speak again. They'd taken another break and were ready to start rolling. The day was growing long, and Kath was tired. But she wanted these interviews to be done. She didn't know how much longer she'd be able to do this.

"Miss Carver," Roger said after staring at his notes. "You wrote at length about your experience in Australia filming *The Sky is Wide*. And you had a few amazing photos you took while you were there. Unfortunately, something devastating happened while you were on location. Gordon Quinn died on Christmas Day, 1971. That must have been heartbreaking for you."

Kath wanted to sigh, but she held herself firm, sitting up even straighter. "The loss of Gordon Quinn was devastating to his family, friends, and multitudes of fans. Of course, it affected me as well. He and I were friends and had made four successful movies together. His death was a great loss."

"But personally, you also lost your closest confidant, did you not?" Roger asked, leaning toward her.

Kath continued unrattled. "I've had many close friends throughout my ninety-eight years. His loss was a tragedy, but so was losing Rock Hudson and Howard Hughes. Many of my dear friends have passed before me. Almost all of them, as a matter of fact."

Roger stared at her, looking annoyed. "The tabloids and newspapers were full of stories for months after Gordon's death about your love affair. Are you really going to sit here and deny that you two were involved all those years?"

Kath stared him straight in the eyes. "A few years ago, the tabloids claimed you were dating a fifteen-year-old girl. As I recall, that story ruined your career as an anchorman. So, was that true?"

Roger turned beet red. "Of course it wasn't true!"

"Then why would you think anything the tabloids wrote about me was true?" Kath asked. She waited for him to storm off the set, but surprisingly, Roger checked his anger and continued.

"The movie you filmed in Australia did extraordinarily well at the box office. After that, you got a few more prime roles. It basically revived your career," Roger said.

"Yes, it did," Kath replied. "And I was thankful for it. I lived a small, quiet life, so money wasn't a problem, but every actress knows her days are numbered as she grows older. I was lucky enough to work well into old age."

Kath remembered those years after Gordon's death. They were difficult, so she kept herself busy by working. Still, the nights were long and lonely.

1974

Kath worked herself ragged after Gordon's death. All she had was her career now, so she was determined to make the most of it while she could. She still hadn't had the courage to visit Gordon's grave, afraid some lone photographer would follow her and start up all the nonsense again. She couldn't bear to be the topic of tabloid fodder again, so she stayed away and paid Scotty to pay for flowers to be put on Gordon's grave once a week.

Alma was a godsend to Kath during that time. She never asked questions—not even about the men's clothing and items in the other guest room, which Kath hadn't yet had the heart to pack up and give away. Alma followed her from project to project as her assistant and never complained about the long hours. But then, Kath paid her well, and they spent a lot of time at the beach house between movies. That was something the young, good-looking woman enjoyed immensely. Kath was thankful for Alma's presence in the house so she wouldn't become maudlin.

Kath was nominated and won her third Oscar for her performance in *The Sky is Wide*. She attended the awards ceremony along with James and Walter, who had also been nominated. Wearing a simple black evening dress with a dusting of beads that shone under the stage lights, Kath accepted the award with great humility. "I actually came this time," she told the laughing crowd. "And I'm so pleased that I did." She held up the statuette as the crowd cheered. Many there knew Kath would have loved to thank Gordon for his years of support and love, but she couldn't. Instead, they all gave her a standing ovation.

Kath brought the Oscar to the beach house and put it on a shelf to hold up a row of books.

"Bragging, I see," Daniel said upon seeing the golden statue. He came to the house on weekends since his job at the Beverly Hills post office was Monday-Friday.

"Hardly," Kath said, flopping down on a sofa. "Use it for a doorstop, for all I care. It's certainly heavy enough."

"We will not," her mother said, slowly entering the room. Catherine was now seventy, and her arthritis had been bothering her knees and hands terribly for a few years. She lowered herself into a chair. "I'm so proud of your accomplishments, Kath. You've worked hard for that award."

Kath shrugged. "It's all glam and glitter. But it's not as important as the work is. I'll be playing a civil rights lawyer in my next film, helping a woman who's been fired for being pregnant to win her job back. It's parts like those that are important—not trophies."

"Bite your tongue, girl," Crandell said as he entered the room. He walked slower these days and was out of breath often. His enlarged heart had, unfortunately, slowed him down now that he was seventy-four. "Trophies are wonderful! I have many from my swimming and rowing teams in college. It means you've succeeded in attaining excellence."

Kath laughed. "Ah, Dad. Yes, for you, they were rewards for your accomplishments. But for acting, I just don't feel that way. If I do a good movie, then I feel accomplished."

"That's a great way to think," Crandell said.

Daniel rolled his eyes. "Well, I was employee of the month once. Maybe I should bring my framed certificate here and hang it up."

"You're welcome to do so, honey," Catherine said.

Alma was there most weekends with Kath, and she got along well with the family. She loved playing volleyball with the younger set now on the beach, and both Crandell and Kath cheered her team on. Alma also helped Mio in the kitchen along with Catherine and Kath. Even though her mother couldn't do much with her stiff hands, she liked being in the middle of all the activity.

The best times for Kath were when Kat and Grant came for the weekend, and she could spend time with Caro. She was now a senior in high school and planned on attending college in the fall. Kath was so proud of the beautiful young lady.

"You and Grant did a great job with Caro," Kath said one evening when the two sisters were hiding out in Kath's old room. "She's becoming a wonderful adult."

"We're very proud of her," Kat said. "And we couldn't have enjoyed these years raising her without you."

"All I did was give birth to her. You did the hard work of raising her," Kath said.

Kat grew silent.

"What?" Kath asked.

"Grant and I have discussed it many times and agree that if you'd like to tell Caro you gave birth to her, we'd be fine with it. Maybe after she turns eighteen."

Kath's eyes grew wide. "Why on earth would I do that? It's a sure way to mess up her life. No. And I don't want you two saying a word either. She's happy and feels comfortable in her own skin—amazing for a teenage girl. Telling her something like that could ruin her perspective on things."

Kat nodded. "We just wanted you to know you can if you ever want to. I don't think it will change her feelings for us. We feel secure enough that she'll still think of us as her parents."

Kath brushed her hand through the air. "Not another word. You are her mother. End of story."

Kat agreed, but Kath did wonder what would happen if anything was said to Caro about her actual birth parents.

Oh, Gordon. You'd be so proud of her," Kath thought. Then she let those thoughts fly away as fast as they had come.

Kath started her next movie and was thrilled to be working with a few of her old industry friends. Scotty had agreed to direct the film, even though he rarely did anymore, and Rock Hudson was playing the attorney opposite Kath's character. Rock had recently been doing a television series, *McMillan & Wife*, which Kath had heard was quite successful. She didn't own a television, so she'd never seen it. But she was thrilled to see her old friend and work with him again.

"We've come a long way from our first movie together, haven't we?" Kath asked him as they hugged hello.

"A long way," Rock agreed. "Everything has changed and surprisingly, I've been happy doing a television series. A serious actor would never have thought of doing that years ago."

"I'm sure you're excellent in it," Kath said. "I made a movie for TV and didn't regret it."

Anthony Crane was also in the picture, a handsome actor Kath had already worked with twice but hadn't seen since 1965. He'd aged beautifully, even though she'd heard rumors that he'd been heavy into drugs in the late sixties. But now he looked clear-eyed and ready to work.

After they wrapped that picture, Kath worked with a whole new cast of young actors in a movie about teaching in inner-city schools in Los Angeles. She loved the role. The younger actors were impressive and it made her work even harder at her craft. Again, she felt she was working on projects that were important social narratives.

Kath took a break over the holidays that year and spent a lot of time with her family at the beach house. She gave Alma time off to spend with her own family, and Kath lazed around the house, enjoying card games with her parents and visits from Kat and Caro.

Late one evening, after everyone had gone to bed, Kath went downstairs to find a book from the many that sat on the shelves. She was surprised to see her father in the living room with the lights turned down low.

"Couldn't sleep?" Kath asked, sitting in a chair near him.

"Sometimes I feel so tired that I can't get to sleep," Crandell said. His brows rose. "That's strange, isn't it? But it's true."

Kath reached over and placed a hand over her father's. She remembered when he was young and strong and would out-race and out-swim all of them even as they became teenagers. Now, he looked thinner and tired. So very tired.

"I can believe that," she said. "How have you been feeling besides tired? Has your heart been giving you trouble?"

Crandell chuckled. "My heart is the reason I'm exhausted all the time. But I'm not complaining. I've lived a good life, and I plan to live a little more before I die."

Kath nodded and patted his hand. She hated hearing her father talk about death. He was the foundation of their family. He was her hero. She'd already lost an important person in her life. She didn't want to lose any others.

"Are you missing Gordon?" he asked as if reading her mind. "I miss his presence here. He was a serious man, but he could also be funny, too. And a good sport."

"I do miss him," Kath said. "Sometimes, I wish I hadn't gone to Australia for that movie. Maybe if I had been home, he wouldn't have died."

Crandell sat up taller and moved closer to Kath. "You can't blame yourself for his death. He would have passed whether or not you were with him."

"But at least I would have been there for him," Kath said. Tears sprung up in her eyes. "He begged me not to go, and I did anyway. I shouldn't have been so selfish."

"Honey. You weren't selfish. You had a life to live, and so did he. He was with family when he died, so you shouldn't feel bad about it. And you, young lady," Crandell said with a grin, "are the least selfish person I know. You give to us and to the rest of the family when they need something. Never confuse living your best life with being selfish."

Crandell sat back as his words fell over Kath. She was about to say something when her father spoke again.

"I've had a lot of time to think over the past couple of years, and there are a few things I regret," he said. "The biggest regret I have is how I treated Graham in his last years. I pride myself on being an independent thinker and a liberal one at that. But I didn't accept him for who he was. I feel like I was responsible for his early death."

Kath couldn't believe what she was hearing. Yet, she was relieved that her dad had come to terms with who Graham actually was. "You didn't kill him, Dad," she said softly. "Drunk driving killed him. If anyone was to blame, it was me. I should have insisted he stay at the house and not drive that night. But he was an adult, and I couldn't force him to stay."

"Kath, dear. He had a mind of his own and made his own choices. Again, you're not to blame for his death or Gordon's."

"It's hard, isn't it, Dad?" Kath said, wiping away her tears. "You think you know everything at a young age, yet the older you get, the more you realize just how stupid you were. I think that happens to everyone."

Crandell nodded. "Well said, dear. I'm glad we can talk openly like this. I can't talk to your mother about these things because it upsets her. And the last thing I want to do is hurt her. She's put up with a lot from me." He smiled.

"She's put up with a lot from all of us," Kath said, grinning back. "She's a saint."

"That she is."

Kath fell into her own thoughts as her father did also. She was happy she and her father could converse this way. And she was also relieved that her father had finally accepted who Graham was.

One month later, the rock of her family, her father, was gone.

Chapter Twenty-Three

Today

"One more day, and I'm done even if he isn't," Kath told Carolyn as they ate breakfast before heading to the studio. "I can't stand looking at his face any longer."

Carolyn laughed. "He is annoying. And he sure likes to push your buttons."

"Yes. He tries, but I always get the best of him," Kath said, grinning. "I've also made another decision."

Carolyn looked up at her. "What's that?"

"Tell the publisher I'll do one appearance. I'll initial as many books as my hand can stand, and I'll do those selfie things. But just the one time, so they'd better make it big and do it right."

"Absolutely," Carolyn said. "I'll tell them exactly what you said."

Kath was silent for a moment.

"What's wrong?" Carolyn asked.

"Do you think anyone will really come?" Kath said, sounding so unlike her usually confident self. "Or read my book?

Or even watch this stupid TV thing? Who cares about an old, useless actress these days? Who even remembers me?"

"Aunt Kath, are you kidding?" Carolyn said sternly. "People will line up around the block to meet you. Your book is already in the top ten in preorder, and your documentary will be watched by hundreds of thousands of people. You're an icon. The tough, strong, independent woman that all women aspire to be. And you did it when women weren't taken seriously. Don't worry. People will be there."

Kath thought about her words as she ate her eggs. Finally, she looked at Carolyn. "Who knew I was so incredibly awesome?"

Carolyn nearly spit out her coffee as she choked back a laugh. "Hearing you say *awesome* is too much," she said, wiping her lips. "But you are."

Carolyn drove her to the studio as Kath wondered what else Mr. Slick would want to talk about. In the years after her father died, Kath managed to make a few more films, but it seemed as if everyone she loved kept leaving her. Certainly, Roger wouldn't want to talk about death. But then again, this was Mr. Slick—of course he will.

Sitting across from Roger, Kath waited for the attack. *One more day,* she kept chanting silently to herself. She could get through this day and never see Roger again.

"Miss Carver," Roger said, smiling his usual fake smile. "You've been fortunate enough to live a long and healthy life. But I suppose the downside to living to ninety-eight is all the loss you endure, losing loved ones."

Kath sighed. *Here we go.*

"Yes, loss is a difficult thing, especially when you feel like the last person still standing," Kath said. "But I'm thankful I've been able to live this long and enjoy so much of my life."

"Your father passed away in early 1975. You must have been devastated," Roger said, trying to look sympathetic but failing. "He was very important to you, from what I gather in your book. How did that affect your life afterward and your family's dynamic?"

Why on earth does he want to dredge all this up? she thought. *One more day!*

"My father was the rock of our family. The nucleus. Of course, we were all devastated when he died. He was always so energetic and healthy that I figured he'd outlive us all. But I was wrong. It was a big adjustment for my entire family."

"And what about your friends?" Roger asked. "Howard Hughes died a year after your father and several other celebrity friends passed away. That must have been difficult, too."

"Howard's death was a shock, but then I hadn't spoken to him the last few years of his life. I learned later that he was constantly drugged for reasons that are only known to him. He was a good friend, and I adored him. I have nothing but good things to say about Howard," Kath said.

"And then the 1980s came along, and with it came AIDS. You must have lost a great many of your friends in that epidemic," Roger said.

Kath sighed. Yes, she did. But she didn't want Mr. Slick to start listing names. It was a tragic time and one she didn't wish to relive.

1975

The year Crandell Carver died was a difficult one for Kath. She didn't work all year so she could spend time with her mother and help her navigate living alone after all these years.

Kath was still paying the expenses on the beach house and Toluca Lake home, and she wasn't sure she'd be able to continue with her income dwindling. Kat and Grant offered to help with the expenses, which Kath was grateful for, but none of her other siblings did, even though they all used the beach house. And now that Malibu was becoming a high-end area for the rich, property taxes were rising by the second. Kath wasn't sure she'd be able to keep up with everything.

"You could move in with me," Catherine said hopefully mid-year. She didn't like living alone.

"Oh, Mom. You know how much I enjoy my privacy," Kath said. She didn't feel she was so old yet that she would lock herself away as her mother's caregiver. Kath still had a few more films left in her. "But we could sell the Toluca Lake home, and you could live at the beach house year-round," Kath suggested. "You'd always have company on the weekends."

Catherine nodded distractedly. "I'd really rather stay here for a little longer," she finally said. "I can still feel your father here."

Kath understood. She'd just have to make the best of it until her mother was willing to move—or eventually had to.

Scotty came up to the guest house to see Kath one day. At sixty-nine, he was basically retired and rarely had the crazy Sunday parties he was so famous for. His last partner had left him recently, and he wasn't in the market for a new one. He looked very serious when he came inside Kath's house to talk to her.

"I had a call today from Lisa, Gordon's daughter," he said.

Kath's heart began to beat faster. "And?"

"She'd like to meet you."

This was so unexpected that Kath was confused. "Why?"

"She said that if all the old rumors were true, it would mean you'd know her father better than even she or her brother," Scotty said. "She'd just like to hear more about his life, his work, and who he was as a person."

Kath had never considered that one of Gordon's children would want to talk to her. But she wasn't against it either. "Did she sound angry?"

Scotty chuckled. "No, but I understand why you'd ask that. She's just curious. She's married and has a daughter of her own, and I think she's finally ready to come to terms with who her father really was. Would you like to meet her?"

"Yes. I'd love that," Kath said. Gordon had rarely spoken about his children, but she knew he loved them despite not being around them much. If Lisa was open to hearing her story, Kath would be willing to share what her life with Gordon was like.

Scotty stood, a small smile on his face. "Good. I'll call her and set it up." He headed for the door, walking slowly.

"Are you okay?" Kath asked, watching her friend struggle to walk.

"I'm fine. Some days, it's harder to move than others."

"It's because you have to walk so far to get around that rambling house of yours," Kath teased. "Maybe you should downsize and move into the other guest house."

Scotty turned around when he reached the door. "That might be a thought. At some point, I'll have to move. I'm not ready to do that quite yet." He left, and Kath watched as he walked down the steps to his home.

Kath had just been kidding, but now she wondered what would happen to her if Scotty did sell. She loved her little house up here in the hills. She supposed she'd have to move to the beach house permanently, but that would take away her privacy.

"A problem for another day," she told herself out loud. Growing excited about meeting Lisa, Kath went upstairs to Gordon's room to look through his things and see if there was anything of interest Lisa would like to have.

On the day of their meeting, Kath was nervous. It took a lot to make her feel this way, but this was momentous. Meeting Gordon's daughter to talk about him meant sharing secrets she never thought she'd tell another person. Yet, it seemed like the right thing to do. A daughter had the right to know everything about her father.

Kath had gathered some photos of the vacations she and Gordon had taken along with a couple of awards Gordon had won for acting and had left with her. She'd also found his favorite book, *The Great Gatsby*, which had been read so many times the pages were dogeared and thin. Gordon lived a minimalist life and didn't keep too many sentimental items around, so there wasn't much Kath could give to Lisa. But the book was a special gift, as far as Kath was concerned.

Kath had given Alma the day off so she could speak privately with Lisa. Alma never asked Kath about her past unless Kath brought it up, and even then, she didn't pry. That was one of the things Kath loved about her. She didn't snoop, and she didn't judge.

A knock on her front door brought Kath out of her reverie. Taking a deep breath, she answered it. There stood a young woman with blond hair and blue eyes. Kath would know those eyes anywhere—they were exactly the same as Gordon's.

"Miss Carver?" Lisa asked. "I'm Lisa Aimes, Gordon

Quinn's daughter."

Kath smiled widely. "Of course you are," she said warmly. "I'd know you anywhere. You have Gordon's eyes. Come inside." Kath moved aside so the young woman could pass her and led her to the living room. "Please, have a seat. I made iced tea in case you were thirsty. Would you like a glass?"

"Um, yes. Thank you." Lisa sat and studied Kath.

Kath poured glasses of tea and moved the sugar closer to Lisa. She could feel the woman's eyes on her the entire time.

"Thank you," Lisa said again. She sat there, slowly looking around. "I have to admit, I'm a bit overwhelmed. I'm not sure what to say."

Kath smiled. "I'll admit I'm very nervous, and it takes a lot to make me feel that way. So, I'll simply ask, what would you like to talk about?"

"This seems blunt, but I'll just say it," Lisa said, her hands smoothing her slacks. "For as long as I can remember, there were rumors about you and my father being involved. My dad wouldn't talk about it, and my mother said to ignore the rumors. But I need to know. Where they true?"

Kath might be able to lie to the press and the world, but she couldn't lie to this young woman. "Yes, dear. The rumors were true. I was involved with Gordon for twenty years. I'm sorry, but there's no way to sugarcoat that, and I'm sure you'd want me to be honest."

Lisa looked stunned for a moment, then seemed to accept the idea. "I guess I always knew since my dad rarely stayed with us, but I had to be sure." She hesitated, then asked, "Were you the reason my parents lived separate lives?"

Kath shook her head. "No, dear. Their marriage was already broken when I became involved with Gordon. He told me the truth from the very beginning. He said he was married, but he and his wife were not together. He lived in the other guest house here on the property for a while. I met him when we made our first movie together, but we didn't get involved until after the second movie we made as a team."

Lisa's hand shook as she sipped her drink. "Then why didn't he divorce my mother if he wanted to be with you?"

"Your father always made it very clear that his first allegiance was to his family, especially his children, so he'd never divorce his wife. Even though he wasn't living with you, he always put you and your brother first," Kath said.

"And you were fine with that?" Lisa asked sharply.

"I had to be. I loved Gordon. We loved each other. If that was all he could offer me, I was willing to take it," Kath told her.

"Wasn't that selfish of him? To be married, but have you too?"

Kath shook her head. "No. He was always honest about it. I accepted the relationship as it was."

Kath watched as Lisa tried to digest everything she'd heard. Lisa was a beautiful woman with a sweet, oval face and long hair that hung down to her shoulders. She was dressed nicely and wore minimal make-up or jewelry. Everything about the young woman showed she had class. Kath had to give Lisa's mother credit for raising such a lovely person.

"Was he happy?" Lisa asked, looking up into Kath's eyes. "He never seemed truly happy when he spent time at home around my mother. I always thought he was a sad person."

The picture Lisa painted of her father broke Kath's heart. "Your father was a complicated man. To be an actor as accomplished as he was, sometimes it takes someone whose feelings are always on the surface. He could be depressed at times. And he did drink when he was sad. But he could also be the man at the party with the funniest jokes or have a sparkle in his eye when he was teasing. I was happy with him, for the most part, and he and I had some wonderful times."

Lisa nodded. She'd known her father enough to understand what Kath was saying.

"I have some photos of him through the years if you'd like to see them," Kath said.

Lisa stood. "Maybe another time. I'm still trying to figure this all out."

Kath stood. "Of course. Please feel free to call me any time you'd like to talk. And here." Kath picked up the book and handed it to Lisa. "Take this with you. It was your father's favorite book. He read it at least once a year. He even spent time talking and drinking with Fitzgerald while he was working on scripts in Hollywood. It was one of your father's favorite stories."

Lisa looked down at the title. "*The Great Gatsby.* I love this book. It's one of my favorites, too. I had no idea my dad loved it so much."

"It's yours, dear. Something to remind you that you are your father's daughter."

"Thank you." Lisa walked to the door and then turned around. "Thank you for being honest with me. My mother would die if she knew I was talking to you, but I had to know."

"I think your father would want you to know who he really was," Kath said.

"I would like to see you again," Lisa said.

Kath took a pen and piece of paper from the table by the door and wrote down her phone number. "Call me anytime. I mean it."

Lisa nodded, then was gone.

Kath closed the door and walked back to the sofa. Staring at Gordon's chair in the corner, she smiled. "Your daughter is lovely, Gordon," she said to the empty chair. "I hope you knew that." Then she picked up the tray of glasses and headed to the kitchen.

After that first visit, Lisa did come to see Kath many times. They became good friends. They shared pictures and stories about Gordon that made them laugh and cry. It was so nice, after keeping quiet for so long, for Kath to share memories with someone of the man she loved. And she felt that, in some small way, it brought Lisa closer to her dad.

The following year, Kath heard, along with the entire world, that the great Howard Hughes had died. She was heartbroken that she hadn't been able to talk to him in years, but so grateful to have known him. She wanted to go to the funeral but learned it was in Houston, and only the family could attend. So, she sent flowers and tucked away another memory of someone she'd cared deeply for.

Chapter Twenty-Four

1985

Surprisingly for Kath, offers for roles continued to come in for her throughout the late 1970s and early 1980s. She rarely played the leading role anymore, but she had good ones in family dramas and historical movies. She was encouraged by the fact that her idol, Katharine Hepburn, was still working and had even won an Oscar in 1982 at the age of seventy-five for her work in *On Golden Pond*. Kath thought if Hepburn could continue working into her seventies, she most certainly could, too.

With the arrival of the eighties came the devasting disease that became known as AIDS, and it worked its way through Hollywood like a cyclone. Kath felt like she was losing friends in the industry daily. She worried about Scotty and begged him to be careful. At one point, he smiled sadly and told her, "Honey. I should have been more careful years ago. Now, time will tell."

Kath had seen Rock a few times through the years and was struck by how much weight he'd lost. When he'd come to visit Scotty in mid-1984, she learned why. Long before it was announced to the world that Rock had AIDS, he quietly told Scotty and Kath he'd been diagnosed with the dreadful disease.

Kath was heartbroken. Rock was one of the kindest men she knew. She couldn't bear to hear he was dying.

"Don't give up on me yet," he told Kath and Scotty. "I'm going to try a new treatment in France that isn't available here. The doctors think it can, at the very least, extend my life, if not cure me."

Kath was happy her friend was optimistic and hoped what he said was true. But, a year later, he came back to the United States from France so he could die at home. Kath and Scotty visited him once at his house and were saddened to see how weak he was. After that, Rock declined any more visits from friends and passed away on October 2, 1985. He requested no funeral and was cremated, having his ashes scattered in the ocean. Kath was saddened she couldn't join friends to mourn his death. Instead, Scotty invited everyone who knew Rock to his home, and they toasted their good friend in their own way.

Not long after Rock died, Scotty told Kath he was ready to sell his house.

"It's just too big and costs too much for upkeep," he told her.

Kath could see that at eighty, Scotty was also declining. He needed a smaller place with less stress. "I'll have to find a new home," she said sadly. "I'll miss being so close to you."

Scotty's eyes twinkled. "I have an idea if you're up to it," he said. "I already checked with the city and county and all the permit people. I can survey off the two acres that the guest houses are on and sell it to you, and then sell the rest to someone else. You'd have to add a separate driveway and build a fence between the two properties. And I'll give you a good deal." He smiled. "I can gouge the new buyers of my house to make my profit."

Kath laughed at his words but was also thrilled about the idea. "Let's do it," she said. "I can't see me leaving this place now, after all these years of renting it."

She bought the property and paid for a new driveway along with a fence and an electric gate at the street for privacy. It was costly, but other than helping her mother with expenses, Kath had been frugal and had the money to do it. It was a good investment, too. Property just kept soaring in the Hollywood hills, and she knew it would continue to do so.

Scotty ended up getting a pretty penny for his house and the rest of the property, then bought a sweet bungalow even higher in the hills where old Hollywood stars used to live. Kath loved his new property. It was right off a narrow street, with a stone wall all around it and a gate. He had a pool and beautiful trees surrounding it for privacy. And on the second floor was a room with nearly all windows where the view was spectacular. This he used as his living room. The brick fireplace kept it cozy, and the view mesmerized guests.

It didn't surprise Kath when the new owners of Scotty's house tore it down completely to build a new, modern home. But it saddened her. How could this younger generation of movie stars not value the beauty of the homes built in the twenties and thirties of early Hollywood? It was terrible, but there was nothing she could do about it. She was so happy she had her home and slice of property.

There were so many changes going on in her life that Kath could hardly keep up with them. Cary Grant, a good friend and the man who'd introduced her to Howard Hughes passed away in 1986 of a stroke. And then, in 1988, dear Scotty died of a heart attack in his small bungalow. Kath was devastated over his loss. He'd made her the executor of his will and given her a nice sum of money, which surprised her. He'd also bequeathed his remaining savings to several charities, with the largest donation going toward research for AIDS. Kath planned his funeral and invited his many friends from his movie-making past. She couldn't find a list of family members to contact, and as far as Kath knew, Scotty had no contact with family. Hollywood was his family, and they were the ones who mourned him.

That same year, Kath talked her mother into selling the Toluca Lake home and moving into the other guest house on her property. Catherine was eighty-four years old and was very frail. She'd fallen once already and, luckily, hadn't broken any bones. She was also confused at times. So, Kath moved her into the house along with her mother's favorite furnishing and hired a woman to cook, clean, and watch over Catherine when Kath wasn't around.

Cleaning out her childhood home was an enormous task. All her siblings came and took the items they wanted, leaving years of old toys, letters, photo albums, and everything else for Kath to take care of. Lillian, now fifty-seven, didn't work and had her days to herself now that her children were grown but refused to help. She took what she wanted and even fought with Kat over a few things just because Kat wanted them. Then she walked away, her nose in the air. Kath was so infuriated she could have slapped her. But Kat just told Kath it didn't matter. Kat hadn't felt well for a while and didn't have the fight in her to worry about it.

"Have you seen a doctor?" Kath asked Kat while they

worked their way through everything in the house. They were trying to decide what to bring to the beach house and what to sell.

"I have. He hasn't found anything wrong," Kat said, sitting down heavily in what was once her father's favorite chair. At sixty, Kat looked worn and tired. She was thin and had dark circles under her eyes. Kath, who was two years older, looked younger than her sister.

"Something must be wrong," Kath said. "Will you go see my doctor? I'll call and get you in."

Kat shrugged. Grant had also begged her to see another doctor. "Sure. But there's nothing wrong. I'm just getting old."

"I'm older than you, and I'm fine. I'll make the appointment," Kath said.

Grant was the only one who volunteered to help Kath move the furniture they wanted to keep to the guest house and beach house. Danny, who had retired from the post office, claimed he couldn't lift anything because of his bad back. It infuriated Kath—who was also trying to work on a movie in between all this upheaval—how lazy her younger brother and sister were. Even Kat, who didn't feel well, was helping with the smaller items.

After moving a leather sofa into the beach house, Grant fell on it with a sigh. "Thank you for offering to get Kat an appointment with your doctor," he said. "She's been feeling so tired for a year now, and no one will do anything."

"I'm happy to do it. She needs to get well so you two can enjoy your retirement." Kath also sat. She was exhausted from moving furniture.

Grant chuckled. "Retirement. That sounds so strange. Weren't you and I just necking on the porch a few short years ago? Didn't I just marry my lovely Katrina yesterday?"

"It feels that way, doesn't it?" Kath said, smiling. "It went by quickly, that's for sure. Gordon's been gone for nearly twenty years. Almost as long as we were together. It's so strange. I feel like I lost him last month."

"Haven't you seen anyone else in all this time? Or have you kept it a secret?" Grant said.

Kath waggled her brows. "A lady never tells." And she secretly promised herself that she never would.

TODAY

Kath sat, waiting for yet another question. Half the time was over. Soon, she'd be finished talking to Mr. Slick forever.

"You didn't mention anyone else you were involved with in your book after Howard Hughes. You claim you and Gordon weren't a couple, so would you mind sharing with us any other men who were in your life?" Roger asked, leaning forward in his seat.

"Yes. I'd mind it very much," Kath said. "If I'd wanted my personal life made public, I would have announced it to the world."

Roger frowned. "You realize that some people suggest that the reason you never shared who you've been involved with is because you dated women in a time when it wasn't acceptable. Do you want those rumors to continue?"

Kath laughed. "Why would I care if people think I'm a lesbian or straight? There's nothing wrong with being either. Frankly, it's no one's business."

"Okay," Roger said, unsuccessfully hiding his annoyance.

"If you didn't want to share the secrets of your life, I'll ask you the question I began this interview with. Why did you write your biography?"

Kath stared at him, her lips slightly elevated in amusement. "And I'll give you the same answer as I did before. For the money."

Roger sighed. "Well, there you have it, ladies and gentlemen. An honest answer from an honest-to-goodness icon." He turned to Kath and smiled widely. "Thank you so much, Miss Carver, for the many hours we spent chatting. I had a wonderful time, and I hope you did as well."

I had a great time sparring with you, Kath thought but decided she'd be polite instead. "Thank you, Roger."

"Cut!" the director shouted, and then the entire crew clapped.

Kath stared around in amazement. Were they clapping for her?

Carolyn came over to help Kath stand, which was difficult after sitting for so long. Roger approached Kath and offered his hand to shake.

"It's been an interesting interview, to say the least," Roger said, his smile finally looking genuine. "You're a tough nut to crack."

Kath shook his hand. "We both had a job to do, Roger. I think we both did quite well."

He laughed. "Good luck with the book. I know it will be a bestseller." With that, he left the soundstage.

Kath let out a long sigh. "It's finally over. We deserve a rest at the beach house."

"I couldn't agree more," Carolyn said as she led Kath to the room to collect their belongings.

That evening, Kath sat on the porch overlooking the ocean instead of helping Carolyn make dinner. Her niece had told her she should rest, and Kath had taken her up on it. She lit her second cigarette of the day as the light ocean breeze came through the window screens. Kath wondered why she even bothered to smoke anymore, other than out of defiance because her doctor said she shouldn't. She could truly be prickly when she wanted to be. This made her laugh out loud. Maybe she'd surprise everyone and quit. She didn't even like the darned things anyway.

Danny joined them for dinner at the kitchen table. He was his usual talkative self, spouting off about nothing that interested Kath. *How can an old man who does nothing but sit around the beach house have so much to talk about?* Kath wondered.

"Aunt Kath? Don't you like your food?" Carolyn asked.

"What, dear?" Kath focused on her niece. She'd been thinking about other things and hadn't even taken a bite. "Oh, sorry. I guess I'm just not hungry. But it looks and smells delicious," Kath told Carolyn. "It's been a long week."

Carolyn nodded. "It has. What about a piece of apple pie? I know you can't refuse that."

"Ah, no, thank you, dear. Maybe later. I think I'll go into the living room and find a good book." Kath stood and teetered a bit before Carolyn came over and steadied her.

"Thank you, dear. I'm a bit wobbly today. But at my age, I have a right to be wobbly," Kath said.

Daniel laughed. "Yes. You've earned being wobbly. You've worked hard these past few weeks."

Carolyn helped Kath into the living room, where floor-to-ceiling bookshelves lined the walls.

"I'm fine now," Kath said. "Go finish your dinner. I'll just look over the books."

Carolyn nodded and left the room.

Instead of finding a book, Kath sat on the sofa, the very last place she'd sat with her father before he'd died. All this reminiscing about her biography and then the interview had made old memories replay in her mind. The first year their entire family used the beach house right after it had been built. The many years of everyone running and playing on the sand, enthusiastically playing volleyball, or having swimming races. So many years of wonderful memories, all because her parents believed deeply in family and being together. It was a wonderful childhood.

And now they were all gone, except Danny and her. Everyone. It made Kath extremely sad.

CHAPTER TWENTY-FIVE

1990

Two years after moving her mother into the guest house, Catherine had a stroke and had to go to a care facility. Kath hated that she couldn't keep her mother at home with her. But Catherine needed constant care, and the doctor didn't think their eighty-six-year-old mother would pull out of her condition. So, everyone came.

Kat and Carolyn, now thirty-three, married, and with a good job as a paralegal in a law firm, came to sit beside Catherine as Kath also kept vigil. Daniel came too, but only for short increments, and Lillian came to pray for her mother, which the other siblings appreciated. Jane visited, too. During her long friendship with Kath, Catherine and Crandell had treated her like a daughter, and she would miss Kath's mother as much as their own family would.

As they sat with their mother, who hadn't awoken since the stroke, Kath noticed how worn Kat looked. Two years prior, after selling the Toluca Lake house, Kat had gone to see Kath's doctor and found she had a tumor in her stomach. After they operated, cancer was found, and Kat went through several rounds of chemotherapy. The oncologist had been very optimistic that Kat could beat the cancer, and once the treatments were finished, they'd proclaimed her cancer-free. But now, looking across her mother's bed at Kat, Kath wondered if it had come back. She prayed not.

"You should go home and sleep," Kath told her sister. "Caro and I can keep Mom company overnight."

Kat narrowed her eyes at Kath. "Don't treat me like an invalid. I'm fine. And I want to be here for mother."

Kath raised her hands as if to protect herself from Kat. "Okay, okay. You don't have to attack me." She smiled at her favorite sibling.

Kat smiled back. "You've been bossy your entire life," she said good-naturedly.

"I was the oldest. I had to be bossy," Kath said. "I was in charge of all of you."

"Tell me about Grandma," Caro said, reaching out to hold Catherine's hand. "I want to know everything. What organizations did she volunteer for? What causes did she march for? She never told me anything about those early years because she called it bragging."

"Oh, sweetie," Kath said to her niece. "Your grandmother did everything she could to raise awareness for racism, for the women's rights movement, and any other cause where she felt people were being mistreated. She even helped with fundraisers for AIDS, despite her getting older and suffering from arthritis. She was a pistol!"

"Mom believed in equality for everyone," Kat said. "She was a very independent and liberal thinker long before it was fashionable. She welcomed people of all races and lifestyles into our home and taught us to do the same."

"And she never judged people," Kath said. "She knew we were all human, and even if mistakes were made, she didn't make people feel bad about themselves. She was a bigger person than me, that's for sure."

"Me, too," Kat said. She pulled Caro closer into a side hug. "Even if we were all half as good as Mom was, we'd be lucky."

Catherine Carver died two days later without waking up. Kat, Carolyn, and Kath were at her side. She was buried beside her husband and her son, Graham. It felt odd to Kath that now she was the eldest member of the family.

Life went on.

Kath continued to do one or two movies a year, small parts but good ones. And in 1996, at the age of seventy, she returned to the New York stage for a run of the play, *The Lion in Winter*, playing Eleanor of Aquitaine. It was the same character that her idol, Katharine Hepburn, had won an Oscar for in the movie version years before. Kath loved returning to the theater, but it was her last time doing a play. The schedule was too demanding for her, and she left after six months. But she was proud to have been able to play such an amazing role.

Over the years, for the most part, Kath stayed out of the public eye. When Kat's cancer returned in 2000, Kath was there for her day and night. Grant didn't want his wife in a nursing home or hospital, so Kath, Grant, and Carolyn took turns caring for Kat as the cancer ran through her. It was heartbreaking for Kath to watch her sister suffer so much. She died in 2002, leaving a big hole in the family. Two years later, Grant died of a sudden heart attack at the age of seventy-nine. Kath always believed that Grant died of a broken heart after losing his beloved Kat.

A year later, Kath received a call from Jane's husband that she'd passed away suddenly in her sleep. Jane—the best lifelong friend a woman could ever have—was gone forever. Kath felt like many pieces of her life were breaking away, taking with them the best parts of her.

Kath's long-time assistant, Alma, retired in 2010, and after that, Kath hadn't felt a need to hire a new assistant. Bringing someone new into her house felt awkward. But at the age of eighty-four, Kath also didn't like to drive around Los Angeles or out to the beach house alone. Kath had groceries delivered, and often, Carolyn drove her to Malibu on weekends. Carolyn and her attorney husband, Mark, had never been blessed with children, so now that Carolyn had retired, she spent more time with Kath. In 2015, when Carolyn's husband died unexpectedly, Kath was there for her niece. A year later, Carolyn moved in with her aunt as her assistant and companion. She didn't need the money because her husband had supported them well, but she wanted to be there for her aunt. It was then that Kath had the idea to organize her journal notes and photos to compile some type of memoir, perhaps about her experiences in Australia or the making of several of her movies—but nothing personal.

Carolyn thought that was an excellent project for them to work on and they began the long process of organizing and typing up her notes on the computer. Little did Kath know she'd have to use this fun project for the backdrop of her biography that she didn't want to write.

TODAY

Kath and Carolyn spent a couple of weeks at the beach after the interviews were completed. It was relaxing to be there despite Daniel's constant presence. Carolyn was in contact with the publisher, making plans for Kath's appearance when the book came out in two weeks.

"When we return home to Bel Air, we should go shopping for something new for you to wear to the book signing," Carolyn suggested one evening after dinner.

Kath was sitting back in the kitchen chair, relaxing after a delicious meal of grilled shrimp, stuffed peppers, and salad. Her brows rose at Carolyn's suggestion. "Why on earth do I need new clothes? My regular clothes will be fine."

Carolyn sighed. "Yes. That's what you said for the documentary, too. But this is a special occasion. Everyone is coming to see a movie star. You should wear something that sparkles like your personality."

Kath snorted. "Since when do I sparkle?"

"Never," Daniel said from across the table. "A wrinkled old suit will be perfect for meeting your fans." He grinned.

Kath glared at him.

"Maybe a new jacket and blouse?" Carolyn asked. "Something with sequins that will twinkle in the light. You'll be taking pictures with people. Don't you want to look nice?"

Kath rolled her eyes. "What are you saying? I should buy clothes from Bob Mackie? I'm not Liza Minnelli, for Pete's sake."

Carolyn shrugged and began clearing away the plates. "Fine. We'll dig through your clothes and find something appropriate from 1940."

Kath chewed on that for a minute. "That's my trademark look, isn't it? Trousers, sweaters, and oversized jackets. That's how everyone has seen me over the years."

Carolyn turned around from the sink and leaned against the counter. "I know. But even a new, fitted jacket would be a nice change. But not if you don't want to."

Kath thought about her words throughout the evening. She was sure the publisher was pressing Carolyn to get her to dress up for the event. As they all sat in the living room, with Daniel watching television and Kath and Caro reading, Kath finally spoke up.

"Okay. You're right. Something new might be nice. But please, no sequins."

Carolyn chuckled. "No sequins, I promise."

When they returned to the Bel Air house, Kath felt relaxed and refreshed. The beach always did that for her. Despite having hated writing her biography and doing the Netflix interviews, it was worth it to Kath to be able to keep the beach house.

Carolyn went to different designer shops and brought home a multitude of clothes for Kath to try. Once the shops knew who it was for and where she'd be wearing it, they offered whatever she kept for free.

"This is crazy!" Kath said, looking at all the jackets, slacks, purses, scarves, blouses, and shoes Carolyn had brought home. "And they aren't going to charge me for what I wear? What's wrong with these people?"

Carolyn laughed. "They do this kind of thing for award shows all the time. They want their products seen on celebrities."

"I'm just an old lady who used to be famous," Kath said. "No one is going to care what I'm wearing."

"Well, the designers beg to differ," Carolyn told her.

Kath looked through the many items and tried on a couple of different jackets. She looked better in rich colors, like deep burgundy or rich purple, so she chose the burgundy jacket that was slightly fitted. They found a cream blouse for underneath and a paisley silk scarf.

"What? No Bob Mackie?" Kath asked, grinning.

"You said no sequins," Caro told her.

"Oh, I do love this leather bag," Kath said, running her hand over the big, dark brown leather Gucci bag that felt as soft as butter. "If I bring it along, will that count as wearing it?"

Carolyn laughed. "Yes, it will. They'll be thrilled you love it."

"It seems silly getting things for free," Kath said as Carolyn packed up the items she was going to return. She had taken a photo of the items Kath was keeping. "I can certainly afford to buy my own."

"It is silly," Carolyn said. "But that's Hollywood."

"Hollywood." Kath said it like it was a dirty word. "I used to be proud to be a part of the land of make-believe. But it's really only about money these days, isn't it? We old-timers never made the kind of money they do today, let alone get residuals for our movies. It's a different world."

"Thank goodness for your book and documentary," Carolyn said. "They'll make residuals for years to come."

"Even that's odd to me," Kath said, resting on the sofa. "Thank you for forcing me to do this, dear. I would have just shown up in an old suit and loafers. You were right. I needed something with a little more pizzazz."

Carolyn laughed. "Yes. That's the word. Pizzazz."

A week before Kath's book signing appearance, a heavy box was delivered from the publisher. Carolyn opened it. Inside lay twenty copies of Kath's biography in hardcover with a gorgeous jacket.

"They're beautiful," Carolyn said, lifting one out to hand to Kath. On the cover was a photo of Kath from the 1940s, and on the back was a more recent picture of her.

"It is nice. And heavy," Kath said, handing it back to Carolyn.

"Don't you want to look through it?" her niece asked.

"No. I'm sure it looks exactly like the copy we approved. It is nice, though," Kath said.

"This book represents two years of work," Carolyn said. "You should be proud."

"Two years of your work, too," Kath said. "I talked, and you typed. You put the manuscript in some semblance of order, too." She thought for a moment. "Open it and see what the dedication says."

Carolyn did and read out loud, *"To my wonderful parents, Catherine and Crandell Carver, who were patient and kind. To my sister, Katrina, who always believed in me. And to my dear niece, Carolyn, without whom I would never have been able to finish this book. I love you all."*

Carolyn's mouth dropped open. "I typed this for you, but I didn't type that last line."

"I still have a few tricks up my sleeve, dear," Kath said. "And I meant every word. This is as much your accomplishment as mine. Maybe even more."

Carolyn wiped tears from her eyes. "It's been my pleasure, Auntie."

The day of the release came. Kath dressed in her partially new outfit, preferring to wear her own trousers and shoes, and filled her new Gucci bag with everything she'd need.

"Ready?" Carolyn asked. She wore a new watercolor print dress that fell to her knees and seemed to float around her.

"What a beautiful dress," Kath told her. "I guess I'm as ready as I'll ever be."

A limo was waiting for them in the driveway, courtesy of the publisher. They slipped inside and enjoyed the posh ride.

The publisher set up a signing as elegant as the silver screen star that Kath was. They rented Grauman's Chinese Theater on Hollywood Boulevard. A bookseller set up a store to sell Kath's book in the entryway, and Kath would sit at a table on stage. While fans waited, they could look over the many hand and footprints in the cement from past stars of the cinema.

A red carpet had been rolled out from the street to the theater's entrance. Red velvet ropes kept a multitude of fans at bay. When the limousine arrived, cheers arose from the crowd loud enough for Kath to hear inside the car.

"My goodness," Kath said, staring at all the people waiting for her to walk the red carpet. Cameramen were there also, waiting to film or snap photos of her. "Are you sure they didn't pay these people to show up?"

"Don't be silly," Carolyn told her. "They're all here for you. Aren't you glad you dressed nice?"

"Sneaky, aren't you?" Kath said, then smiled. She took a deep breath, feeling the old nervousness of years past when she'd attended large events. "Let's go."

A handsome man in a tuxedo helped Kath out of the car and offered his arm as her escort down the carpet. Another man in a tuxedo did the same for Carolyn. Lights flashed, and fans called out as Kath walked by. When they were halfway down the carpet, an older woman called and waved at Kath to stop and look.

"Your hand prints and shoe prints!" the woman yelled, pointing to the very spot where she stood.

Kath stopped and looked. It had been decades since she'd encased her hands and shoes in cement for the theater to display. She smiled at the woman and nodded as the camera flashes continued.

Once inside, the gentleman escorted Kath down the left aisle to the stage, where a group of women were waiting for her. Kath thanked the young man and approached the women. A small table covered with a red velvet tablecloth stood in the center of the stage with a nice sturdy padded chair next to it.

"We're so happy to meet you," the lead woman, Haley, said, shaking Kath's hand. "We're from your publisher and will be helping with the signing and pictures today. Our job is to ensure everything goes smoothly so you aren't here any longer than necessary."

"That's wonderful," Kath said. "Thank you."

Carolyn helped her aunt sit in the chair, which was quite comfortable for being so simply made. She asked Haley for two water bottles and a glass or mug to pour it in. Haley sent a woman off to get them for Kath.

"Once the line of people come inside, we'll have them come up to the stage one at a time," Haley told Kath. "The bookseller out in the lobby can sell books to anyone who wants a copy. I hope it's okay to take photos with people who don't buy a copy. Some people just want to meet you. Many times, they've already purchased an eBook online or will buy a copy later."

"That's fine," Kath said. "That's the reason for this, isn't it? To sell more copies."

Haley smiled. "Yes, it is. It's a great promotion. We'll be in the newspapers and magazines everywhere with pictures of you walking the red carpet to your book signing. It's great publicity."

"Well, then. Let's get started," Kath said. Her nervousness had left her, and now she was excited to meet the people.

They brought out a chair so Carolyn could sit near Kath and help. One of the other women was available to take photos of Kath with fans.

"They are quite organized, aren't they?" Kath whispered to Carolyn, very impressed.

"Yes, they are," Carolyn said.

"I've been in line since five this morning, so I could be one of the first people here," a middle-aged woman said to Kath, handing her a hardcover copy of the book to sign. "I've loved watching your movies since I was a child."

Kath stared at the woman, shocked that she'd be that dedicated just to meet her. "That's incredible," Kath told her. "Thank you for doing that. I'm so happy to meet you."

The men and women kept coming, books in hand as well as phones, hoping for a photo as well. A young man told her she was his idol, the way she was so independent and fierce in her roles. An elderly man and woman said they were at the premiere of Kath and Gordon's first movie together, standing outside the theater just to see her. Two young girls with their grandmother shyly asked for a photo with Miss Carver. Kath figured this was more for the grandmother than the girls, but she was happy to do it.

The line went on and on.

Carolyn requested a break for Kath each hour so she could stand, stretch, and use the bathroom. Each time she stood, the people in line gasped, afraid she was leaving.

"I promise, I'll be right back," Kath called out to them. The crowd sighed with relief.

"Tell me when you've had enough," Carolyn told Kath during their third break. "You've already been here longer than I thought you would."

"I'll try to get through everyone," Kath said. "If I can't, maybe I can walk past everyone in line and at least say hello. I don't want to be rude."

Carolyn grinned. "Well, look who's being Miss Sociable."

"Oh, stop it," Kath grumbled but smiled too. In truth, this was the most fun she'd had in a long time. If it made the people waiting happy to see her, then she was determined to meet them all.

After five hours, the women organizing the event went outside to end the event. They apologized to anyone who was still waiting and said that Kathleen Carver had stayed longer than anticipated, and they didn't dare ask her to do more. But before leaving, Kath came outside and, with Carolyn's help, walked down the line of people behind the red ropes and shook hands or took selfies with each person who wanted to.

"I'm sorry I had to stop for the day," she called out to her fans. "I'm an old lady, and I wear out quickly. But you can't even imagine how heartwarming it is for me to see all of you here, and I thank you all from the bottom of my heart."

The audience cheered.

One of the tuxedoed gentlemen finally escorted Kath to the limousine and helped her in. But before she moved to sit inside, she waved to the crowd and blew kisses to them. The people erupted in cheers once more, and then Kath and Carolyn were gone. The day that Kath had dreaded the most was the best day of Kath's life.

Chapter Twenty-Six

TODAY

By the time the limousine dropped Kath and Carolyn at her Bel Air home, Kath's hand was stiff from writing, her throat sore from talking, and her back hurt from sitting so long.

"Do you want to soak in a hot tub?" Carolyn asked. "It might help the stiffness."

"I think I just want to change into my comfy old clothes, have a bite to eat, and then go to bed," Kath said.

Carolyn brought her clothes downstairs and helped her change so Kath wouldn't have to climb the stairs. Then she left her on the sofa with a cup of warm tea while she prepared a small dinner.

Kath sat staring at Gordon's empty chair. "Well, old boy," she said. "You never would have believed the turnout today after all these years. I guess I'm still relevant." She chuckled. "And people talked about you, too. See? Old stars never die. They keep burning brightly in the hearts of movie lovers."

Carolyn stuck her head out the kitchen door. "Did you say something?"

Kath shook her head. "No, dear. I was just talking to myself."

She glanced at Gordon's chair, nodded knowingly, and returned to the kitchen.

"You seemed to have a good time today," Carolyn said as they ate dinner in the kitchen.

"I did have a good time. I forgot what it was like being out with the public. Honestly, dear, I never believed anyone still cared for this old lady. So, it did my heart good to meet all the people willing to wait in line just to say hello or take a photo."

"It was fun to watch, too," Carolyn said. "It gave me a glimpse into your early years of Hollywood. Was it as glamorous as it seemed?"

Kath chuckled. "Glitter and tinsel made it look glamorous, but working in movies was just that, work. And those of us who survived it didn't necessarily work harder, we just weren't willing to give it up. You had to be tough and stubborn."

"Your two best qualities," Carolyn said.

"You've got that right," Kath said proudly.

After dinner, Carolyn helped Kath upstairs to her bedroom and change into pajamas. Kath got under the covers and sat back against her fluffy pillows. She loved this room. It looked much the same as it had in 1949 when she'd moved in. The room had been repainted a couple of times and the comforter and curtains had been changed every few years, but otherwise, it hadn't changed. Kath liked that. She felt comforted by keeping things the same.

Kath watched as Carolyn hung the new clothes she'd worn that day and gather the items that needed washing. When her niece turned to say goodnight, Kath smiled.

"What are you smiling about?" Carolyn said. "Still thinking

about how famous you were today?"

Kath laughed. "Famous for a day. Yes. I like how that sounds."

Carolyn studied her aunt for a moment, then asked. "I'm curious. Why did you write your biography and do that documentary? I know you told Roger that it was for the money, but there's more to it than that. You like your privacy and have your secrets. Why now?"

Kath's face softened. "I wanted to save the beach house for the next generation. That much is true. But the real reason I did all of this was for you, dear."

"Me?" Carolyn looked stunned. "Why?"

"You know that you'll inherit everything I have, even my half of the beach house, don't you?" Kath asked.

"I suspected so, yes. You had me sign papers at the lawyers years ago. And I do appreciate it. But you could have easily sold the beach house and split the money with everyone instead of working so hard these past few years. It's worth a fortune," Carolyn said.

Kath nodded. "Yes, it is. But the beach house is worth more than money to me. It's a magical place where you can relax and enjoy life. My father built it, and we all had such happy times there. I wanted to ensure you had it to enjoy until you no longer want it. I wanted to take care of you. Because I was unable to do that properly, the way I should have."

Carolyn walked over to the bed and sat down. "Take care of me? I have more than enough and will have more than I need in the years to come."

"I know," Kath said. "I just wanted to finally do things right."

"I'm still confused," Carolyn said, frowning. "Why?"

Kath stared into her niece's beautiful blue eyes, thinking of the man she'd once loved who had the very same eyes. It was time to tell the truth.

"I need to tell you something important, and I hope you won't hate me afterward," Kath said softly.

Carolyn smiled. "I could never hate you, Aunt Kath."

"Well, we'll see," Kath said. "A long time ago, in 1957, I gave birth to a beautiful baby girl with auburn hair and blue eyes. I was in France with my sister, Kat, and her husband, Grant. It was all planned from the start. Since I was single, I'd give my little girl to them to raise as their own. I knew I could never give the baby the kind of home that they could. But I've loved her all these years, even when I wasn't with her. I've always loved you, Carolyn. Because you're my little girl."

Carolyn stared at her but remained silent. Then, she sighed. "Now it's my turn to be truthful. Mom told me you were my mother right before she died. Dad said it was true. But they asked me not to tell you I knew. I had always hoped you'd tell me yourself."

Kath took a breath as tears welled in her eyes. "So, you knew? All this time? And you still came to help me all these years."

Carolyn smiled. "I came to help you to get to know you better. I've always loved you as my aunt. And now I can love you as my mother, too."

"Oh, sweetie," Kath wiped the tears from her eyes. "I'm so glad it's out in the open now. I can die happy, knowing you know my biggest secret and you don't hate me for it."

Carolyn drew close and hugged Kath. "I can't blame you for giving me up. It would have been impossible in those days to keep your career and a child. And I had amazing parents and wonderful grandparents, and an incredible aunt. What more could I have wanted?"

"Thank you, dear. I feel like a tremendous weight has been lifted off me," Kath said. "I'm assuming you know who your father was."

"Mom and Dad never said, but it's an easy guess. It had to be Gordon Quinn. You two were together for twenty years," Carolyn said.

Kath nodded.

"I do have one difficult question," Carolyn said. "Wasn't it hard staying with a man who wouldn't leave his wife and marry you so you could keep your baby? Did you ever resent him for that?"

Kath sat back against her pillows. "No. I was upset with him for a while, but the truth was, he was always honest with me about never divorcing his wife. So, when I became pregnant with you, I knew I only had two choices. Give you away or keep you and lose my career. I never expected Gordon to marry me. But that doesn't mean he didn't care about you, believe me. Even though he and I rarely talked about the baby I gave away, I would see him watching you when we were all together. His eyes were always sad. I think he would have liked to have known you better. I wish he'd had the chance."

"Well, if you can forgive him, then I can, too," Carolyn said. She smiled. "You know, you really are the strongest person I've ever known."

"Oh, honey," Kath said. "You have more strength in you than I ever did. And I'm proud to call you my daughter."

Carolyn hugged Kath again and then stood. "I need to let you rest. It's been a long day."

Kath's eyelids were already drooping. "Yes, it has. But it's been the best day of my life."

After Carolyn left, Kath turned out her bedside light and lay there, nearly asleep. She smiled. "Our daughter finally knows the truth, Gordon," she whispered into the dark room. "Now we both can rest." She closed her eyes and fell into a deep sleep.

The next day when Carolyn went to Kath's room to wake her, she was gone.

Epilogue

Kathleen Randall Carver died peacefully at the age of ninety-eight. The news was a shock to family and friends but even more so to the many people who, just the day before, had seen her be so talkative and vibrant at Grauman's Chinese Theater.

Flowers were laid out at the theater by those who'd visited her there until the outer sidewalk was covered in a rainbow of bouquets. Old movie channels ran her films twenty-four hours a day, and celebrities who'd worked with her in a movie or play were booked on morning and late-night shows to talk about Kath.

Kath's funeral was a quiet service attended by family only. All that was left was Carolyn, Daniel, and Lillian's grown children, Jonathan and Lauren. Lisa, Gordon's daughter, also attended. In the weeks to come, she and Carolyn would spend a great deal of time together reminiscing about Kath and their shared father, Gordon.

Kath was interred next to her parents and Graham and near where Katrina and her husband Grant were buried. Carolyn would have liked to have buried Kath next to her only true love, Gordon Quinn, but he was in another cemetery with his family. Carolyn knew that even in death, Kath would have found it inappropriate to lie near her long-time love.

On her grave marker, Carolyn had placed the words she'd heard her aunt say to Gordon that very night before she died.

Old stars never die. They keep burning brightly in the hearts of movie lovers.

It seemed a fitting end to an illustrious career.

-End-

Thank you for reading my novel. If you enjoyed this story, you may also enjoy the following historical novels:

Mrs. Winchester's Biographer

The Ones We Leave Behind

The Secrets We Carry

The Women of Great Heron Lake

Author's Notes

Kathleen Carver is a fictional character I created that was influenced by my favorite classic female celebrities including Lauren Bacall, Ginger Rogers, Lucille Ball, and Katharine Hepburn. They were beautiful, smart, sharp, witty, and tough, and that's why audiences loved them. While I had fun creating Kath's life out of thin air, I also paid homage to many real celebrities—Rock Hudson, Howard Hughes, Cary Grant, Marilyn Monroe, and many more. I researched these real-life characters to ensure I kept as close to their true life and personalities as possible.

As a teenager living in Southern California, I drove through Beverly Hills, Bel Air, and Holmbly Hills quite often, staring in wonder at the beautiful homes of the rich and famous. I've walked the Hollywood Walk of Fame and seen the stars on the sidewalk and have visited Grauman's Chinese Theater to see the many celebrity hand and shoe prints in the cement. Hollywood, at one time, seemed magical.

The studio system of old Hollywood wasn't perfect. But studios did protect their stars from nosy reporters and gossip columnists. Once celebrities no longer had the studio to protect them, they were fair game for the tabloids. Secrets in Hollywood are hard to keep.

I loved writing this story about a woman who lived a long life and kept her secrets. I hope you enjoyed the story too.

Deanna Lynn Sletten
March 25, 2024

About the Author

Deanna Lynn Sletten is the author of MRS. WINCHESTER'S BIOGRAPHER, THE ONES WE LEAVE BEHIND, THE WOMEN OF GREAT HERON LAKE, MISS ETTA, FINDING LIBBIE, and several other titles. She writes heartwarming women's fiction, captivating historical fiction, a murder mystery series, and romance novels with unforgettable characters. She has also written one middle-grade novel that takes you on the adventure of a lifetime.

Deanna is married and has two grown children. When not writing, she enjoys peaceful walks in the woods around her home with her beautiful Australian Shepherd, traveling, photography, and relaxing on the lake.

Deanna loves hearing from her readers.

Visit her at www.deannalsletten.com

Made in the USA
Coppell, TX
09 June 2024

33300604R00155